BENEATH
LOST
GROUND

By

G.D. Higgins

CHAPTER ONE

July 18th, 2019

He slouched as he descended the station steps. A phone call from inside interrupted Detective Sergeant Conal Brophy from his meandering thoughts of how to deal with the humidity in his stuffy two-bedroom country house. He was loath to spend another night there alone with his nightmares and ghosts. The heat was sweltering. He wiped the sweat from his brow.

The call came from Garda Finch, requesting his assistance in interviewing a local drug addict. Patrick 'Packo' Lenihan, one of the station's most frequent offenders in recent years, had been brought in and processed. Having been arrested dozens of times, his charges through the years ranged from possession of class A's to vandalism, theft, and indecent exposure. Brophy instantly regretted not turning off his phone, as he had planned to do as soon as he got into his black Saab.

He returned to the dim central corridor of the city's headquarters, which didn't get any natural light. It was unusually busy, with several uniformed gardaí racing in the opposite direction to Brophy. A thought crossed his mind, which delivered a pang of guilt as soon as he'd had it, that the N25 heading eastbound might be impeded by a rush-hour accident, preventing him from getting back to his isolated dwelling on the Copper Coast.

Brophy entered Interview Room Two, a growing chip on his shoulder; he wasn't in any kind of mood to deal with Packo's lip. Two uniformed gardaí stood in opposite corners, half-poised to make a grab for Packo if he stirred. Brophy knew something wasn't quite right. For all his indiscretions, Packo was never violent or dangerous, as such. His five-foot-six skinny frame would rarely give any garda cause for caution. But this time was different. Packo sat at the square, bolted-down table, his back straight, growling and drooling, a look of sheer terror in his eyes. He didn't even register Brophy's arrival.

Garda Finch approached Brophy from the back corner, glancing down at Packo a couple of times as he moved, and whispered into Brophy's ear, "Thanks for coming back in, Sergeant. He was brought in twenty minutes ago, kicking and screaming, talking about winged demons out to get him if he didn't find a pot of monarch butterfly wings, quickly. He was found in someone's back garden over in Saint John's Estate. On his hands and knees, he was, digging with bleeding fingers. Scared the life out of two sisters inside watching cartoons, six and eight years old."

"Thanks, Garda. I'll take it from here."

Brophy sat on the chair opposite Packo and glanced at the fresh plasters covering all of his fingers. Six-foot-one and broad-shouldered, Brophy slumped in his seat to get to eye-level with the much smaller Packo, so as not to intimidate him too much, an old academy trick he never gave much credence to but had become accustomed to, nonetheless.

"Packo, you're looking a bit worse for wear over there. Can I get you a coffee or something?"

Packo's eyes darted around the room, tracing along the outline of the triangle of light cast by the single shaded bulb overhead, still not having registered Brophy's presence. He reeked of ammonia-like body odour.

"How many arrests is this now, Packo? Sixty? Seventy? The judges are going to lose patience soon and send you down for a few years."

Packo laughed, a guttural dreg of a cackle. After finishing in a viscous sniffle, he half-focused on Brophy for the first time. "They'll never put away an upstanding citizen like meself."

"Oh yeah?" said Brophy. "And why is that, then?"

"Because all the bleedin' prisons are full to over-capacity in this lawless nation of ours."

"Who told you that?" Brophy questioned, attempting to act combative, and not show he completely agreed with what Packo was saying.

"That ride of a blonde one on the news told me. She's on about it nearly every day. Since you mad peelers locked up all the big time gangs, the Joy and the Portlaoise Hilton are all booked out for years to come."

"Maybe you should become a crime correspondent yourself. You seem to know so much about what's going on."

"Yeah. And I know the shower of yee made it wicked hard to get sorted these days."

"You seem to have managed, all the same. What is it you're on, anyway? Doesn't look like the usual coke high with prescription downers."

"Me? I'm just high on life, man. Had a couple of tins of cider to celebrate the success of you lot."

"Well, your latest escapade has left two little girls traumatised. Do you care about that?"

"Traumatised? Traumatised?" he said, incredulous, his eyebrows raising in hideous arches. "What about my childhood trauma, Bottler?"

Up to that point, Brophy hadn't been sure Packo even recognised him. His entire body tensed up at hearing the word. "Don't call me that, you little rat."

Packo lit up a little, perhaps from knowing he had touched a nerve with Brophy. The two uniformed gardaí shuffled uncomfortably in the background.

"I remember when I was six years old, All-

5

Ireland hurling final day — our first crack at that title in fifty years. In the pub, I was, with the aul fella and his mates. My little signed Waterford jersey on, swinging a hurley around like a wild caveman, all those stoned bastards laughing their arses off at me."

Brophy took an audible breath, his lips pursed tightly.

"Devastated, I was when our star player didn't show up. No injury, no explanation. Nothing. And then, the biggest ever defeat in an All-Ireland final. You talk about trauma. I never got over that day. In fact, it's what drove me to the drugs." He smiled, then seemed to get confused about what he'd just said.

"You're a little scumbag, Packo. And I'm going to see to it that you go down this time."

Packo sniggered, momentarily lowering his head, and Brophy noticed a large red blotch under his tightly cropped mousy hair.

"You'll bottle it again, Brophy," he said, a demented look swiping across his face.

Brophy sprang to his feet and pressed his hands on the table and came face to face with his tormentor.

"You listen to me, you scabby little junkie. We're testing your blood to see what you're on, and when I find out, I'll make sure whoever is supplying you knows that you're the biggest little rat in the city."

"You'll do no such thing, Detective Brophy,"

he said, moving in close enough for Brophy to see tiny flecks of blood on his cracked lips. "You need me for-"

A uniformed garda burst in the door, disturbing Packo's train of thought, but Brophy never took his eye off him.

"Sergeant Brophy," called Garda Sinéad Mallon with some urgency.

"I'm busy here, Mallon. Get someone else."

"Inspector Bennett was just on the phone. You're needed urgently. There's been an incident."

"You heard the young lady, Brophy. There's been an incident."

Brophy glanced back at Garda Mallon, biting his lower lip, then turned around to face Packo. "I'm not finished with you yet. The Hilton might be full, but we have plenty of space here." He looked up at Garda Finch. "Make sure our guest here has a comfortable stay in the penthouse. The toilet hasn't been fixed yet, has it?"

"No, sir. Still as blocked as a stuffed pheasant," said Finch with a smirk.

"Well then, that's about all for now. We'll continue this in the morning."

"Ah here, don't be like that," pleaded Packo as Brophy turned to head out the door. "I have to babysit tonight."

Brophy shut the door behind him, oblivious to Packo's last words. "What's so urgent Garda Mallon?" he said, noticing the worry in the rookie's green eyes.

"There's been a murder out in Woodstown. A husband and wife shot in their dining room whilst having dinner. Sounds like a real mess. Bennett wants you there, pronto."

CHAPTER TWO

Despite the siren and the reckless driving of Garda Mallon, it still took over twenty minutes to make the eight-kilometre journey. She sped through the Waterford city evening traffic and the winding country roads that led to the picturesque seaside village of Woodstown. Brophy assumed the heavy traffic was due to people returning from the beaches of Tramore and neighbouring areas. Mallon had no further details on the unfolding incident than what she had told Brophy at the station, so a contemplative silence pervaded the speeding squad car. Brophy considered what his role might be in such a big case, and assumed Mallon, who was only months out of the academy, was anxious about seeing her first murder scene. It was only natural; they all experienced it at some time or another.

Brophy's ascendancy up the ranks during his early years on the force had been commendable, but in recent years his career had stagnated, and he wasn't too bothered by it, either. When he made detective sergeant at twenty-nine, the department handed him every big case concerning suspicious deaths or missing persons. Nowadays he was content to play second fiddle to Detective Inspector Bennett, assisting in, rather than leading the big cases.

As they turned off the Dunmore Road, heading towards Woodstown, Brophy felt himself become light-headed and for a moment panicked about what could be happening. A sensation that usually only occurred in confined, stuffy spaces. He quickly realised it was the blistering heat and lack of functioning air-conditioning in the squad car that made him feel disorientated. He pressed the window button on the passenger door and sucked in a few deep breaths, drawing a confused look from the now pale Garda Mallon.

"We're nearly there, Sergeant. Just another kilometre," she said whilst turning onto a narrow country road, flanked by dense Sitka spruce trees. "What's it like, Sir?"

"What's what like?"

"I mean, the first time you see dead bodies at a crime scene."

Brophy looked at her and was caught off guard by how very young she looked, her shoulder-length brown hair up in a neat ponytail, her sallow skin smooth and unblemished. He guessed she couldn't be more than twenty-two, a year younger than when he joined the force.

"I'm not gonna lie to you, Garda Mallon. It stays with you for a while, but you get used to it, I promise. It just becomes another part of the job."

He observed her smile uneasily and

appearing unable to get out what was on her trembling lips.

"Just try not to look into their eyes, if they're still opened."

"Okay, Sergeant. Thanks."

Mallon indicated right, and Brophy had to do a double-take to spot where she was about to turn in to. She headed towards a driveway that looked more like a logging route for lorries and heavy machinery than an entrance to a house. The trees shaded most of the mid-evening summer sunlight, and Mallon turned the lights on full. After crawling along the bumpy lane for a minute, it opened into a large clearing, and they turned onto a tarmacked driveway on a large two-acre green patch that led down to the beach on the far side. At the end of the driveway was an expansive modern dormer bungalow.

Five squad cars were parked at varying angles in front of the house, and the large white van of the Technical Bureau was surrounded by people in white hooded overalls. Mallon stopped the car behind the van and they both got out. The entire scene felt silent and haunted, only the low toned murmurs of gardaí speaking through their light blue facemasks to be heard. Those who weren't talking, moved around in a sombre haunch, going about their tasks, examining the crime scene.

Brophy shut the car door as silently as he could, not wanting to interfere with the deliberate silence. He saw Inspector Bennett near the front door, talking to a uniformed garda, in his early fifties, he didn't recognise. He approached the two men with Mallon in-tow.

"What have we got, Inspector?" he asked Bennett.

"Thanks for getting here so quickly, Sergeant. I know you were on your way home, as was I." Brophy gave him a faint nod. "This is Garda Sergeant Gough, from the local station. He got a call about an hour ago; someone on the beach heard gunshots and a scream."

Brophy glanced towards the shoreline at the end of a fifty-metre-wide garden. *Must have been some scream.*

"How are you, Sergeant Brophy?" said Gough, wide-eyed, clearly out of his depth as a countryside, one-garda operation. One of the few small stations around the country to avoid closure during cutbacks in recent years. "I got a call just before seven. The caller was walking his dog on the beach. Lives in the next house over, about half a mile away at the far corner of the woods. Said he heard four or five shots and thought he heard a scream, too, but couldn't be sure. He's a man who's done a lot of hunting through the years and knows what a gunshot sounds like, so I took it seriously straight away. Got here within seven or eight minutes and found the two of them... well, you'll see for yourself when you go inside."

Mallon returned after a few moments, having retrieved two sets of white overalls and handed one to Brophy. They got suited up and were about to enter the house when Bennett called Brophy back.

"There's one more thing I should tell you," he said with a cold glare.

"What's that?" said Brophy.

Bennett nodded at Gough in a gesture that said, 'divulge.'

"They have a ten-year-old son."

Brophy's heart thumped off his chest wall.

"He hasn't been located yet. They're conducting a room to room search now."

Without saying a word, Brophy headed towards the house and put on shoe covers at the front door before entering, followed by Mallon. They found themselves in a large reception area, tastefully decorated, with a painted family portrait, with four adults and a small child. A blue Persian rug covered a wide section of the centre of the foyer.

"Don't stand on that," said one of the forensics team, "and keep to the right along the hallway. We want to limit the contamination area," he seemed to add for Mallon's benefit, whose apprehension was visible in her eyes, the only part of her exposed.

Brophy looked to the right at the stairs and saw two pairs of white pants passing by the landing, searching for the boy, no doubt.

They proceeded left, down the hall, keeping close to the wall on the right, as instructed. At the end of the hall, they entered through double French doors into a spacious dining area that opened out into a large glass conservatory. Most of the many windows were wide open, which might explain how the scream was heard, but it would still be a stretch.

Brophy took a few steps in and looked to the right where he saw a long, solid wood dining table. At the end of the table, slumped over, head on a dinner plate, was one of the victims: the father, a hole in the back of his skull, where the bullet had exited. A pool of blood darkened and glimmered around the man's head. Brophy glanced at Mallon and saw the familiar look of terror at seeing such a sight for the first time. He briefly considered excusing her but decided against it. She had to go through this at some stage.

Brophy noticed another three places set at the table, two that had been cleared of the plates, and the other had an empty dish and wine glass still in situ. He crouched a little to get a better look at the body and was able to determine the man had been shot at least one more time, in the chest. Maybe it was how a trained killer might have done it. A first for Brophy. The few murders he had seen in his eighteen years on the job were mostly crimes of passion, domestic abuse gone to the extreme, or suspicious suicides. Waterford and the South East simply weren't the places where this kind of criminal activity happened. There was never a major problem with gangs. That sort of stuff seemed to be confined to Dublin or Limerick.

He looked towards the conservatory and saw two people crouched down by where the wall met the glass, and a door on the adjacent wall looked like it led into the kitchen. He walked around the table, starting to feel the layer of sweat on his back drip down. He saw the second victim, lying in a twisted scrawl, her upper body facing down, whilst her lower body jutted upwards. He and Mallon were quickly instructed to keep several feet back, and he soon saw why. Scattered around the body were the remains of the shattered plates and glasses she must have been carrying to the kitchen at the time she was shot. Knives and forks were also on the wooden floor, nearby. Unlike the untouched set at the table, those looked used, and so would provide a hotbed of fingerprints and DNA if they happened to have been touched by the shooter. Unlikely as that might be, they couldn't rule anything out at that stage.

On closer examination, the woman appeared to have had the same gunshot wounds as her husband— one in the chest, and one in the head.

"No sign of the boy, Detective," came a voice from near the door.

Brophy turned to answer but quickly saw it

wasn't he who was addressed. It was Detective Sergeant Christine McCall. The tall, athletic blonde sergeant had entered the room unknown to Brophy who was subsumed in a sort of dark tunnel, with only the elements of the brutal crime present in his seclusion. A state of mind he often got into at crime scenes in recent years. He agonised over whether it was a good thing, a focusing strategy to help him take in the scene, or a hindrance, his unconscious mind telling him he was growing further imprisoned by a job he was not sure he wanted any longer.

"Okay, Sergeant Halpin. Proceed with the search around the perimeter. Focus on the woods and the beach, and quickly. It's about to get dark soon."

"Yes, Sergeant," said Halpin and turned on his heel to leave the room.

McCall approached Brophy. "What a mess we have here, Detective. Are you all right, Garda Mallon?" she said before Brophy had a chance to reply.

"Yes, Ma'am. Just a little hot."

"You can go out and join the search now. There's no need for you to be here."

"Yes, Sergeant McCall."

Mallon swiftly left the room.

"That was a bit harsh, Brophy. Making her witness this."

"She has to see it at some stage."

"I've certainly never seen anything like this

in my ten years."

"What do we know so far?" asked Brophy. The tension between the two equally ranked detectives was palpable. McCall had had a similar career trajectory to Brophy, making detective and then sergeant before the age of thirty. But unlike him, she was still ambitious.

"Shots fired just before seven. Local garda was on the scene a short while later. Front door was left wide open, so he came in and found these two like this," she said, glancing at each of the victims.

"What do we know about them?"

"Jordan and Maura Walters. He owns Bioford Laboratory in the industrial estate. Employs about seventy people, mostly high-skilled technicians and researchers."

"And the wife?"

"Maura Walters, née Roache. Housewife and well-known in social circles in the city. Heavily involved in charity work around town, chairwoman of the Waterford Regional Cardiac Unit Fund."

"Surprised I haven't heard of her before."

"Maybe you should get out more often then. The family are big fish around the city. The lab was started by Jordan's father, Kevin Walters, in the eighties. He ran it right up until his death a few years ago."

"You haven't wasted any time, have you?"

"Your man, Gough seemed to know a bit

about them, being the most prominent family in his district, and all."

"Didn't happen to know if they had any enemies who'd wanted to shoot them in the head and chest during dinner?"

"Afraid not. That's going to be up to us to find out. The state pathologist is on her way down from Dublin now."

"Not leaving it to the local coroner, then?"

"This is too big for that. The media are going to be all over this one. And Bennett's going to expect results, and fast. He won't want the Dublin units coming down here and taking over. Not when the South East Headquarters plan is in review."

McCall went over to take another look at Jordan Walter's body whilst Brophy crouched to take a closer look at Maura Walters. He couldn't help but think how glamorous and beautiful she must have been in life, a life that was snubbed out so viciously. His thoughts turned to the missing boy, and he became engulfed by the dark tunnel once more. He couldn't make sense of it. Why would someone kill the parents and take the boy? Was he even there when his parents were slain?

Before he had a chance to form a single theory, an earth-shattering scream that arose from the front of the house wrenched him out of the darkness. He locked eyes with McCall, their curiosity registering identically in their eyes. *Who the hell was that?*

They headed out of the dining room and down the hall towards the front door. When Brophy went out, he saw Bennett and Gough holding back a blonde woman who looked to be in her mid-thirties. She was screaming, and her eyes bulged in despair.

"What happened? Where is my Seán? Let me go. What's going on?"

CHAPTER THREE

The Incident Room in Waterford Garda Station was like any other in a large town or city across the country. Desks packed with files and folders took up most of the floor space, and each had a computer standing idle in the corner, guarded by a stained coffee mug at that late hour on a Thursday night in July. Filing cabinets jostled for most of the remaining space, particularly by the walls. Except for the back wall, which was panelled in light coloured wood with a long table situated in front. That was where the team would assemble to discuss ongoing cases, using the wall to tack up various exhibits of evidence, and photos of suspects and their victims.

Tonight the wall was bare, and a dozen or so officers took up positions, either seated at the table or standing against the cabinets awaiting the senior investigating officer, Detective Inspector Bennett. He finally arrived, pacing across the room, talking angrily into his mobile.

"Keep that shower away," Brophy heard most distinctly, knowing the pressure Bennett would be feeling to handle the case locally and not have a specialist unit come down from Dublin, undermining their efforts, and to Bennett's mind, making a fool of him. Brophy secretly hoped they'd arrive as soon as possible and had little doubt it was only a matter of time before they did.

Bennett rounded the table and stood against the panelled wall. His six-foot-three frame imposed an aura of authority, matched only by his ceaseless ambition. He took off his hat and ruffled his sweat-soaked black hair.

"Sergeant Kenneally, you're the inside officer on this case. What do we have so far?"

Brophy wasn't surprised Kenneally would coordinate things on the inside. He had a great touch for collating information but didn't like to get his hands dirty on the outside. Brophy wasn't sure if he could fit in the front seat of the squad car at that stage, having ballooned in weight since his wife had their third child a year ago.

"Two victims and a child unaccounted for. Male victim is one Jordan Walters, forty-one years old. The female victim is Maura Walters, thirty-eight. Obviously, a wealthy family. Made their money mostly from agricultural and food testing, GMO and nutrition analysis, and the likes. That's what they do in Bioford, their lab in the industrial estate, that employs about seventy people. Walters seems to be a quiet family man. Came up clean on the PULSE system. Not even a parking ticket. Had trouble with a couple of burglaries about a year ago. Nothing much taken. Thieves never apprehended," said Kenneally.

"How about the wife?" asked Sergeant McCall.

"Used to be a lab technician in the same line of business but gave it up when they had their child, Seán."

"So, he was her boss?" asked McCall, her contempt visible as she stood, legs firmly apart, hands clasped behind her back.

"No," said Kenneally. "This is where it gets interesting. Her mother's maiden name is Donahue, making her the niece of Barry Donahue. He owns Qualchem Labs over by the Waterford Crystal Centre. That would make him Walters' main competitor in the city."

"Okay. That's good. We need to look into that first thing in the morning. I'm sure he's been informed about his niece by now. Give him the night to let it sink in, then see if there's anything between him and Walters," said Bennett. "Any word on CCTV images?"

"Got a call from Garda Neven a while ago," said Detective Paul Dunford, in a thick West Cork accent. A young detective with cropped ginger hair and a square jaw who looked like he should be playing in the back-line of the Irish Rugby team. "She said they tracked down the nearest camera to the village, two kilometres away. There's a pub-cum-supermarket there with a small car park. One of the two cameras covers the entrances to the pub and shop, and the other is faced on the car park, but also catches a bend on the road coming from the direction of the house. She said we should get a clear view of the cars, but it was busy today. Loads of people from the city at the beaches out there today. They're some of the most popular in the county, apparently."

"And the search for the boy?" said Brophy, worrying that a quiver might be detected in his voice.

"There's a team in the area now, made up of Civil Defence volunteers and some locals, but nothing yet," said Garda Lonergan, a balding uniformed Garda in his fifties, who sat at the end of the table. "They've covered most of the area, but there are eight square kilometres of it, so they can't be sure. Tech team will have a closer look in the morning."

"What have Tech come back with so far?" asked Bennett.

"Nothing official, of course," said Kenneally, "and the state pathologist should be arriving shortly, but unofficially, the victims were shot twice each, head and heart. No sign of forced entry, and the front door was left open."

"Maybe the boy did a runner, and he's still going," added Brophy.

"Let's hope so," said Kenneally before looking at his notes and adding, "The dining table was set for four, but only three people ate. Apparently, there was enough for five more people in the oven."

"And family in the area?" said Bennett.

"Walters has none. Both his parents have

passed away, and the extended family are mostly from Dublin. We need to look into that a bit more. There's a few Donahues in the city, but not many. Maura Walters has no siblings. Jordan Walters has one sister, Ciara, who I believe made an appearance at the house and is waiting in Interview Room One with Garda Mallon, as we speak."

Bennett looked to Brophy. "When we're done here, you and McCall interview her, see what you can get."

"Yes, Sir," said McCall, whilst Brophy remained silent and looked to the ground, scuffing his brown leather shoe along the thin blue carpet.

"Okay, everyone. There's not much we can do tonight, but first thing in the morning, I want you all on your briefs like flies on shit. Let's wrap this one up quickly, show them what we're made of at this station. Eyes are on us, and if we want this to be the headquarters for the South East, we need to show that we're closers."

They all nodded and spoke in affirmative monosyllables and shuffled away from the Incident Room, all lost in their thoughts, knowing the next few days would be amongst the most intense they've had on the force. Brophy hung back at the behest of a nod from Bennett. McCall hesitated, as if she expected to be kept firmly in the loop but turned and headed out with a barely restrained scowl as Bennett gave her a patronising wave to usher her on her way.

"Conal, I need your A-game on this one. You're the best investigator of the lot of them, but I want your head in the right place."

"Sir, maybe McCall would be more suitable to lead things on this. She's well switched on."

"What are you talking about?" said Bennett, grimacing with disgust at the thought. "She's a maverick, out only for herself."

Some man to be making that accusation, Brophy thought.

"Wrap this up like I know you can, and soon enough, you'll be able to run the show like you should have been years ago."

"That's your job, isn't it?"

"Only by default, Conal, and we both know it. I'll never understand why you turned down this position, but as soon as this place is upgraded, Superintendent Russell will retire. I'll take his place, and you're the new detective inspector."

"*If* this place is upgraded," sniped Brophy.

"You heard there's been talk about them making Carlow station the HQ," said Bennett uneasily. "That's just another way of them saying everything will still be run from Dublin. Let's catch the shooter on this one and find that poor boy."

Brophy bowed his head at the mention of the missing boy.

"Don't get personally involved. You work

much better that way. Now, go and interview the Walters woman, see what she knows."

The two men, who used to be close friends, and had a solid partnership back in the day, looked at each other awkwardly.

"Dismissed, Sergeant Brophy," said Bennett.

Brophy couldn't get out of there fast enough.

CHAPTER FOUR

Brophy glimpsed in the small Plexiglas window on the door to Interview Room One. Garda Mallon sat on the brown leather couch with her arm around an inconsolable, Ciara Walters.

"Shall we get this over with?" said McCall who had joined him outside the door.

Brophy opened the door and slowly stepped into the brightly lit room, keeping his eye on Garda Mallon. The young garda moved to stand up but was held down by the sobbing aunt of the missing boy.

"Ms Walters?" said McCall in a voice softer than Brophy had ever heard her utter.

Ciara Walters raised her head from Mallon's shoulder and looked at McCall and Brophy with blood-shot watery eyes. Brophy couldn't help but notice the lack of make-up streaks despite all the tears.

"I'm Detective Sergeant McCall and this is Detective Sergeant Brophy. I know this is an extremely difficult time, but the sooner we get some information from you, the better a chance we have of catching who did this and of finding your nephew."

Walters took in a deep, composing breath, smacking her lips and wiping under her eyes with her thumbs.

"Of course," said Walters in an easily recognisable South Dublin accent. "Have you any idea what happened yet? Oh, God, please find him," she said, struggling to hold back another sob. She inhaled another gulp of coffee-scented air.

"We have a large team out looking as we speak," said Brophy. "But the next twenty-four hours are crucial, so we need to know as much as possible if we're to find him and figure out who's responsible for this."

"I was supposed to take him to Dublin with me for the weekend. That's why I was coming down. I was meant to be at dinner with them, but I got delayed."

That would explain the extra food, well, some of it, at least.

Brophy and McCall sat on the armchairs at either end of the couch. Walters straightened her back and pulled an expression of determination like she was going to do what was necessary to help the detectives. People often froze at that early stage of an investigation, either because of suspicions directed at the police or because they were too crippled with grief at hearing of the loss of a family member.

"Firstly, Ms Walters," said Brophy. "Is there anyone you would immediately suspect of doing this to your brother and sister-in-law? I mean, did they have any enemies you know of?"

Walters face softened, and Brophy couldn't

help observing her sheer beauty, like a perfectly ageing Hollywood actress. "Jordan was very reserved, even by our family's standard. He'd do anything to avoid confrontation. He ran our father's business and kept his head down. As far as I know, he didn't even socialise that much in recent years."

"How about Maura?" asked McCall.

"Maura was the opposite, in many ways. A bit of a go-getter. Gets along with everyone. I can't imagine her having enemies, though."

"How was their marriage?" asked McCall, drawing a quizzical look from Ciara Walters.

"Their marriage seemed great. They've always been very committed to each other and were great parents. Oh, please find Seán. He must be terrified wherever he is."

"We'll do everything we can," said Brophy. "It's come to our attention that Maura was the niece of one Mr Barry Donahue."

"That's right."

"Are he and Jordan serious rivals?"

"I wouldn't say that," she said, expressing she knew what they were getting at by a flick of her eyebrows. "My dad and Mr Donahue would have been much bigger competitors. They both started their labs in the eighties when this kind of work would have been scarce enough. They would have outbid each other on some contracts, but these days there should be more business than they can keep up with. It's a thriving sector."

"Do either of them have any friends you've ever been suspicious of?" asked McCall.

Walters' poise faltered, and she looked to the ground for the briefest of moments.

"What is it, Ms Walters?" asked Brophy.

"I don't know if I should say it. It might be nothing."

"If anything creates the vaguest amount of scepticism, then you shouldn't keep it back," Brophy replied.

"Something my dad and he argued about many years ago. Jordan went to private school in Blackrock, you see. The same private school as Bobby Quilty."

Brophy and McCall glanced at each other, McCall's nostrils flaring. Bobby Quilty, born to wealth and privilege, went on to become the head of Ireland's biggest crime family, smuggling most of the cocaine to be found in the country. He was now living in the lap of luxury in Bahrain after evading capture and arrest, when the rest of his crew were brought down in operation, Swift Downpour, or wiped out by their rival cartel, the Doyles.

"They were close in school, and I think they remained friends afterwards, but Jordan would never admit to it," Ciara Walters added.

"Okay. That's good to know. We should look into that," said McCall.

"Is there any chance your nephew wasn't at

home when the incident occurred? Maybe he was at a friend's house or something?" asked Brophy.

"I'm pretty certain he was there waiting for me to arrive. The kids are on summer holidays at the moment, and he was at hurling camp in the city during the day. He loves his hurling, all sports for that matter."

"Where is the camp being held?" asked Brophy.

"I think it's in Saint Xavier's, but I'm not too sure."

"Thank you very much, Ms Walters. You've been extremely helpful. We won't take any more of your time for now, and we're very sorry for your loss," said McCall.

Brophy watched on with pity as the last few words made Ciara Walters realise the horror of what had happened that evening and broke down crying, once more.

He and McCall left quietly and allowed Garda Mallon to care for the bereaved woman.

CHAPTER FIVE

Brophy made the twenty-minute journey to his house, along dark winding roads, guarded by imperious overgrown deciduous trees. The bright cloudless night did nothing to clear the foggy thoughts threatening to plague his mind, thoughts that never quite take enough form to haunt him directly. As always, oblique foreboding imaginings, lying in wait for their opportunity to catch him unawares.

The countless farms and well-lit houses barely registered as he pulled into his driveway, having forgotten he made the journey at all.

Brophy's two-bedroom bungalow would appear abandoned and derelict to passersby, not in the know, but he found solace there, nonetheless. The old grey stuccoed walls, the peeling brown window frames, the faded and stained white front door, all a reminder of what his life had become in recent years. His ex-wife kept the house they bought together fifteen years before, moved her new partner in five years ago. With his daughter living with her mother full-time, she hardly spoke to her old man, or was it he hardly spoke to her? He couldn't quite tell anymore.

The front door led straight into the living-room if one could call it that; a foldout couch, always set up as an unmade bed, a wide-screen TV still in its box in one corner, strategically placed to hide the damp stains on the wall, but not very successfully. He threw himself down on the couch and was out in seconds.

"You know, you could have been a lot more than this," came the voice of his mother, father, coach, and professor, all rolled into one claustrophobic echo chamber. "You always bottle it at the last moment, don't you? Your hurling career, your university, your marriage, and now your fucking job," the last words shouted at him in a deafening roar.

Brophy, a small child now, tenacious and brave, waves his arms in the blinding darkness, looking for anything, a wall, a way out. But nothing. He's trapped. He can't remember if he fell or was pushed. But he's a brave boy, the bravest of his group of friends. That's why he came in here— to show the others that he was courageous enough. And now he's smothered in the unseeing thickness of the pit.

This was the place of childhood horror stories amongst his friends on Park Lawn Terrace, the housing estate where he grew up. The old Georgian house that stood on six acres of walled-off land, and separated his estate from the nearest beach, was the hiding place of a mysterious, wealthy family, the Phelans. Brophy and his pals always dared each other to go further and further up the tree-lined long entranceway and seek out the hidden tunnel that led to a secluded part of the beach they could only reach across the rocks.

He gets down on his hands and knees and feels around for the steps he's sure he came down just seconds before. The stone ground is cold and greasy. Stars appear before his eyes. He touches the side of his head. It's wet. And it stings. Panic sets in as he realises it's his blood. That's what's making the ground seem greasy. *But was I pushed, or did I fall?*

Drowsiness is overpowering. He lies on the ground and isn't sure if his eyes are open or not, but he drifts off.

"Detective Brophy. Help me, please?"

An unfamiliar voice unsettles him from his slumber. Maybe just as well. He needs to find a way out of this pit. He blinks furiously, trying to force some light in. It's working— the outline of something, a person. The stranger is face to face. But he's also lying in the pit.

"Who's there?"

"You haven't found me yet. Keep looking." A girl's voice, sweet and gentle. "Why have you stopped searching? I'm right here in front of you. I've always been right in front of you."

"Who are you? I can't see a thing. I want to go home."

"I want to go home too. But I haven't been found..."

Brophy woke, drenched in sweat, expecting

to roll over and find a dry spot and go right back to sleep, but soon the predawn light eased through his thick brown curtains and brought him fully out of his slumber. He felt as though he'd just fallen asleep, and now it was already time to get up and face a new case he wanted no part of.

He stumbled to the bathroom through the door at the other end of the living room, pondering yet another stifling day ahead. He got into the shower and turned the cold water on full.

CHAPTER SIX

"Any news on the boy?" Brophy asked Kenneally.

"Nothing yet, I'm afraid. The search party aims to step it up at nine o'clock and widen the search to the neighbouring beaches, and more woodland in the area."

"Keep me updated of any developments," said Brophy.

"Will do. Hey, I hope you're not on that phone whilst driving again," said Kenneally through a chuckle. "That's illegal, you know?"

"Stupid arsehole," said Brophy under his breath after swiping at the red button on his phone.

He rolled down the windows of his Saab as he sped along the N25 towards Waterford City, and a blast of hot air hit him. A layer of sweat already made its way across his back. The weather was unrelenting and set to last another week or two, according to reports. People up and down the country revelled in the mid-summer heatwave, but Brophy would have preferred to roll around naked on arctic ice-sheets than endure this torture.

He'd always had a preference for colder weather, especially in his sporting days. He felt more alive, driven to achieve physical optimisation in the wintry conditions, while he struggled through the warmer climes of the championship months. That's why many people believed he'd missed the big game sixteen years ago. But he never gave an answer to demands for an explanation. He just quit. He checked out and focused on his police work. Withdrew from all forms of public life, except for those he served.

After half an hour of stopping and starting through the morning rush hour traffic coming into the city, he finally reached his destination, Saint Xavier's Secondary School, just off the Cork Road, behind the Waterford Crystal Recreation Centre. The largest secondary school in the city, and one of the biggest rivals of his school and club teams, Dunabbey, his hometown, in the west of the county. He'd played there many times growing up, mostly on the losing side. The school ran hurling camps all through the summer, and kids came from all corners of the county, hoping some of those winning ways would rub off on them.

He drove past the main school building, turned the corner on Gleann Fia Road and headed down towards the beautifully kept GAA ground of the local Saint Xavier's School and club. A high chain-link fence separated the field from the road. Brophy saw the coach had kids of all ages already doing laps of the pitch at a quarter to nine in the scorching morning heat. Seeing the coach standing at the goalposts with his assistant at the far end of the field, Brophy cursed at the thought of having to tread across the perfectly manicured grass to get to the man he needed to question.

He rounded the outer fence to the side entrance and tried to ignore it was his first time stepping onto a hurling pitch since he scored the winning point against Cork that brought his team into their first All-Ireland final in half a century.

He headed towards the eastern end, the sun beating down on him. Though he wore his thinnest white shirt and brown slacks, he felt as if he was stepping into the depths of a giant furnace. His heartbeat raced, his skin singed, and he realised that the onset of a panic attack was gripping him tightly. *It's this damn field. I should never have taken a single step onto it.*

"Oi! You! What are you doing on this field?" The hoarsely shouted words came from the direction he was headed.

Brophy tried with all his mental energy to focus on the silhouetted figure growing in size before his eyes. Raising his hand to shield the sun from his vision helped a little.

"I don't believe it. Look what the cat dragged in—if it isn't Conal Brophy. How's it hanging, sham?"

Brophy was beginning to recognise the voice that spoke to him, but the 'sham' sealed it. Jerry Cunningham. Corner-back on the Waterford squad for the great team of the naughties. Rarely got a game but was an ever-present source of commentary and catch-phrases. The years hadn't been kind to his waistline or his hairline, but he still looked like he could go a few rounds in a boxing ring if push came to shove.

"How's it going, Jerry?"

"It's going good, lad."

Brophy's panic attack was averted, and he was now almost fully focused on his old teammate.

"So, are you here for a game, or what? Sixteen years late, but I reckon you'd give a few of the kids here a good challenge."

Cunningham broke down at his quip. Brophy remained expressionless.

"I'm here to get some information about Seán Walters."

Cunningham scanned the perimeter to try to pick the ten-year-old out from the pack.

"Information? What do you mean? What's happened?"

"He's gone missing."

"Jesus."

"You obviously haven't heard the news yet this morning, so I might as well tell you."

"Tell me what?" said Cunningham, concern evident in his tone.

"His parents were murdered in the family home yesterday evening, and the little boy is nowhere to be found."

"Holy God above. What do you need to know?"

"Was he here yesterday?"

"He was, yeah."

"Anything strange about his behaviour?"

"Not that I could tell. But I don't know the kid that well. He's done our camps the last few summers and came back on Monday to start a two-week camp this year. God, I can't believe it. How were they killed?"

"I can't discuss that with you, Jerry."

"Oh, no. Of course not."

"What time did he leave, and who picked him up?"

Cunningham gripped his chin and lowered his head, a gesture of recollection Brophy was accustomed to seeing.

"Come to think of it; he left a little bit early. Said he was off to Dublin for the weekend and wanted to buy something in town first."

"Can you remember who picked him up?"

"I can't be too sure. We had a rough aul game on the go when he left."

"You didn't see if someone was waiting for him?"

"Sorry, Conal. I wasn't looking. But nothing seemed out of the ordinary if that's any good."

"Well, if you remember anything, you give me a call."

Brophy reached into his pocket and pulled out a business card with his and the station's details.

Cunningham took the card and examined it closely. "Will do, Detective Sergeant Brophy. Good to see you, man. It's been too long." He glanced over to his young charges and shouted, "Get a move on, you lot, or there'll be two more laps." He turned back to Brophy, a thin smile appearing on his podgy face. "What a team we had. Those were the glory days, weren't they, Conal?"

"If you say so," Brophy curtly replied, and as he turned to walk away, he said, "Make sure you get in touch if you remember anything."

"No worries," said Cunningham.

After a few paces, Brophy turned back, momentarily dazzled by the sun once more. "What's the lad like?"

"Walters? He's a decent player. Good speed and power, but not the kind of skill you had at that age. He'll be a fine player, though."

"I meant his personality. What is he like?"

Cunningham looked almost puzzled by the question like it was something a coach should never be bothered about. He paused for a few beats. "Bit arrogant, truth be told. Likes to take-on the bigger kids and push the smaller lads out of his way. Great attitude for the game, really. Actually, he got into a bit of a scuffle yesterday when practising blocks. Only lasted a few seconds." He paused as if something just popped into his head. "Hey, come to think of it, I do

41

remember seeing him getting into a car after he left. The memory isn't the best these days. I looked up towards the fence there, and saw him getting into a black car," he said, gesturing to the other end of the pitch.

"Did you see who was driving?"

"Nah. Was too far away, and I think the windows were darkened with that tint stuff."

"What kind of car was it?"

"Not a hundred percent sure, but something big and fancy. Maybe a Mercedes. And he was laughing as he got into the car. That's all I remember. Hope it's helpful."

"Thanks, Jerry," said Brophy, nodding in acknowledgement, then he turned away.

He couldn't get off that pitch fast enough.

When he reached his Saab, in the general vicinity of where Cunningham said he saw Seán Walters get into a black car, he looked down the field and saw the boys assemble around their coach. As much as he'd never admit it, the sight brought him back to easier times, when the next game was all he cared about. Now it was the thing he dreaded the most.

As he was about to get into his car, his phone buzzed.

He answered.

"McCall here. Are you still around Saint Xavier's?"

"Yeah. Just finished with the hurling coach now. What's the craic?"

"One of the neighbours mentioned they'd seen a Ford Fiesta around a few times, driven by a dodgy looking character not from the area; we found it on the CCTV from the shop. Got a clear look at the plate. Get this. The car is registered to Michael Delaney."

"Jesus Christ. What would he be doing around there?"

"Who knows? Might be just a coincidence, but we need to check it out as soon as possible. As you're already in the area, there'll be a squad car with a couple of uniforms waiting for you down the road from his house. You're advised to approach with extreme caution."

"Okay. I'll get there in five minutes."

CHAPTER SEVEN

Michael 'Budgie' Delaney was one of the highest level local dealers in Waterford City. Not much more than a common street dealer, but he seemed to have the kind of connections that ensured he always had the best cocaine in the town and the muscle and bad attitude to ensure no other back-alley dealer invaded his turf. Six-foot-three and built like a middle-aged bricklayer who'd been hauling heavy loads since he was a wee lad, Delaney had fallen off the radar recently. Like most dealers, due to the massive operation that brought down the country's two main cartels, his supply had run short to non-existent. Brophy had hardly heard mention of his name in three months and was certainly unaware the local man could even drive in his late twenties.

Brophy swung around a few bends until he was brought back out onto Cork Road. After a few seconds, the Waterford Institute of Technology appeared on his left. The sprawling council estate, Gleann Fia, came into view, across a two-acre playing green, on his right. The south -eastern city, the oldest in the country, had fewer than a hundred thousand inhabitants, and over two thousand of these lived in the notorious Gleann Fia estate. Fifteen of the twenty assaults against gardaí reported in the city the previous year took place there and sixty percent of drug busts, thirty percent of burglaries, and on and on. It housed many of the city's working-class families, and with youth unemployment at a worrying high since the financial crisis, boredom and idleness, as always, led to the worst kind of apathy.

Brophy drove slowly past the estate's squalid playing green. After a couple of turns, passing countless multi-coloured semi-detached houses, he ended up in the interior of the estate and soon spotted the squad car. It was parked around the corner at the end of Delaney's street, out of sight. But that didn't matter. If Delaney was home, he knew well by now they were parked in his neighbourhood.

He slowed down as he approached the squad car and waved at the uniformed gardaí to follow him to the house down the street.

He pulled over and parked two houses down, knowing there was always a possibility of having something thrown at his car if left in front of his assailant's. After he got out, he scanned the rows of houses on all sides and saw a dozen, or so, people staring out windows at the latest sighting of trouble. He briefly wondered why the place was devoid of children running around on a hot summer's day, then remembered it was still quite early in the morning.

He shimmied the latch on the thigh-high

rusted iron gate, eventually getting it opened and took a few steps to reach the blue front door. He noticed the two upstairs windows had their curtains drawn, but the downstairs ones were pulled. The glare from the sun made it impossible to see in, especially from their position.

Brophy gave a loud, unmistakable police knock. *Ratt, tatt, tatt.* "Hello, anyone home?" *Ratt, tatt, tatt.*

They waited for a response. Brophy glanced at the two young uniformed gardaí, who he'd barely acknowledged until now; he wasn't sure if he recognised either one of them.

"Who's there? What do you want?" came the raspy voice of who, Brophy assumed, was Delaney's mother.

"It's the gardaí," he said, attempting to sound soft-spoken and non-confrontational but failing miserably at both. "We need a word with Michael, and we know this was his last registered address, so please open up."

He'd scarcely spoken the final words when he heard the mewing sound of a baby, winding up for a full-on bawl. The chub-lock clanked open, a chain rattled over and back against the door and frame, and the door was pulled open a couple of feet. A girl in her mid-twenties stood before them, rocking the baby gently in her arms, a look of anguish on her freckled face that said she couldn't take another screeching baby outburst at that moment.

"He's not here, all right. But if you do find him, tell the bastard to get home and help out with his baby daughter."

The baby, who looked only a couple of months old and was dressed in a vomit-stained, pink babygrow, began to quiver, winding up for another attempt at waking up the entire neighbourhood.

"Would we be able to come in for a word?" interrupted one of the young gardaí, whilst trying to look around the woman and see inside the house.

Brophy instantly felt like telling him to clear off back to the station and learn a bit of subtlety.

The tall, dark-haired mother pushed the door closer to the frame, rocking her baby and scowling at the uniformed garda. "Do ye have a warrant? Ye can't just come in here and demand to see who's in the house. At least that much I know."

"We're not trying to invade, Ms...? said Brophy, cracking a half-smile, trying to sound reassuring. "We just need to talk to Michael about someone he knows who might be hurt. We'd really appreciate it if you could tell us where we could find him."

She glared at Brophy, the dark circles around her eyes, giving nothing away about her mood at that moment. "Like I said, he isn't here, and I don't know where he is."

"Okay, I believe you. Could you tell me when was the last time you saw him?"

She paused, and a look of suspicion wasn't far from the surface.

"Tuesday morning, he took off, running out the door like the house was on fire or something. Haven't seen or heard from him since. I'm beginning to hope I don't hear from him again, either."

Brophy heard a door opening upstairs. "Who's there, Sandra?" a woman's voice shouted, hoarse and aggressive. "If that's the cops, don't say a bleedin' thing to them." Barging down the stairs. "Don't dare let them in. They have no right to be here."

The door swung open fully and almost struck the baby, were it not for the young mother jumping back out of the way.

"What the hell do ye want this time? Will ye ever leave that boy alone. He hasn't done a damn thing. One little mistake ten years ago, and you assume anything that happens must be his fault. Will ye ever clear off and leave us alone?"

The smell of cigarettes and booze erupted from the skinny, short-haired woman, who looked to be in her sixties but could have been a decade or more younger. Brophy fought the urge to react and take a step back.

"Mrs Delaney, we're not-"

"It's Ms Foley, actually. I haven't carried that man's name in twenty years," she said, her wrinkled face contorting into a toothless sneer.

"I beg your pardon, Ms Foley. Look, we're not here to take him in. We just need to ask him a couple of questions."

The baby howled in the brief silence following Brophy's words.

"Get that baby inside, will ye. And feed her, for fuck sake. She's obviously starving."

The young mother dropped her head and disappeared into one of the doors at the end of the gloomy hall.

"We haven't a clue where he is, and that's the truth," his mother said, an involuntary look of worry passing across her face. "But you tell him to get back here as soon as ye track him down. That young one hasn't a clue what she's doing with that baby. Jesus, she's only a baby herself, just nineteen years old." She said under her breath, "Me bleedin' nerves."

"What kind of car is he driving these days, Ms Foley?" asked Brophy.

"He's still got that shitty little Fiesta, hasn't he? I've been telling him to change it with ages."

"And when he left on Tuesday morning, was it in the Fiesta?"

"Well, it's not here now, so I presume so."

Another door opened upstairs, and the three gardaí poised. *Maybe it was Delaney*, Brophy thought to himself.

"Mam, who's there at this bloody hour?" shouted the newly broken voice of a teenager.

"It's okay, Connor. Go back to bed. It's only the law looking for that useless brother of yours."

"Tell them to piss off and get a warrant if they want to come in," shouted the boy, then slammed the bedroom door shut again.

A rolling screech emanated from the baby in the other room.

"Look, I have to go and take care of this little one." Her tone softened. "But if you see him, please tell him to come home. He's not usually gone this long without contact. Truth be told, I'm starting to worry a little bit. Tell him I don't care what he's after getting himself into. He can still come home."

"I'll do that, Ms Foley. Thanks for your time," said Brophy with genuine empathy, thinking of all the parents he'd come across over the years who had to suffer in silence, not knowing where their child was.

The three men turned and walked through the postage stamp concrete yard and out the rusted gate. Brophy nodded for the young garda who spoke out of turn to come closer.

"Listen, if you want to get anywhere with people, don't be so eager. Sometimes we only have one chance with these people, and if they shut the door in our faces, we have nothing."

"Sorry, boss. I won't let it happen again."

"I know you won't. We all have to learn some-"

Brophy's train of thought was cut by a vision

drawing closer to where they stood. A dishevelled, gaunt little scrote hobbled down the street towards them, head down, hands tucked into his pockets. *Packo Lenihan. He must have just been released*, thought Brophy, and he clearly hadn't spotted the squad car.

When he was about twenty metres away, he finally raised his head. His bloodshot eyes popped, and he flinched as if considering doing a legger.

"Packo, don't even think about it," said Brophy, and no sooner had he finished speaking than the two uniformed gardaí fast stepped and reached Packo within seconds.

"Ah, for fuck sake."

Brophy approached slowly, rubbing his face with one hand, the four or five days of stubble rasping loudly in his ear. This was an old reflex of his that preceded the adrenalin rush brought on by taking a penalty or making an arrest by physical force.

"Packo, what are you doing here? Shouldn't you be at home sleeping it off?"

"Ah sure, no problem Bott... Detective Brophy. I got great rest in that penthouse you put me up in last night."

"Were you charged?"

"Too right, I was. Have an appointment in the courthouse on Tuesday morning."

"Listen, Packo. If you tell me where Budgie is, I'll make the charges go away."

"You mean he's not home now? Fuck it, anyway," declared Packo, making no attempt to hide the reason why he was there.

"It doesn't take a genius to figure out where you got whatever muck was in your system when we took you in yesterday. Why not tell us now and save yourself a bit of trouble? The pharmacology results will be in by Monday, before your date with Judge Andrews. It'll do your case some good if you cooperate now."

Packo looked as though he struggled to take in what Brophy had said to him. He swayed from side to side, almost banging into one of the two young gardaí on a couple of occasions. He looked up at Brophy, his eyes clouding in and out of focus.

"Hey! Aren't you yer man who used to play the hurling for Waterford? Jeez, you were some player, man. I wasn't bad meself, in my days."

Brophy gave the two uniforms a look that said, "this is pointless; let's get out of here."

"Get yourself home," said one of the gardaí. "There's some serious shit about to go down here. You don't want to be around when it does."

"Ah, sound out, Garda. I'm just headin' into one of me friends houses to play a bit of X-box. We'll see ye later."

Packo turned and walked in the direction in which he'd come, oblivious to his doubling back.

CHAPTER EIGHT

Brophy skirted the city, curving around the corner of The Mall where Reginald's Tower stood, a medieval fortification built by early Viking invaders and the most famed and revered landmark in Waterford. He edged along Parade Quay, looking across the breadth of the River Suir to Ferrybank, his destination, and the home of Maura Walters' uncle, Barry Donahue.

Fifteen minutes later, the GPS on his phone, having guided him away from the town's more built-up area, took him to the leafy suburb, Turanore. The neighbourhood was dotted with over-sized houses, their large gardens landscaped and manicured to perfection. He'd forgotten such a place existed in the city, a sign its crime rate in the last two decades was near zero. Another few minutes of driving and the city seemed like a distant memory.

At the end of a Cul-de-sac, he spotted McCall leaning against her car, smoking a cigarette, whilst chatting on the phone with gestures that suggested it was most certainly a work call. As he drew closer, he observed she had on a pair of slightly tight blue jeans, with a blue shirt and brown and white boating shoes. Brophy briefly thought she could have almost passed for one of the locals, a high-powered businesswoman come-good, or the heiress to old money. But Brophy knew better. She was as working-class as he was but always seemed to carry more of a chip about it than he. Or was that just what he told himself?

"Any signs of life inside?" said Brophy on reaching her at the car.

McCall tossed the half-smoked cigarette to the ground, a little too close to Brophy for comfort, stepped closer to him and stubbed it out with the ball of her foot.

"This place gives me the creeps," she said, staring over his shoulder. "And yes. It looks like all the family are there, and they've gotten a couple more visitors in the ten minutes I've been here."

"Any sign of Donahue?"

"Haven't seen him. How did things go with that scumbag, Delaney?"

"Not present. His family says they haven't seen him since Tuesday morning."

"Interesting. Wonder what he's hiding from?"

"His girlfriend has just had a baby."

"Maybe that's what he's hiding from then?"

"Could be."

"How about the hurling camp? Did they have anything useful?"

"The kid left a little early yesterday. Said he was going into town to pick something up before going to Dublin to stay with his aunt. Left in a black car. Possibly a Mercedes."

"What did the parents drive?"

"Father, a black Mercedes. The mother, a blue Audi SUV."

"We'll get Tech to check out CCTV in the area, see if we can get a positive ID. But probably the father. The industrial estate where the lab is isn't far from Saint Xavier's."

"Shall we do this?" said Brophy, a shudder almost surfacing. One of the things they all hated most about the job, was going to interview a bereaved family member under the suspicion that they could possibly have had something to do with the crime. It was impossible to disguise the approach as anything other than what it is.

They walked across the road to the high cast iron black gate. McCall's hand had just reached up to press the call button on the intercom on one of the towering redbrick pillars holding up the gate when a mechanised sound initiated the opening of the gate. Brophy had a glance around and saw at least two cameras strategically placed on the underside of the pillars overhead.

"Taking no chances, are they?" said McCall.

"Can never be too careful. It's a rough neighbourhood," he replied with a smirk.

McCall let slip an involuntary half-smile, something they'd both tried to avoid in recent years. Another workplace tryst was the last thing either of them wanted, and so coldness generally pervaded.

They walked along the cobbled path, taking in the garden that was tastefully tended to with rose bushes, ferns, and the likes. They crossed the front of the house, a spattering of brickwork facades and windows until they reached the arched, lightly-varnished door. Brophy rang the bell and was greeted in seconds by a tall, slender man in his early sixties, greying black hair, wearing a black v-neck jumper over a white shirt and navy slacks. The first thought that struck Brophy, and probably McCall too, was how grief-stricken the man looked. The lack of visible blood vessels in his eyes told that he likely hadn't cried, but he appeared distraught, nonetheless.

"Barry Donahue?" asked Brophy.

"Yes, I'm Barry Donahue."

"Good morning, Mr Donahue," said McCall. "I'm Detective Sergeant Christine McCall, and this is Detective Sergeant Conal Brophy."

Donahue turned to scrutinise Brophy, surprise evident in his expression. "Conal Brophy? Well, well. My niece and grand-nephew are big fans of yours."

The mention of them appeared to send another wave of grief through him, and he sighed, needing to rein in the sigh from breaking down in tears on the spot.

"Do come in, please. Anything I can help you with, I will to the best of my ability."

"We're so sorry for your loss, Mr Donahue."

Donahue stepped back and gestured them

in. Brophy strode across the large ornate foyer in the direction of murmuring sounds of mourning and disbelief.

"This way please, Sergeants," said Donahue, his outstretched arm guiding them to the other end of the hall. "I'm afraid my family are far too devastated to face strangers right now. I hope you understand."

"Of course," said Brophy, his ears automatically poised to pick up anything out of the ordinary coming from the living room.

Brophy and McCall sat on a plush sofa, their backs to the opened window, a welcomed draft sweeping across them. Donahue had taken them into his library, a small room, the wall adorned with bookshelves full of periodicals and science books. A mahogany desk was positioned near the back wall, where Donahue stood, fixing himself a drink from a bottle he'd pulled from under his work station.

"Can I offer you a brandy?" he said to the detectives.

"No, thanks," said McCall.

He took one large gulp, then refilled the glass, wheeled his desk chair closer to them, facing the detectives and slumped into it.

"This has all come as a devastating shock. I sincerely hope you're close to catching whoever did this and bringing back my nephew."

"We're doing all we can, but the next twenty-four hours are crucial," said Brophy, wanting to get straight into the probing questions but deciding on a little tact instead. "I believe you were very close to your niece, Mr Donahue?"

"Of course. She was like one of my own. And my kids always viewed her as a big sister more than a cousin. Her mother, my sister, passed away when she was thirteen, you see. Breast cancer. And her father wasn't very present in the proceeding years. Then he passed away about seven years ago."

"Did they not have a good relationship?" said Brophy.

"No, nothing like that. She adored him, and he her. But his work took him all over the Middle-East, China, Korea. He spent a couple of months in Ireland a year, and that was about it. She was here for most of her teenage years, and my wife and I loved having her around. She was great with the kids when they were young."

"Mr Donahue, I need to come right out and say this, but do you know of anyone who would want to do this to your niece and her husband?"

Donahue eyed them both for an unusually long time, then spoke. "No, of course not. They were both so hardworking and very family oriented. I can't imagine who would want to inflict this on them."

"Did Jordan have any serious business rivals?" asked Brophy.

Donahue gave a brief scoff before returning to a picture of grief. He took a small sip of brandy.

"I see what you're getting at Detective, and I understand why you need to ask these questions, but it's a waste of time. It's true that maybe twenty-five years ago, his father and I jostled to get ahead of each other in the industry. One could have even argued that we were the best of enemies, but truth be told, I always looked up to Mr Walters. He showed me what could be achieved in a small city like this. Then, by the time Jordan got into the business, there was so much work to go around, our rivalry became obsolete. After Maura married him, we became quite close. We even make recommendations of contracts to each other. So, you're barking up the wrong tree there."

Brophy listened to the explanation but felt there was something a little rehearsed about it. "Sorry, but I had to ask. We'll move on from it."

"That's quite all right, Detective."

"You must be terribly worried about your grand-nephew" said McCall, trying to throw him off and gauge his reaction with such an obvious statement, a tactic Brophy knew well.

Donahue looked directly at her, his cold blue eyes momentarily darting out the window behind her. Brophy followed his sight-line with his own. "Are you expecting someone else?" asked Brophy.

"No. Well, yes. Maybe more family and friends will arrive later to pay their regards." He looked down and nodded, then took another sip. "I was just thinking, if Seán was here now, he'd be out in that garden, whacking a ball off the wall with his hurley."

"Do you know who collected him from hurling camp yesterday?" asked Brophy.

"His mother, I assume. She usually did. Jordan would be far too busy. Even though he runs the place, he's very hands-on in the lab. Sometimes he stays all night."

"When was the last time you saw them?" McCall again.

"Tuesday evening, they came over for dinner. Only Maura and Seán. Jordan was working late again. They stayed till about nine."

"Who was here?" said Brophy.

"The two of them, my wife and I, and my youngest, Aidan."

"Did they seem normal to you?"

"Yes, they were both in a great mood. Seán was raving all through dinner about doing another camp with Jerry Cunningham and about going to Dublin with his aunt this weekend. They were going to some concert in the O2 Arena on Saturday. Seán sat in the living room with Aidan after dinner, looking at videos on YouTube of the singer he was going to see, and we stayed in the kitchen chatting and drinking tea."

"Did Maura drink any alcohol that evening?"

"She may have had a glass of wine or two.

Does that really matter?"

"Probably not," answered McCall.

"Do you know if they were expecting anyone for dinner last night?" asked Brophy.

He hesitated. "From what I understand, Ciara was supposed to be down early in the day and take Seán into town after camp to get a new pair of jeans for the concert. But apparently, she got held up at work." He said the last line with a certain amount of scepticism in his voice, Brophy couldn't help noticing.

"Was it like her to cancel like that?" said Brophy.

"I'm not sure. I don't know her all that well. But Seán certainly thinks she's his guardian angel or something." His face twisted as though he was contemplating saying something else but held back. "I believe she intended on joining them for dinner and then planned to drive Seán up to Dublin straight after they'd eaten."

"She never made it, though," said McCall. "Had to work late."

"So, I've been led to believe."

Brophy and McCall made brief eye contact.

"Mr Donahue, one of the possibilities we have to consider is that Seán saw or heard what was happening in the house and ran off and hid somewhere."

"If that were the case, he would be smart enough to go to the local police station in the village. As he didn't turn up there, I don't believe for a second, that's what happened." He looked about ready to crack at this point. "Someone has taken him, for Christ's sake," he said with a raised voice. "Please, find him before it's too late."

"Sir, we're doing everything we can," said McCall. "We're sorry if this line of questioning is distressing."

"That's quite all right," he said and polished off the two fingers of Brandy left in his tumbler in one lip-curling gulp.

"Just one more question before we leave," said Brophy as he saw McCall ready to get up. "Did Maura ever mention anything about Jordan's friendship with Bobby Quilty?"

Donahue's face dropped, truly caught off guard by the mention of the name. *Bingo*, thought Brophy. *He knows something.*

There was a long pause followed by a stuttered, "Isn't he that drug kingpin I hear mentioned on the news a lot?"

"That's correct. He's currently living in exile in Bahrain. It's come to our attention that he and Jordan go back a long way. There's probably nothing there, but under the circumstances, we need to explore all avenues... So?"

"So what?" asked Donahue, seemingly trying to hide his heavy breathing.

"Has Maura ever mentioned their friendship?"

"No. I don't believe she has. That's

something I think I'd definitely remember."

"Okay, thank you for your time, Mr Donahue. And again, we're really sorry for your loss," said McCall rising to her feet.

"Please, don't get up," said Brophy after Donahue began to follow him up. "We'll let ourselves out."

Not so much as a step taken after gently closing the door behind them, and they heard Donahue break down in anguished sobs.

Whilst Brophy and McCall retraced their steps out of the house and back along the garden path, they gave each other a look that signalled they needed to discuss Donahue's strange behaviour as soon as they got away from that place.

The potential complexity of the case, along with the increasing heat of the day, made Brophy's head spin. He had no doubt that if any of Ireland's major drug cartels had even the vaguest involvement, the NBCI would be down from Dublin to take over the case.

He would never voice his welcoming of that possibility, as he knew every other detective, including Bennett and the Superintendent, would be dead set against any interference in what could be the biggest investigation in the region for many years. Bennett's ambition was matched only by McCall's, and he believed they were both beginning to sense his own growing discontent with being on the force.

A bead of sweat trickled down Brophy's forehead and his thoughts turned to how he should probably get a haircut that week. No sooner had an alternative idea entered his mind, that this case wouldn't give him a minute to spare in the foreseeable future, than he and McCall were nearly blown off their feet by a sudden flash of black metal careening, at high speed, into the driveway.

McCall, never one to hold back when she felt she was wronged, shouted, "Hey, watch it," to the driver through the opened car window.

Brophy's initial observation: it was a C class black Mercedes.

"Watch what? You're the ones walking on *my* driveway," answered the young man, after slamming on the brakes. His eyes were puffy and bloodshot. He'd been crying. "Who are you, anyway?"

"We're detectives assigned to your cousin and her husband's case, Aidan."

The young man's omission to correct Brophy about his name, let Brophy know he'd gotten it right.

Aidan stared at Brophy and sighed, his knuckles white from how hard he clutched the steering wheel. "Have you had any luck finding who did this yet?"

"We're working on it, but maybe you could help us out," said Brophy. McCall was still scowling at Aidan Donahue.

64

He furrowed his eyebrows. "How can I possibly help?"

"Were you aware Jordan Walters was friends with Bobby Quilty?"

Aidan Donahue's expression turned from one of belligerence and sadness to one of nervousness. He broke eye contact with Brophy, facing forward for a moment, thinking of what lies to tell, Brophy surmised.

"I had no idea. And I'm shocked to hear it. Look, I must go and be with my family. This is a terribly difficult time. Please find these people."

With that, he eased the Mercedes slowly past the detectives, and they observed him pick up his phone and make a call before they continued out the gate.

When they reached McCall's car, after a few moments of silence, she said, "Something's definitely going on with these people."

"I agree. Let's give them a day; then we'll attempt to get them into the station."

"Black Mercedes."

"And he didn't even ask about Seán. We need to look into-" Brophy's concentration was cut by his phone vibrating in his pocket. He took it out, immediately noticing it was Bennett. "What's happening?" he said upon answering.

A few seconds passed, and McCall looked on impatiently. Brophy felt the blood drain from his head and became dizzy at the news he'd heard. He pressed the phone off and eyed McCall.

"They've found a boy's hurling jersey with blood on it in the woods near the house. We need to get over there at once."

CHAPTER NINE

The air circulated in a spiralling rush as he raced along the R711, all four windows down in the Saab, the strong breeze still doing very little to settle the mangle of thoughts going through Brophy's mind. The prospect of another missing-young-person case had haunted him for over a decade, and now that nightmare had become a reality. The guilt he'd carried for his own perceived negligence in the investigation into the disappearance of Mel Fanning from Ballyhale village, had burdened him immensely.

As he passed the train tracks on his approach to Waterford's Plunkett Train Station, the words of one of the chief suspects in her disappearance, Maurice Scanlon, echoed in his ears, "Why don't you try the old track? She loved to tease the lads down around there."

He considered calling one of his connections in the NBCI, there and then, to ask if they were already taking an interest in the case, but resisted, knowing there was no conceivable way they weren't. They'd probably have a couple of detectives at the station by the time he'd get back that afternoon.

The journey through the city was less restricted now. Most people had reached their workplaces and the peak shopping time still a couple of hours away. He was rolling down the wooded driveway to the Walters' house within fifteen minutes, paying callous disregard for speed limits.

The area around the house was more crowded than the previous evening. Having passed a few news vans parked outside on the main road, he knew it was only a matter of time before they gained access, and photos of the crime scene made their way around the globe. Such a murder was rare in Ireland. Most murders those days were gangland killings, dealers and hitmen wiping out people with debts, or those who dared encroach on their turf. But this was different. A well-to-do family, gunned down in cold blood, their ten-year-old son nowhere to be found.

He parked at the back of a row of about ten cars, marked and unmarked, and made his way towards Bennett and Halpin, the head of Tech, standing by the white van, talking to McCall. He wasn't surprised she'd made it there before him. She was a rally driver in her free time and came from a family of mechanics. Driving fast for her was as trivial as having a smoke.

"What have you found?" he asked Halpin on reaching the trio. Halpin was a short, thin man, shrewd, and born to do this job. Studied forensic criminology in Britain and worked for the Met in London for ten years before moving back to Ireland to take up a position in the Waterford headquarters.

Halpin went to the back of the van where one of the two doors was opened and returned seconds later, holding a plastic evidence bag. What appeared to be a light blue with dark blue trim garment was folded inside it. *A Dublin jersey.* The family was originally from the capital, and they seemed to maintain strong connections from what he'd observed so far.

"Is there much blood on it?" said Brophy.

"More than a little dribble down the front centre," answered Halpin. "Consistent with a head wound rather than from the body." Brophy's heart sank. "We'll take it back to headquarters soon. Should have more on it by tonight." Halpin had seen it all in his tenure in London but couldn't disguise the disdain on his face.

"Where was it found?" McCall this time.

"Beside a tree, about a hundred and twenty metres west of the house."

"Any other blood sighted around?" Brophy asked.

"None that we've been able to find. But we'll be bringing in the dogs later and scanning the area more thoroughly during the day. Jesus, this heat is unreal," said Halpin, pulling down his white hood and wiping his brow with the back of his hand.

Bennett, who'd been quiet and pensive until then, spoke. "What have you two found out so far?" He eyed Brophy as he said it.

"I talked to the hurling camp coach. Said Seán was there yesterday and nothing unusual about him. He left a little early. Left in a black Mercedes. We assume it was the father's, but we're not sure."

"What?" said Bennett aghast. "The coach didn't see whose car he got into?"

"He said he saw the kid laughing as he got into the car."

McCall said, "The uncle, Barry Donahue, also has a black Mercedes. We saw his son driving it a while ago. They all seemed to be very close to the kid."

"What's the story with this Donahue?" Bennett asked, again looking at Brophy.

"He was definitely distraught, but there was a glimmer of something when we mentioned Bobby Quilty."

"Ah, fuck! Please don't tell me there's a connection with that rat," said Bennett with a slight hiss.

"It's something we can't ignore," said Brophy.

"That'll mean there's no way Dublin won't be involved. We need to crack this one ourselves, Brophy. The upgrade hangs in the balance, and if we want it to go through, we have to show them we don't need their help with big cases. That's imperative. Get to the bottom of this quickly."

Bennett gave Halpin a nod, and the two men

turned on their heels and headed in the direction of the front door of the house.

"Does that wanker even realise I'm a detective?" said McCall, gritting her teeth. "He doesn't trust my judgement one little bit."

"Don't mind him. He's just used to deferring to me. We've been together a long time."

"And it should be you as DI anyway, and he bloody well knows it."

Brophy said nothing, just bit his lower lip.

"Don't let this one get to you, Brophy. It's nothing personal. Keep a distance, and we'll close it together. Find that poor kid. He has to be somewhere." Brophy didn't answer and stared into space. "What are you thinking on this one? I know you have a theory, and it would be good to hear it now before we move on."

Brophy focused on McCall, her blue eyes conveying an almost motherly affection. "I don't have a theory yet. But one thing I'm sure of, and that's the whole Quilty connection has something to do with it. Maybe Walters knew something he shouldn't, or maybe he has some kind of debt he couldn't pay. Can you give your connection in the Drug Squad a call and see if Walters' name has ever come up?"

"Sure. I'll get right-"

Before McCall had a chance to finish, a chorus of yells travelled over from the direction of the converted-barn garage at the opposite end of the house. Brophy and McCall gave each other

71

a quick look then started jogging towards the sound. The garage was a large two-storey building; the walls painted the same magnolia as the main house. The entrance was two well-restored wooden doors that opened out onto a gravelly yard. McCall entered, followed by Brophy.

Brophy immediately felt claustrophobic in the open dark space and had to focus on the light coming through an upstairs window to reorient himself. A mixture of smells struck him. Motor oil from the John Deer sit-down lawn-mower on the far side of the massive room. A faint smell of livestock, from a bygone era, the kind that always stayed in a building like that, no matter how much time has passed. And something more pungent, like raw chemicals mixed with methylated spirits. Trying to catch his breath in the baking heat and blinking rapidly to regain his vision through the raised dust, he attempted to locate where the shouts had come from. A uniformed guard burst in the door after them and almost stumbled to the ground with the sudden change in light from the outside.

"The stairs by the back wall," said McCall and quickly headed in that direction.

Brophy followed, and soon they were scaling ancient rickety stairs that creaked under every footfall. Ascending the stairs, visions of a broken and bloodied body of a child sent a convulsive thud down his legs. His stomach clenched, his heart slowed to resemble the tick of a clock, counting down the horror that awaited them.

McCall reached the top first. Brophy followed right behind, his eye-line revealing a dusty old attic space full of clutter. McCall approached the far corner of the space where the flashlight beam was visible behind a stack of sealed boxes.

"What is it?" asked McCall, and Brophy felt the bile rising in his throat.

"Take a look at this, Detective," came the muffled reply of the white-suited, masked guard who was crouched down, looking into a bygone-era child's pram.

Brophy reached them at around the same time McCall was bending down to take a look at where the light was shining. "What is it?" he said. The question was accompanied by the realisation there was no way a ten-year-old boy could have fit in there.

The white-suited guard pulled back a filthy old cotton blanket further to reveal what looked like a cellophane bag of damp brown sugar. The chemical smell wafted up and coursed through the dead air, making it bitter and strangely antiseptic. Brophy leaned in for a closer look. More footsteps emerged from the creaky stairs.

"Looks like heroin," said McCall.

"Or methamphetamine," replied Brophy. "One of the samples at the DS seminar in Templemore smelled identical to this.

"Jesus Christ. Meth?" said McCall. "That's a first. Are you sure?"

"The stench would certainly point to it being some kind of amphetamine," said the garda. He gently removed the blanket entirely from the pram, revealing four more bags of a similar size.

"Must be about five or six kilos, by the looks of it," said Brophy.

The guard cut in. "More like ten."

"What have we got here?" came Halpin's familiar voice with the London twinge he never quite shook off, despite having left there eight years ago.

"Possibly up to ten kilos of methamphetamine," said McCall.

Bennett appeared over Halpin's shoulder, and now there were six of them huddled into the small corner of the garage attic, staring down at a discoloured pram. "What is it?"

"Class A narcotics. Approximately ten kilos worth," said Brophy.

"Ah, fuck!"

CHAPTER TEN

Back at the incident room, urgent murmurs rose from the gathered group that had doubled in size since the previous night. DS Sally Reagan and Detective Garda Vincent Hogan from the drug squad were now present. They fervently discussed the contents of the bags found by Garda Walsh, the member of the Tech Bureau, who discovered the bags of drugs in the pram. Brophy stood by the filing cabinets watching Kenneally add more signs and photographs to the wall.

"This is turning into a real shit show, is it not, Brophy?" said Kenneally.

Brophy didn't reply but instead focused on the picture of Seán Walters, in his school uniform, directly under snaps of his deceased parents.

"Have they come back with any CCTV on who picked up the boy yesterday?" said Brophy as Kenneally tacked a picture of the bags of amphetamine to the wall.

"I think they might have something, but I'm not sure what yet. If Bennett ever gets the finger out and arrives on time like the rest of us, we might get started and get all the information we need."

Kenneally had barely uttered his last word

when Bennett came storming in through the back of the room, a raging ball of negative energy, wound-up for his usual outbursts of rebukes and rebuttals.

"Okay, everybody, gather round quickly," he said in a volume just shy of all-out shouting. "The NBCI are on their way, and I want to get things straight before they arrive."

Not wanting to add fuel to the fire, those sitting at desks and huddled in small groups immediately dropped what they were doing and formed a horseshoe facing the wall. Brophy stepped to the side to allow Bennett to take centre stage, a position he'd always relished.

"As you're all well aware, there was a large quantity of class A's found on the property of the victims." He half-turned to look at the exhibit photo of the drugs, an involuntary snarl raising his upper lip. "This is by far the biggest ever drugs seizure in the city, so now we have a double murder, a missing child, and what could be a few hundred thousand worth of synthetic amphetamine. A detective from Murder and one from Narcotics are on their way. I want you all out of here, following up on leads by the time they arrive. Is that clear?"

"Yes, Sir," came a few hushed replies from some of the younger members of the squad.

"Sergeant Kenneally is going to give a full rundown of what we know of the time-line, so far, then the rest of you can add what you know.

I want you all to focus, and don't forget a single detail. Write down what you think is important, and don't be shy with suggestions." The last comment forced Brophy to restrain an ironic scoff. They all knew full well how Bennett reacted to ideas, not in line with his thinking on a case, and the abrasiveness that would be directed their way should they dare offer something contrary. It was much more likely the lower ranking detectives and junior gardaí would consult with either Brophy or McCall after the meeting.

So, what are you waiting for, Kenneally, a fucking standing ovation? Let's get this thing going."

"Yes, Sir," said Kenneally, awkwardly getting to his feet and positioning himself in front of the board in such a way he could keep his distance from Bennett, but still be able to point at the exhibits he would talk about easily. A difficult task for a man of his bulk. The heat was almost unbearable for everyone. Kenneally wore it the worst.

"Aright ladies and gentlemen," he started, wringing his hands, as he usually did. But this case wasn't the one to be joking around with. Bennett cut him a vicious look. "Ahra, yesterday morning, Thursday, July 17th, Jordan Walters," he said with a nod to the top of the board where Walters' picture was hung, "arrived at his company, Bioford Laboratory, in the industrial estate, at the usual time of 9 a.m. This has been corroborated by CCTV footage and witness testimonies gathered by Detective Dunford and Garda Mallon this morning. The detective will fill you in on the details of that a little later. We have CCTV footage of Maura Walters passing the local shop, heading in the direction of the city, at around half-past eleven. She returned home at approximately two forty-five. Due to the angle of the camera, the tech team can't be sure if she was alone or had passengers in the vehicle. We can't even be certain it was her driving either time but close up analysis has put it at a high degree of probability."

"Based on what?" chimed Brophy.

"Hair colour and the colour of the clothing she was found in at the crime scene."

Several people in the room made a note of that detail.

"Jordan left his company at eleven-thirty, a little earlier than he had the previous three days, presumably to collect his son from hurling camp at Saint Xavier's field. He returned to the office at about one o'clock. This would have given him enough time to drop the kid home in Woodstown and make it back, no problem. However, his car wasn't picked up on the CCTV during that time. Now, he could have come and gone from the other direction, but that would have meant going through Dunmore East, which wouldn't make a whole lot of sense unless he had something to do on the way."

"Were there any other black Mercedes spotted on the CCTV during that time?" asked Brophy, drawing a quizzical look from Kenneally and a furling of the forehead from Bennett. "I spoke to the hurling coach this morning. Said the kid left training early and got into a black Mercedes. Couldn't be sure who the driver was from the distance he was away."

"Maura Jordan's uncle, Barry Donahue, who they're all very close with, also drives a black Merc," added McCall.

"We'll have them recheck the tapes as soon as possible on that one," said Kenneally.

"Back to the time-line," instructed Bennett with growing contempt.

"Erm, of course. We haven't picked up on what Maura Walters was doing at that time yet, but every camera in the area is being checked. We're experiencing the usual delays with the phone company, but the court has issued the paperwork, so we should hear back on that soon. Hopefully, get a better read on where she was. Jordan left the lab at five-thirty and was captured on the pub CCTV returning home sixty-seven minutes later."

"It's a twenty-minute drive to Woodstown. Are the other forty-seven minutes accounted for?" demanded Bennett, clearly frustrated with the lack of information on the victims' movement during the day.

"Again, we're working on that. Hopefully know more by the end of the day. After that, all we know is the gunshots were heard by the neighbour out walking his dog. He called the local sergeant who was there within minutes. And we know what happened from there."

"Thanks, Sergeant Kenneally," said Brophy, giving him a look that suggested he sit down as quickly as possible.

McCall took a few steps forward, readying herself to address the small crowd with what she and Brophy had learnt that morning. Bennett turned dramatically, half-blocking her approach and said to Brophy, "Detective Brophy. Can you fill us in on what you found out this morning?"

Brophy cut McCall a regretful look as she stopped in her tracks, sullen and stony-faced.

Brophy hesitated for a moment, felt a cold chill trailing up his back. His vision became starry, and the thought of all those eyes on him, in his current predicament, exacerbated the slow descent.

"When you're ready, Brophy. We haven't got all day," said Bennett.

The comment snapped Brophy out of it. He focused on Garda Mallon in the background and took a deep breath. "This morning, at nine-thirty, I paid a visit to the family home of Michael 'Budgie' Delaney in the Gleann Fia estate. It was reported that his Ford Fiesta was seen several times on the CCTV in the pub yesterday. He wasn't present when I called to the family home, and his mother claimed not to have seen him since Tuesday morning."

Again, many in the room made a note of this information.

One of the Drug Squad interjected, "I heard he knocked up a Polish girl recently. Might be worth looking into."

"His long-term girlfriend has just had a baby, too. She was furious he wasn't around to help out." Brophy momentarily felt familiar walls of dark shadow close in on his periphery and took another breath to keep composed. "Before that, I went to Saint Xavier's to talk to the hurling camp coach. The boy attended all week but left early yesterday. Apparently, he was going to town to pick up new clothes for a trip to Dublin with the aunt, Ciara Walters, this weekend. Ms Walters was late coming down from Dublin, and we're not a hundred percent sure who picked up the boy at quarter to twelve. It was likely his father, but we need to be sure of this. He was laughing, getting into the car, so definitely someone known to him. And, as Detective McCall already mentioned, the uncle, Barry Donahue also has a black Merc. His nineteen-year-old son drives it too, so we need to look into their whereabouts at lunchtime yesterday. We went to the family home of Barry Donahue this morning. McCall can fill you in on the details," he said, giving her the nod.

"That won't be necessary," said Bennett, his impatience now a ticking time-bomb, ready to wipe out the whole room. "Continue as you were, Brophy."

"The Donahue's live over in Ferrybank, in a very exclusive community. He's in the same line of business as the Walters' family and was the main competitor of Jordan Walters' father, now deceased, when they both started out in the eighties. As you all know by now, Maura Walters is his niece and lived with Barry Donahue's family for much of her teen years. Her mother passed away when she was young, and her father travelled a lot for work. Now, also deceased. When interviewing Ciara Walters last night, she mentioned her brother was a long-time friend of Bobby Quilty."

An audible gasp and a trickle of hisses permeated the air in the ever-increasing stuffiness of the overcrowded room.

"When we asked Donahue if he knew anything about this, he became visibly uncomfortable. He then denied any knowledge of the friendship. In light of the discovery in the Walters' garage today, the connection with Quilty will be one of our main lines of enquiry. Quilty has been hiding out in Bahrain for over six years now. He did a runner when the NBCI was said to have accumulated a fair amount of evidence implicating him and one of his crew in the murder of Detective Sergeant Ross O'Malley in a drug raid in the Drogheda in 2012. We need to trace-"

Bennett interrupted, "DS Reagan," he said into the assembled crowd, yet barely acknowledging Reagan's presence, "Has there been any sign of methamphetamine on the streets recently?"

"Sir, we haven't made any arrests of anyone in possession of meth, but we've been starting to hear whispers from a couple of informants and some worried parents. We also took in Packo Lenihan yesterday, and he was out of it, but not in the usual way."

"Well, that's hardly something new, is it?" hissed Bennett. "Where is he now?"

"We released him this morning."

"That's just fucking great," said Bennett. DS Reagan lowered her head.

"I bumped into Packo as I was leaving Budgie Delaney's house. Looked like he was heading straight towards Delaney's place but thought better of it when he saw me. I think it was the right choice to release him. Now we can keep an eye on him, see if he leads us to the whereabouts of Delaney or anywhere else useful. I assume a blood test was taken, DS Reagan."

Reagan perked up again. "Yes, Detective Brophy. It's due to go off to the lab this afternoon."

"Let's prioritise that, get it done as soon as possible, see if it matches the haul we found in the garage," said Brophy.

"Detective Dunford. Yourself and Garda Mallon went to Bioford this morning," said Bennett, his tone softened, talking to the young detective he'd taken under his wing. "Can you fill us in on what you learnt there?"

"Of course, Inspector." Dunford didn't bother moving to the front but instead puffed out his chest, making him even more imposing than he already was. Everyone turned to face him at the back of the group. "Firstly, there was mostly shock amongst the employees of Bioford. People were standing around, crying, or scratching their heads in disbelief. The receptionist, a fine young thing from Limerick, seemed a bit too upset if ye know what I mean? Like she'd lost the love of her life or something, which was odd, as she's only been working there for the past three months. Worth following up. There's four senior managers under Walters. Three of them are older gentlemen and have been there since the old man founded the place. They were in utter disbelief. But the other one, a Dublin 4 chap, who knows Walters since school, had a very different reaction." Dunford glanced at Mallon, who was nodding in agreement at his statement. "Came across as though he wasn't all that surprised, wouldn't you say, Garda Mallon?"

"That was certainly my feeling," she replied.

"David Hughes. He's been with the company since 2008."

"Okay, that's good work, Detective," said Bennett. "Once we've made a bit more sense of this whole thing, we'll follow up with Mr Hughes and the receptionist."

Dunford nodded to Mallon as if giving her permission to speak. Bennett cut her a sharp look.

"What is it, Garda Mallon?" said Brophy.

"There was one more thing. We were looking around, and I walked into one of the labs. There was a white-coated technician in there, working on something when I stepped in the door unbeknown to him. When he turned and caught sight of me and the uniform, he dropped a test tube and looked like he was considering bolting out the nearest window. I asked him what he was working on, and he could barely answer through the stuttering. Eventually said he was testing a food product from a local meat processing facility. When I asked him what he thought about hearing Walters had been killed, he became somewhat defensive and claimed he only knew him a little, was just an intern, and Walters didn't give him the time of day. Maybe he just doesn't like the police, but he was far too nervous for someone with nothing to hide."

"Well done, Garda Mallon," said McCall. "If Walters was producing narcotics in the lab, he surely would have needed some assistance. Finding that person, or people might be the key to unlocking this."

"Detectives Reagan and Hogan, after we receive a full analysis on the drugs, I want you two to interview the intern," ordered Bennett, directing the order more to Hogan than to Reagan. "Okay, everyone. I expect you all working overtime this weekend. We can't waste a single second on this. I'll be doing a press conference with Superintendent Russell in a couple of hours. If any of you learn something significant before then, let me know immediately. If you can't get hold of me, pass the information on to Detective Brophy."

Brophy knew exactly what that meant. Bennett would be acting as if he were leading the investigation and taking all the credit, whilst Brophy would be the one heading up all details of the case. A nod that usually would have cast a certain amount of frustration over Brophy, but this time he thought it irrelevant, given that the NBCI was on the way and would take over anyhow.

"I believe you've all been given your briefs," said Bennett. "We've plenty of hours of daylight left today. I suggest you make the best of them."

"And let's make finding the boy a top priority," added Brophy. Bennett gave him a look as if to say that was obvious.

"Every known druggie, every street thug, every sex offender is to be treated with suspicion. Question as many of them as you can," said

Bennett. "And needless to say, tracking down that hard-man arsehole, Budgie Delaney, is imperative. I want him off the street and in here for questioning. The eyes of the country and possibly the world will be on us on this one. Let's show them we're more than capable of bringing these scumbags down. Alright, that's it. Dismissed." After a few silent beats, he shouted, "Well, what are you all waiting for? Get out there and solve this damn thing."

Most of the twenty or so people in attendance turned and headed for the door, leaving only a few detectives hanging back.

"Reagan and Hogan have something to tell us before you all head back out there," said Bennett. "This information comes from the top and is to be kept in this room for now."

DS Reagan perked up and glanced back towards the door to make sure everyone else had left. "We've been working closely with the Drug Squad in Dublin the last couple of months due to several sightings of Clarence Veale in the area recently. Veale is said to be Quilty's right-hand man and has been for many years but has always done well to keep himself out of the public gaze. His name has hardly been mentioned, even by some of the more bottom-feeding tabloids."

McCall asked, "Has he been seen with anyone in particular?"

"Not really, no. He was tailed leaving Dublin, but officers there didn't want him to know he was being followed, so let him go and put the word out to other drug divisions in the south to keep an eye out for him. He was picked up on a traffic camera just outside the city, and then again passing the bus station."

"Why the hell wasn't I informed of this?" said Bennett, his face reddening.

"Orders from the top, Inspector," interjected Detective Hogan. "We were instructed to tell absolutely no one about it and to just keep our eyes and ears open. The Superintendent knows all about it. There's been a big operation against him for years. He's an elusive beggar."

"And there's been more sightings of him?" said Brophy.

A couple of unconfirmed reports from one of our informants, but nothing concrete. There hasn't been any more footage since those two times," said Reagan.

"Can they bring him in for questioning? Find out where he was last night?" asked Bennett.

"Not gonna happen, Sir," said Hogan. They're afraid he'll do a runner like Quilty if they put the fear in him too much. They'll only bring him in if they have something solid that can put him away. Getting to Quilty somehow is their main objective. Ross O'Malley was a popular copper in Drogheda. Came from a long line of gardaí. They're determined to get someone for it."

"We're all aware of who the O'Malley's are,

Detective Hogan," said Bennett with a sharp edge.

"The Narcotics detective coming down from Dublin said he'd give us more details when they get here."

"Okay, back out there with ye," said Bennett. "It's forecast to be a roaster this weekend, and the city is going to be thronged with people. Try not to make a scene, but if ye have to, then bust some heads."

Everyone nodded in agreement without saying a word.

"There's one more thing, Inspector," said Reagan.

"What is it?" asked Bennett.

"Veale has only one conviction to his name. When he was eighteen, he was done for molesting a nine-year-old boy. There's been rumours about him ever since."

Brophy made eye contact with McCall. They'd surely had the same thought.

CHAPTER ELEVEN

"What's the plan of action, Boss?"

"I told you before not to call me that," said Brophy with a forced smile at McCall, who he knew was trying to get a rise out of him. "We're equal in rank, so how about you lead the way this time?"

"We could head out to Woodstown and have a chat with the local sergeant. I'd like to hear his view on what's happened."

"Good thinking. I thought he might have been at the briefing here today."

Voices were being raised, as a dozen other officers were getting into squad cars where Brophy and McCall stood talking in the station's car park. There was partial relief from the heat outside the stuffy incident room, but Brophy still felt agitated.

"I can't wait to see Bennett play second fiddle to the Dubs. That prick has it in for every woman in this place."

"Don't let him get to you," said Brophy, then rubbed a bead of sweat from his forehead.

"I'll try my best, but it's hard with some of the shit that creep gets up to."

"What do you mean? What has he done?"

"Nothing. Forget about it."

Brophy knew better than to press her any

further.

"Drink after talking the Gough?"

Brophy's stomach tensed, and he broke eye contact with McCall.

"Sorry, can't tonight. Having dinner with the folks."

"Oh. That's nice. Tell them I said 'hello.'" She looked over his shoulder, and the smile that had crept across her face talking about Brophy's parents dropped to a tight-lipped scowl. "Speaking of the arsehole himself, here comes trouble."

Brophy looked back and saw Bennett coming out the rear door of the station and heading in their direction. By the time he looked back, McCall was already on her way to her car.

"See you at Woodstown Station in twenty," she said, then threw Bennett brief dagger eyes.

"Conal, wait up a moment," called Bennett from twenty feet back, stopping Brophy's attempted dash for his car.

He turned slowly, not sure if the sigh was audible or not. "What is it, Inspector? We're just about to head out and talk to Sergeant Gough."

"Gough? Why would you bother with that? We've gotten all we can out of him."

"You never know. There's often a detail, no matter how small, that we can miss. I want to have another look around the house too. It's been swarming with people every time I've been there so far."

"Fair enough. Whatever you think will help close this thing." Bennett looked around awkwardly. "Look, I wanted to have a word about these Big City Coppers on their way down."

Brophy was momentarily distracted by the raucous revving of McCall's Audi, and her erratic screeching of tyres, pulling out of the car park. "Don't worry about them. They're not going to push us aside just like that."

"That's not what I wanted to talk about." He clenched his mouth shut and took a deep breath. "I heard they'll be keeping a close eye on you during this investigation."

"On me? Why, what have I done?" Brophy asked aghast, and nervous at hearing the news.

"You haven't done anything. That's not why they're interested in you."

"What's up with them, then?"

"From what I understand, the assistant commissioner has had an eye on you for a while, and he's considering making you an offer."

"An offer?"

"To join some new squad, they're putting together in the capital. Little is known about it yet. Top secret kind of stuff. Bloody wankers, think they're the FBI or something. So, what do you think?"

"I don't know. It's a bit of a shock to hear this now. No. I'm not up for it."

"That's what I like to hear. We can't lose our

best investigator when this upgrade hangs in the balance. The inspector position has your name on it as soon as I'm made superintendent. You know that, right?"

"About that, I'm not sure I'll still be here by then."

"What the hell are you talking about? Did you get another offer?"

"No. I'm thinking of getting out. Leaving the force. I have enough of all the bullshit."

"I can't believe what I'm hearing. What would you possibly do? You were made for this job. All you need is a drinking problem and a scar across your face, and you'll be the complete copper."

Brophy let out a dry laugh, and for a fleeting moment, remembered why they had been good friends way back when they first joined.

"Really though? Are you honestly thinking of quitting?"

"Yes, I am."

"I don't know what to think right now." Bennett suddenly became serious and authoritarian. "Well, you can't leave. Not until this upgrade is done. You'll be letting every young officer in this place down if you hightail. For some reason, they all seem to look up to you. Maybe because of your Munster final medals. But don't bottle on us before things are settled here."

Brophy gritted his teeth and had to fight off

the urge to chin him there and then. He couldn't believe Bennett used that word against him. He knew it was calculated and intentional like most things Bennett did and said those days.

"Don't worry. I'll work night and day assisting the NBCI with you on this one."

Bennett took a step closer to him, now face to face, and looked down his nose with utter contempt at the shorter man. "You be very fucking careful what you say to me."

Brophy clenched his fists, ready to engage with his physically more imposing superior officer. "This is exactly why I want out, you see? Out there, we have to deal with all kinds of scum, and in here, it's not much different."

Bennett rotated his body slightly to the side as if lining up to take a swing. As his shoulder budged to raise his arm, a familiar voice shouted down from the third-floor window behind them.

"Detective Inspector Bennett. Get in here now. Our guests arrive in ten minutes," blared the superintendent, the fury in his voice echoing around the yard.

Bennett took a step back, but Brophy didn't budge. "I'll be right there, Sir."

He turned, keeping a stinging glare at Brophy for a few seconds, then headed back the way he came.

CHAPTER TWELVE

The Woodstown Garda station was a small two-storey house, painted pale yellow, and set back from a narrow country road, in a small garden. It could have been mistaken for just another house, were it not for the blue and gold insignia of An Garda Síochána, nailed to the wall beside the blue door. The white squad car was parked in the single space next to the building, so Brophy pulled up behind McCall, who was parked on a grassy patch across the road, smoke billowing out her window.

"I've been sitting here for almost ten minutes. What kept you?" she asked as he approached the open window.

"Speed limits and civic responsibility."

"Speed limits don't count in urgent police matters."

"What's your excuse the rest of the time?"

"What did Inspector Tool want, anyway?"

"Not much. Just asked me to keep an eye on you."

"Yeah, that wouldn't surprise me in the least. Probably thinks I might break a nail and get all emotional."

Brophy opened the driver's door. "Shall we?"

She chucked the lit cigarette down near his

feet, slid out her seat in a swift movement, and began crossing the road. Brophy slammed her door shut and stubbed the cigarette. "You'll start a forest fire in this damn heat. Put out your smokes properly."

"Is that an order, Boss?" she said without a hint of irony.

On reaching the door, they found it locked, not unusual for such a station in the sticks that likely also had rudimentary living quarters. Brophy rapped the heavy brass knocker against it. Almost twenty seconds had passed before they heard footsteps shuffling towards them.

"Detectives," said Gough on opening the door, "Sorry to keep you waiting."

"No problem, Sergeant Gough. I hope it's not a bad time," said Brophy.

"It's a terrible time, Detective Brophy. Two people have been murdered on my watch, and an innocent young boy is missing."

Gough bowed, clearly dejected by the events of the last twenty-four hours. He was a large man with just a few tufts of black hair rounding the back and sides of his block head. He looked as though he might have been an athletic specimen in his day, but the years were catching up on him fast. He wore his uniform, but the shirt was untucked, and Brophy guessed he'd just been having a nap.

"Please come in, Detectives. I'm glad you're here. I've been kept pretty much in the dark today, which hasn't helped matters in the least."

They entered a tiny reception area with a small counter and a narrow hall flanked by a narrower staircase. It felt crowded with the three of them standing there.

"Come in here to the meeting room," said Gough and ushered them down the hall.

They entered what felt more like the living room of a shut-in. A bare, polished teak table sat in the middle with four fold-out chairs surrounding it. Little light penetrated the small sole window, but the one-foot squared window opened at the top, whipped up a surprisingly pleasant draft, all the same. Brophy could easily imagine the appeal of working in such a station.

As if reading Brophy's mind, Gough said, "There used to be three full-time guards here back in the day. Someone at the station twenty-four hours. They'd have known the names of every man, woman, and child in a five-mile radius. They'd take calls any time of night, whether it was to break up a fight between quarrelling brothers or assist the local vet delivering a foal. Now?" he scoffed, "Lucky if we know half the people who live a five-minute walk from here. Come next or near their houses, and they get all defensive. No sense of community in this country anymore."

"Were the Walters like that?" asked McCall, the abruptness of the question snapping Gough out of his pining.

He looked at her, his eyes full of sorrow. "No, actually. They weren't. They were some of the most decent folks around here. Always salute you with a smile coming down the road. The few times I had to call into their place, they were very welcoming, always offering tea and biscuits. And the lad-" He folded in on himself and seemed half his formidable stature. "A grand little fella, he is."

"Sergeant, have you ever spotted Michael Delaney out here before?" asked Brophy.

"Can't say I have. We get that type out here from the city, the odd time. They head into the woods or down to one of the beaches to smoke their reefer. I've busted a couple of them over the years, but they generally park in a way that they can see me a mile off and get rid of the stuff. But this Delaney fella, I haven't seen."

"How about any 'D' reg cars? In particular, high-end vehicles."

"We tend to get quite a lot of them passing through, alright. Especially in this weather we're having. A lot of wealthy folk from Dublin have summer houses around here. Others come down for the weekends and stay in Dunmore or Tramore. Why do you ask, Detective? Is it something to do with the hubbub around the house today?"

"Have they not told you what they found, Sergeant?" asked McCall.

"No, they haven't. What did ye find?"

McCall glanced at Brophy, and his expression gave the go-ahead to explain.

"In the Walters' garage, in an old pram, a few kilos of amphetamine was found. Nothing is certain yet, but it's suspected that Jordan Walters may have been manufacturing it in his laboratory in the city."

Disbelief and dismay sagged Gough's already drooping features. He slumped into one of the chairs. "Well, Jesus, Mary, and Joseph. I suppose it should be no great surprise at this stage, but God Almighty, why would a family who has it all get involved in something like that?"

"That's what we're hoping to find out," said Brophy. "Did you know Jordan's father?"

"I didn't. I only took up this role a while after he passed."

"Where were you before that?" asked McCall.

"Drogheda. Almost twenty years after doing my first few years in Dublin. Just like yourself, Detective Brophy. I knew your Sergeant Cusack in Store Street. Spoke very highly of you, he did."

Brophy hoped the cringing sensation he felt inside wasn't projected to physical manifestation. "We were told the Walters reported some burglaries a while back. Can you shed any light on what happened?"

Gough's eyes shot up, deep in thought. "Not much, Detective. They called me around last

September, I believe it was. Said the door had been left open and some things were clearly out of place, but nothing was missing. A similar thing happened about three weeks later, but this time a laptop and some jewellery were pinched. I advised them to install a camera system. Heaven knows they could afford it. They said they would, but it seems they never got around to it. Pity really."

"Don't suppose there were any clues as to who it might have been?"

"Unfortunately not. But it wouldn't surprise me if it was some of the aforementioned city druggies. There's easy access to the property from the beach."

"What's the closest car park to that beach?" said McCall.

"It's a long beach, about a quarter of a mile. The car park is on the far end."

"And you say the neighbour was out walking his dog at the time?"

"That's right, but I doubt he would have driven to the car park to go for a walk. He only lives down the road and usually cuts through the woods to get onto the beach."

"His name, again?" asked Brophy.

"Sam Harrington. Old gentry, gone poor since the family's money ran out a few decades ago. Decent sort of chap, though."

"I think we should have a chat with him soon," said McCall. "Can you tell us what he said when he called, Sergeant Gough?"

"His tone was very casual. I don't think he suspected anything untoward, but he knew the Walters weren't gun people at the same time. Told me he heard four or five shots and a scream. Expected it was someone in the wood, arsing around. But my internal sensors buzzed the moment I heard it. No one had ever gone into those woods shooting, as far as I know. I bolted outside into the car and was there in a few minutes, and, well, you know what I found."

"Thanks, Sergeant Gough," said Brophy. I hope we can work closely together on this."

"Absolutely, Detective. I'm going back out on the door to door interviews in a moment. I was out earlier but had to come back for a quick rest. Didn't get much sleep last night, you see."

"That's understandable," said McCall. "We'll let ourselves out."

Gough sprung to his feet and shook hands with the two detectives before they headed out.'

CHAPTER THIRTEEN

Brophy's childhood home was in a housing estate, built in the seventies, on the outskirts of Dunabbey, the county's largest town besides Waterford City. He sat at the dining table, as he had as a child, and his mother served him a lukewarm dinner from the oven — beef stew with carrots and potatoes, his favourite of his mother's many dishes growing up. Having promised his parents he'd be there by seven o'clock, he arrived just after eight-thirty. His mother was glued to the latest reality dance contest on TV when he finally turned up but was delighted with his appearance, giving no sign of annoyance at his lateness.

"Where's Dad?" he asked after devouring the first half of his generous helping of stew, without a word spoken.

"Where do you think he is? Out in that shed of his, pottering about. I'll call him in after you've finished."

"No need. I'll go out to him. How are the rest of them?"

"Molly's doing great in Sydney. I don't think she'll ever want to come home. Why would she want to come back to this place anyway? Nurses are treated a lot better out there."

"And the lads?"

"They're all doing great. Busy out with the kids and work and all the rest of it. But they still have time to call us at least once a week," said his mother, tongue in cheek. "The only one of our four kids around, and we speak to you the least often."

"Sorry, Mam. They have me working crazy hours these days."

"That's what you always say. Laura was here all afternoon."

Brophy shut his eyes tight and cursed under his breath, having just been reminded his seventeen-year-old daughter was also due to have dinner with them.

"When was the last time you spoke to her, Conal? Poor girl's heart is broken."

"A few days ago, I think. I'll give her a call tomorrow. I promise."

"Why wait until tomorrow?"

He started spooning more of the stew into his mouth to avoid answering.

"I saw Bennett and Russell give a press conference on the six o'clock news. Terrible what's happened to those people. I suppose they have you working on it?"

"I don't want to talk about it right now. It's a bloody mess, and there's a child missing."

"You never know when they'll go," she said, looking down and wringing her hands.

A surge of unspeakable feelings caused tension throughout Brophy's jaded body, and how much he wanted to comfort his mother, he couldn't tell. He rose warily to his feet. "I'll go out and have a chat with Dad. Thanks for dinner, Mam. It was lovely."

"Oh, just leave it there," she said as he attempted to take the plate from the table and set it in the kitchen. "Go out to your father. He'll be glad to see you."

Brophy went out the back door to the small yard that was half taken up by a low-ceilinged shed his father built by himself in the eighties. He opened the grey plywood door and entered the dimly lit workspace. His father was bent down over a wooden work desk, made out of discarded pallets and offcuts of wood he used to build cabinets in all the three bedrooms of the house.

"Hey, Dad."

"How's it going, Conal? Did you have a bite to eat?" he said without looking up from what he was pinpoint focused on.

"I did, yeah. What are you working on there?"

"Laura was here earlier."

"I know. Mam told me."

"She has her driving test in a couple of weeks."

That was news to Brophy. "Yeah? I think she mentioned something about that."

"She said you were supposed to take her out for a few lessons."

"You know how it is? I'm mad busy with

work at the moment. I'll give her a call tomorrow and arrange something."

"That'd be nice. Pass me that half-inch chisel there?"

Brophy handed his father the chisel from its place hanging on the wall. "A bishop?"

"That it is." His father held the light-brown stone up to the light and examined it with one eye closed. "Nearly have a full set complete."

"What will you do with it?"

"I don't know." He lowered his head and started shaving fine layers off the stone once more. "I can't play chess and I have no intention of learning. Maybe I'll donate it to the Lyons Club charity raffle in September. Stuff like this sells for a high price."

"Why not sell it yourself and keep the money. Take Mam over to see Ger in England."

His father stopped in the middle of what he was doing and looked at his son like he had lost the plot. "But sure, I can take your mother to England any time." He turned back to what he was doing.

"I wanted to ask you something."

"Ask away."

"Remember that time I went missing when I was eight?"

"You were nine. And yes. Of course, I remember it. You were gone for over twenty-four hours. A parent doesn't forget something like that."

"Did you ever talk to Tim Phelan about what happened?"

"We asked him at the time how a child could have gotten locked in his coal bunker in the middle of winter without him noticing. He said he didn't light the fire that day and never heard a single thing coming from the bunker."

"Did you believe him?"

His father looked up at him and creased his brow in a look of confusion. "Why wouldn't I believe him?"

"I don't know."

"You kids were always messing around on their property in those days. Taking a shortcut down to the beach or playing hide and seek in the trees. You must have taken a look in the bunker, and the door slammed shut and locked you in for the day. Why are you asking me about this now, anyway?"

"It's just I have dreams about it sometimes."

"Since when?"

"Recently enough. In the dream, Mr Phelan pushes me into the bunker and shouts down that he's going to teach me a lesson, then slams the metal door shut. It's made me question what exactly happened that day."

His father stood up straight and turned to fully face him for the first time. Shorter in stature than his son, he was an imposing figure when serious. "Listen Conal. If I ever thought for a second Tim Phelan did something like that to you, or any of my kids, he wouldn't still be in the land of the living." His nostrils flared as he said it. Then he took a deep breath to. "Is this about that young boy who's gone missing? Or maybe that girl who was never found? These things can come back and play tricks on a person's mind, you know? You need to take care of your mental health, son. That's what everyone says these days, isn't it? Be compassionate to yourself and all that bollocks."

"I suppose so."

"Any idea who might have killed those people and taken the kid, then? Your pal, Bennett, didn't seem so sure of himself on the news this evening. Probably expects you and the public to do all his dirty work for him again."

"He's not so bad. He's got a lot of pressure on his shoulders."

"Yeah. Pressure doing the job that should have been yours. I'll never understand why you signed up with that shower of maggots, anyway. You could have made a fine solicitor."

"It wasn't for me, Dad. I didn't want to talk about the law for a living."

"I know that. Pass me the polishing rag there."

Brophy handed him a small black square of sponge-like material, and his father began delicately rubbing it against the handcrafted bishop piece in his hand. "Did you see the Sunday Game on telly the other day?"

"No. I never watch it."

"They had a small feature about the Munster final in '03. Showed you making the block and scoring the point, twice."

"Jesus, will they ever get sick of showing that? It's done a hundred times a week on fields up and down the country."

"Not in Munster finals, though." He looked up at his son from his crouched position, the uplight reflecting off his glasses. "That's your problem, Conal. You don't know how to see any of the good in what you do. I can only hope I didn't make you like that."

"I best be going, Dad. I have a busy weekend ahead of me. They have us working overtime until we catch whoever murdered those people."

"Well, off you go then. See you next Friday, yeah?"

"Yeah, I'll be here."

Brophy headed out of the shed without another word.

As he circled the housing estate, he thought about the events of the day; all the people he'd interviewed, the briefing back at the station, and for a brief moment, felt overwhelmed by the complexity of the case. The heat had somewhat subsided, but the blazing redness of the sky beyond the stretches of fields leading out to sea before him predicted yet another scorcher the next day.

He turned the corner onto Strand Road, and before he could register what had happened, the brakes of his car screeched, and a thud from the front of it striking something reverberated in the warm air.

"Slow down there, young Brophy," came a familiar yet increasingly croaky voice. "You're not on the playing pitch now, charging down some Corkonian wild-man," he said and chuckled at his cleverness, his clipped accent doing nothing to help the irritation Brophy was feeling at not having looked at the road ahead of him.

Come to think of it — he always drifted to another place whilst driving on the road where the Phelan's estate loomed on the horizon. The hundred-metre long, high stone wall flanked by age-old conifer and sycamore trees was the scene of his most troubling childhood memory.

Brophy pushed the button to open his window further. His hand trembled. "Mr Phelan, I'm sorry about that. I don't know where I was just then."

"I know where you were. You were behind the wheel of this automobile, driving like a madman." Phelan leaned his six-foot-four broad body down towards the open window. His eyes were a piercing cold blue, and his wild curly hair shot out at all angles from underneath his peaked cap. "I should probably call the police and tell them there's a joyrider in the neighbourhood, causing havoc." The power of his laugh automatically straightened his body, and then he came back down for more. "Although I guess you'd have the connections to get yourself out of that one. How are you keeping anyhow, young Conal? We don't see you around these parts much anymore."

"I keep myself busy. You know how it is." Brophy wanted nothing more but to get out of there.

"Terrible business, what's going on down near the City, isn't it? It's all over the news. Even saw it on Sky News before I came out for my evening stroll. Any idea who did it? Or wait, actually. Don't tell me. That'll ruin the surprise, won't it? I love a good mystery," he said, looking more and more menacing by the second. "It's not the same around here these days, you know, Brophy? No kids running around like they used to. You and your posse used to be a right bunch, I tell ye. Racing around my place, tormenting the life out of me."

"We were only children, Mr Phelan. I'm sure we couldn't have been that bad," Brophy said and instantly regretted engaging in the kind of double-talk exchange Phelan thrived on.

"Oh, you think so, do you? My elderly mother probably wouldn't have agreed that you weren't too bad. Scared the life right out of her half the time."

"I have to be getting on anyway, Mr Phelan. Busy weekend ahead of me."

Phelan leaned down more and rested his arm on the window frame. His large head seemed to take up the entire opening. "You were always the ring leader, Brophy. Always the popular one everyone wanted to follow around. The hurling star who couldn't do a thing wrong. Little fuckers like you got away with everything," he hissed, his jagged yellow teeth now showing, "just because you could hit a ball with a stick whilst a bunch of like-minded Neanderthals chased after you. Well, I taught you a lesson good and proper, didn't I?"

"And what lesson was that?" Brophy said, a surge of reptilian fight or flight bracing his body for action.

A broad smile lit up Phelan's face like a demented clown who was never out of character. "I told your mother and father, and they gave you a right talking to, I'm sure."

"Always nice bumping into you, Mr Phelan. I hope you have a nice summer."

"You too, young Conal," he said, then stood up straight and backed away from the car. "Now go and find that boy. You never know where someone might have hidden him. Sometimes it's in the most obvious place."

Brophy released the clutch and pulled away from Phelan, slowly at first, cruising past the play place of so many happy memories of his youth, and one that spoiled them all.

CHAPTER FOURTEEN

The first light of morning delivered a shock of searing heat, a cold realisation the young boy was still missing and likely terrified, and an acute pulsating headache. Brophy's car journey along the coast road, towards the city, was like driving through a pitch-black tunnel, with images of faceless victims rushing at him from a distant pinhole of light. The beaches and coves along the route were already beginning to receive their first weekend guests, basking in the heatwave sweeping the country. His phone started to vibrate in its dashboard holder. He was glad for the distraction.

"Morning, Sergeant Brophy," said the recognisable voice of Garda Mallon. "There's just been a sighting of Packo Lenihan by a guard coming off night duty. He tailed him for a while but didn't want to scare him off. He last saw him heading into People's Park. He's known to kip-out there, near the playground or the skating ramps. Thought maybe he might know the whereabouts of Michael Delaney."

"Good thinking, Garda Mallon. I'll head over there first thing."

After ending the call with Mallon, he pressed McCall's number and told her of the change of plan. They agreed they'd both reach there in about fifteen minutes. Brophy would enter from the Park Road entrance, McCall from the opposite side via the People's Park Bridge, in an attempt to cut Packo off if he caught sight of them and tried to escape.

Brophy parked by the cover of the stone wall perimeter and couldn't help glancing back at De La Salle College. Built on an incline, soaring above the city, the century-old five-storey building was the largest all-boys secondary school in the county, and the grounds on which many of his best youth games were played, on its pristine hurling field.

Brophy decided on a thin, light blue cotton polo neck that morning, hoping to avoid the drenching of wearing a heavy button-down shirt as the previous day, but already it was sticking to his back and upper chest. He pulled it in and out several times to ventilate inside, to little avail.

He turned to face the park and made a quick scan of the expanse of the area. He only spotted a few people out walking their dogs, three individuals stretched out on the lawn sunbathing, and two Spanish-looking students firing a Frisbee to each other at a great distance with impressive accuracy. The skatepark was in full view. No sign of Packo.

Trying his best to sight McCall on the far side of the park near the bridge, he entered without locating her position as arranged. He headed down a tarmacked path with flowerbeds running along the sides, and after turning a corner around some densely leafed trees, the playground came into view. Conscious that his position was visible from most of the surrounding area, he sidled up against a tree trunk and took stock of the vicinity around the playground.

His phone buzzed. McCall asking where he was, an expletive, the only word fully spelled in the text. He called her back and told her to head around the back of the playground, near the water fountain, and he'd wait until she was in sight before he'd make a move.

Brophy was startled by two eight-year-olds darting past him on bikes, cackling in high pitches at the sight of an old man hiding against a tree, staring at the playground. Worried his cover was blown, he strolled towards the playground as casually as possible. Finally, Brophy saw McCall turn a corner and emerge in the distance behind the fountain. She had a much better view of the area from her angle, and he noticed her stake it out with the precision she was known for. He soon made eye-contact, and she gave a non-discerning nod. Brophy felt the tension flow out of him. Half disappointment, half relief.

McCall reached the swings before him and sat on one and started swinging gently, all the time examining her surroundings. Brophy reached her and leaned against the yellow frame of the swing-set. They almost looked like a couple out for an early morning romantic walk. Only their glum expressions gave the game away.

"No sign of the little fucker," said McCall. "He must have gotten away just before we arrived. I'll radio in to keep all eyes out for him today. Someone will surely spot him at some stage."

"We need to find him fast. If anyone can lead us to Delaney, it's him. As much as he's out of it all the time, he always knows where lowlifes are in this city."

"Wait a sec. What's that over at the skatepark?"

Brophy followed her eye-line, and at first, couldn't make out what she was talking about. He squinted through the brightness of the sun-drenched morning and focused on an area just above what looked like a section of level ground on the concrete course. Circling and curling up from the depths was what appeared to be a plume of smoke.

"Gotya, ye little rat," said Brophy. "You come in from this end, and I'll circle around and head him off at the far side."

McCall was up and moving by the time he finished speaking. The skatepark was a hundred metres away, and from the playground, the ramps and inclines were visible. They had just realised, however, there were also a series of hollowed-out sections for the skaters to dip into and do their tricks. Packo must have been lying in one of them, out of sight of anyone in the park.

McCall reached the edge of the skatepark first but waited for Brophy to arrive at the back side before stepping onto the hard ground. Brophy guessed this was so as not to alert Packo to their presence. Nodding, he signalled for her to approach as he did from his side. Brophy glanced around to make sure Packo didn't have an ally who'd alert him. Then he recalled Packo usually travelled alone and got most of his information through gossip and eavesdropping when he was out of it in the company of other junkies.

They tiptoed to the circular edge of the one-metre deep pit and stretched their heads over just as he was putting the glass pipe to his lips.

"Lovely morning for a stroll in the park, isn't it, Packo?" said Brophy

"Ah, fuck. Not you again, Bottler."

In a sudden movement, not without a vent of frustration, Brophy jumped into the pit, just missing Packo when his feet stamped down with a thud on the graffitied concrete. He pulled Packo up by the scruff effortlessly with one hand and frisked him with the other. He patted him down on the outside first to make sure there were no sharp objects, then put his hands inside his jeans pockets. Just then, the stench registered in Brophy's mind, and he had to fight back retching on the spot. Packo was in the same filthy clothes as two days ago and had probably worn them a lot longer than that. Within seconds he felt a small plastic package in Packo's left pocket.

"What have we got here?"

He held it up before Packo's eyes. The baggie was all but empty but covered in slightly off-white powder.

"It's just a bit of baking soda I borrowed from a friend," he slurred, eyes foggy and face drooping. "Me mam's making a loaf of brown bread later. She asked me to sort her out with some," he said and sniggered at his stupidity.

"Is that right? So when we analyse it in the lab, we won't find it's the same methamphetamine as was found in a murdered couple's house, will we?"

"I've no idea what you're talking about, murdered couple."

"But I thought you were an avid follower of current affairs. Surely you're aware there was a double murder in the city two days ago." Brophy glanced back at McCall and said, "And now I think we might have our first suspect."

"What are ye talking about, man? I'm no suspect. Wasn't I in the station getting a teardown from you when them murders happened?"

"So, you do know about it," said McCall.

"And those people were slain a couple of hours before we had our little chat. And as I recall, you were well out of it at the time. Makes me think, you could have paid a visit to that family, pulled the trigger a few times, then searched around and found what you went there for."

"Ah, here now. That's a load of bollocks."

"Sounds plausible enough, doesn't it, Sergeant McCall?"

"More than plausible," she replied, moving in closer to crowd the now terrified Packo.

"But your boys in blue found me digging for treasure in Saint John's Park. I wasn't anywhere near that house in Woodstown."

"And now he admits to knowing the address," said Brophy.

"Everyone knows the address. It's all over the news."

"You wanna know what I think, Packo? I think you had an accomplice who was the driver for the operation. And do you want to know why I think that?"

"Why?" he said, shaking, his pale podgy skin turned a sickly shade of grey.

"Because your best pal, Budgie Delaney, was caught on CCTV several times driving around the area that day. And it looks like he's done a runner and left you to take all the flack for the double murder."

"You're out of your friggin' mind, Brophy. I had nothing to do with it. I was off me trolley in the city that day, ye know well."

"We're gonna take you in for questioning, anyway," said McCall. "If your story checks out, which I doubt it will, we'll set you loose. But I wouldn't like to be you when the big boys get wind of the fact that you've been questioned in connection with this murder."

Packo squirmed in Brophy's grip, and it took him a few seconds to realise why. "Ah, for fuck sake, man. You just pissed on my shoe. That's another thing I'll have to book you with."

"Look, you can't pin this murder on me. I'll be torn apart limb for limb."

"I don't see how we have a choice," said Brophy, taking a step back to avoid getting anymore overspalsh on his shoe. "You're in possession of the narcotics that were found in the house and likely the cause of this whole mess, and I'm willing to put my house on it being the same junk you were out of your head on the other day."

"So, Packo," said McCall, "are you going to tell us where Delaney is, or do we have to pin it all on you?"

"I haven't seen that mad bastard in weeks. He's off playing Daddio with some Polish one. No one has seen him, even his own family."

"That's not going to work for us," said Brophy. "You tell us right now where he is, and we'll give you twenty-four hours to clean yourself up before Drug Squad pat you down."

"I swear on me mother's life. I don't know

where Budgie is."

"I'm beginning to think your poor misfortunate mother is immortal with all the times you've sworn on her life with absolute lies. Now tell us where he is, or we're getting a squad car over here to take you in."

"Not before I get that swarm of reporters that are plaguing the city about this story first, though," said McCall.

"What's it gonna be, Packo?"

"Honestly, man. I have no idea where he is. I never have anything to do with that scumbag. Last time I met him, he gave me a right beating over twenty Euro."

"Then, where does the Polish girl live?"

"How the hell would I know that?"

"Okay, play it your way," said McCall. She reached into her pantsuit pocket and took out her phone.

Packo squirmed and shook uncontrollably. "Please don't do this. Those fuckers don't mess around. They'll come after me little one. I'm not joking ye."

"But you have to give us something, Packo," said Brophy, his patience wearing thin. "I'll give you one last chance then. If you don't answer immediately, Sergeant McCall will dial you in. Is that clear?"

Packo nodded profusely.

Brophy held the baggie up before Packo's eyes. "Where did you get this?"

He hesitated a few beats, and Brophy tightened his grip on his tracksuit top. "Some young-fella in the city centre. I think he's a student in WIT."

"Where do you go to meet him?" asked McCall.

"He comes to meet me. Usually around John's Street or Red Square Shopping Centre."

"How do you contact him?" asked Brophy.

"Whatsapp. Ye send him a message, and he gets back saying where he'll be, usually within half an hour."

Brophy gave McCall a look that said, 'we've got a result.' He fished around Packo's tracksuit and pulled his phone out of an inside pocket. "It's time you got another fix then, isn't it?"

"Ah, no way, man. Then they'll know it's me who squealed. You said you'd let me go if I told you."

"We'll get you out of this," said McCall, "but you have to do it our way. Now set up a meeting with him, and we'll jump on him when he arrives, and make it look like we were tailing him and not you. But you have to do exactly what we say."

"Ah, Jesus. This can't be happening."

"Message him now," said Brophy and released Packo and handed him the phone.

CHAPTER FIFTEEN

The city was already teeming with people by the time they received the dealer's reply and headed towards the centre to meet him. Brophy and McCall had decided not to call in any reinforcements lest it aroused suspicion and scared the man away.

Shoppers and summer holiday school kids jostled for space around Red Square Shopping Centre in the heart of Waterford. Random gangs of teenagers loitered on street corners, many with their tops off, revealing paper-white bodies with slightly tanned forearms and necks. Just like any other Saturday in summer, Brophy told himself. A merry-go-round, set-up in the middle of the square, twirled with joyful screaming children, waving their arms and kicking their legs. The entire city centre was pedestrianised, so they knew there'd be no quick getaway by car should things go haywire and the dealer eluded their capture.

Brophy stood at a coffee counter to the left of the mall entrance and ordered a black coffee from the listless teenage barista. It took a couple of awkward moments before he realised she had no idea what a black coffee was and ordered an Americano instead. McCall was positioned inside, sitting on a bench by the central water feature. She feigned a girls'-talk type of conversation on her phone, something Brophy wasn't used to seeing from her. Packo was between the two of them, standing in the middle of the ground floor, looking as shifty and out of place as usual.

The routine was when Packo saw the dealer coming in the back door, he'd head for the nearest toilet, then his fix would follow him in and make the deal. Brophy hoped Packo wouldn't get kicked out by security before their mark had a chance to arrive.

His coffee was set before him and minutes passed without any movement from inside. His phone rang, and he checked the screen to see who it was. DI Bennett. Brophy would have pressed the red button to hang up only he was anxious in case there was any news about the boy.

"Where are you, Brophy? You're wanted at the station?"

"Wanted by who?"

"By Superintendent Russell and the NBCI boys."

"What do they want?"

"They want you to stop asking dumb questions and get over here."

"I'm afraid I can't be there for a while. We're in pursuit of a dealer who might be flogging the same meth that was found yesterday."

"Jesus. Who is he?"

"We don't know yet, but he might be able to lead us to Delaney."

"Why haven't you called in for back-up?"

"No time."

"Give me your location now, Sergeant. I'm sending the DS and a few squad cars. We can't look to be acting like mavericks on this-"

The last words faded into obscurity as Brophy noticed Packo squint towards the back entrance then head towards the toilets as planned.

"Look, I have to go."

He hung up and took a sip of his scalding coffee and waited. The young man who came into view looked little more than a child. Short and skinny with a boyish face, he confidently strolled towards the toilets, with McCall just a few paces back. As soon as the young dealer turned the corner leading to the restrooms, Brophy shot through the automatic doors. Within seconds, he was in the hallway and peeked around the corner to make sure he hadn't yet copped that he was being apprehended. McCall stood at the entrance to the men's toilet and waved him on. Almost ten seconds had gone by now, and according to what Packo had told them, the deal would be done in a jiffy, and they'd be on their way.

Brophy reached the door and burst in without hesitation, shouting, "Police. We've got you surrounded. Don't you dare fucking move an inch."

At a urinal in mid-stream, an elderly gentleman's mouth dropped open. McCall was quickly in behind Brophy, and for a second, he thought he'd been duped by Packo, and there was an alternative exit. Then the old man gestured with a sideways motion of his head towards one of the cubicles.

In one brutish movement, Brophy bolted for the door and ran right through it, crashing into both men and sending the three of them bouncing around the cubicle. The dealer's hand reached for the hanging string toilet flusher, and Brophy swiftly grabbed his arm rather than the string. It felt like holding onto the wrist of an eight-year-old, and the boy let out an agonising yelp of pain.

"Ah, Jesus. You're breaking my arm. Let me go."

"Let the string go," shouted Brophy.

The dealer complied, then Brophy reached down and fished two baggies out of the bowl. As he was doing so, Packo pushed with all his might and ran out of the cubicle. Brophy heard McCall letting out a scream of anguish as Packo escaped altogether, and Brophy knew the plan had worked. It all seemed natural enough for the dealer not to suspect Packo was in on the sting operation.

McCall half leaned in the cubicle door. "Sorry, Boss. The little toe-rag got away. I got a good look at his face though. We'll get a few squad cars to hunt him down. He'll be hauled in by the end of the day."

"That's no problem, Detective. We've got the main man right here. The big dealer we've been tailing for months. Now we can finally put him away for a long time."

At the sound of that, the young man began sobbing uncontrollably. "Ah, please no. I'm just a college student. I'm only eighteen. I can't go to prison."

Brophy shook off some of the toilet water from his arm and held up the two baggies. "Eighteen, you say. That's an adult, and these are class A drugs. Your life has just gone right down that toilet, young man. What's your name?"

He could barely squeeze the words out through the tears. "Daithí O'Byrne."

"Do you realise how serious this is, Daithí?" said McCall. "A young good looking fella like yourself wouldn't do well in Mountjoy."

"I can't go to Mountjoy. I just finished first year in college. My parents will kill me."

Brophy gave McCall a quick smirk. "Mr O'Byrne. Please believe me when I say you only have one single chance to get out of this mess. If you hesitate for a second, we'll call in the uniformed officers to take you away. Do you understand?"

"Yes," he said wide-eyed and trembling.

"Who's supplying you?"

"He's a Waterford lad. Michael Delaney."

Bingo.

"Where can I find him?"

"Tramore. He's in a flat near the amusement park."

"Address?"

"B-2-5 Plunkett Court on Gellwey's Hill."

Brophy looked at McCall, and she gave him a nod. She knew the place.

CHAPTER SIXTEEN

Despite the bumper-to-bumper traffic all along the fifteen-kilometre journey to the beach town, Tramore, and having decided to take McCall's car, they reached Gellwey's Hill in little over twenty minutes. They parked outside a colourful pub with a toucan painted on the gable end, near the bottom of the hill. The newly constructed and presumably very expensive three-storey block of flats was clearly visible on the top of the hill.

They walked up, planning their move on Delaney. It was decided they'd both approach the front door as opposed to one of them waiting downstairs in the event he made a run for it — mostly because of Delaney's size and reputation for being liberal with the distribution of punches and headbutts. Brophy looked down to his left at the sprawling Tramore Beach, at two kilometres, one of the longest in the country. It was already packed with day-trippers and holidaymakers from every corner of Ireland.

They arrived at the sand-coloured building. Balconies dotted the entire sea-facing side of the flats, so they'd have to head around back to find the front door. O'Byrne had told them the flat was on the second floor, and Brophy had a good look at the second-floor balconies, thinking the jump would be risky but certainly doable should

Delaney decide to make a run for it. There was no way to know which flat was his from this side, so they made their way around the back of the building as fast as they could. A separate stairway led up to each of the second and third-floor flats, and they quickly scanned the numbers on the doors to figure out which one was B-2-5.

McCall nudged Brophy, who was looking at the opposite end to which she was signalling. Briskly, they made their way to a stairway at the far end of the flats. Brophy observed there was no way Delaney was getting past them at the front door, and the two windows at this side would be too small for the tall and well-built dealer to fit out and make a quick escape.

On reaching the top of the stairs, they paused for a couple of seconds to listen for any sounds of movement. There were none. McCall rang the doorbell, one of those loud gongs with a long pause between the initial sound and the closing chime. A thought popped into Brophy's head. *What if Delaney was still in possession of the gun he might have used in the double murder?* Brophy quickly regretted not signing out a gun from the station the previous day, as he had considered doing on several occasions. Within their rights to carry one at all times, the detectives of Waterford rarely did.

After ten seconds, McCall rang the bell once more. Almost as soon as she'd pressed the brass button, a thick Eastern European accent impatiently called out, "Who is there?"

A look of imminent indecision passed between Brophy and McCall.

In his best Dublin accent, Brophy said, "It's Clarence Veale. I'm here to see Budgie. Open up now."

A crescendo of whispers rose from somewhere in the depths of the flat. It was followed by mutedly restrained shouting by the girl on the other side of the door. Brophy gave three solid knocks.

"All right, Vealo, I'm coming," came the aggressive tone of Delaney's thick Waterford accent. I'm just puttin' on me pants."

They heard him draw nearer, and Brophy braced himself for a physical altercation. The dull clang of two chains being taken off the latches gave further pause to the situation. Then a deadbolt thunked open. The door opened slowly, and there was Delaney, his head down, doing up the last of his buttons with one hand.

"How's it going, Budgie? We've missed you in the city," said Brophy.

Delaney's eyes sprang to alertness as he looked from Brophy to McCall and back again. In a sudden and rash movement, he tried to slam the door shut, unaware that Brophy had wedged his foot forward as soon as it opened. Delaney tried with all his might, but it was useless.

"Fuck you, Peelers. I didn't do a god-damn thing," he shouted, and no sooner had he finished than he turned and made a run for the back of the house. Brophy barged in, followed by McCall.

A blonde girl stood in the hallway, cradling a sleeping baby, a look of fear turning to shock as Delaney brushed off her running past, nearly knocking her and the baby to the terracotta tiled floor. McCall reacted quickly and stopped her fall. Brophy rushed in the living room door after Delaney and instantly saw he was in the process of swinging his long muscular legs over the railing of the balcony.

"Stop," shouted Brophy. "We just want to talk to you."

Rage and guilt were painted all over Delaney's face, and he motioned like he was about to say something. Instead, he looked down and jumped. A heavy thud, accompanied by a hoarse scream of pain, came back in the patio door towards Brophy as he made his way to the balcony.

He looked over the railing, and Delaney was scaling the wall leading onto Gellwey's Hill. Brophy knew he hadn't a second to lose if he was to catch up with him. He put one hand on the wooden crosspiece and leapt over without a thought for the impact that awaited. The ground came at him like a hammer blow, and he feared he'd sprained an ankle, a sharp pain searing up his leg. He took a couple of steps and recognised the feeling from his sporting days. It wasn't sprained but would surely swell up and give him a couple of days' discomfort.

He pushed the pain to the back of his mind and shot for the wall. Delaney was already well and truly over and probably halfway down the hill by now. Brophy sprang over the wall in one laboured movement and saw Delaney was almost down by the pub. He looked back to see where Brophy was and sprinted across the road and out of sight on the far side of a Chinese restaurant.

Known for his speed and agility, unbecoming of his height and bulk, during his playing days, Brophy sprinted down the hill and reached the Chinese restaurant in seconds. The back of the restaurant opened out onto a vast car park that was practically full of cars. He walked hurriedly towards the first line of parked cars, unable to see his mark, fearing he'd lost him. Either way, he knew where he was headed from there. The Tramore Amusement Park — a seasonal local attraction that was a hub of activity on a piping hot day like that. Past the amusement park, on the far side of the road in front of it, was the sprawling Tramore beach.

At least twenty rows of cars separated him from the first of the rides, and he began to lose hope. Just then he spotted Delaney popping his head up from a crouching position in front of a blue Mitsubishi SUV. Delaney caught sight of Brophy and swivelled, making his way for the park. Brophy upped the pace and broke into a laboured run, needing to zigzag between groups of people and parked cars. He was making up some ground while Delaney looked back on several occasions, appearing more agitated the closer Brophy got. His passage was impeded by two teenage boys. Delaney didn't hold back in sending one of them flying over the bonnet of a car, drawing shouts of protestation from a couple of middle-aged women nearby. He reached the metal railing and hopped over into Tramore Amusement Park.

Brophy reached the railing a few seconds later and followed suit. Delaney was weaving through the crowds, knocking over more people as he went. He ran around the bumper car course and stopped to see Brophy at the far end, still on his tail. He changed direction and flew towards the Mystery Hotel, disappearing through the entrance.

Drenched with sweat and his ankle in agony, Brophy was at the entrance within a few seconds. He stopped at the door and looked around to see if there were any other entrances Delaney could slip out of when he went in. There didn't seem to be. He stepped through the maroon velvet curtain and was momentarily blinded by the contrasting darkness of the interior. Old-style out-of-tune piano music started to play, and an American woman's southern drawl beckoned him further into the attraction. His heart pummelled the inside of his chest when a costumed monkey came flying at him, crashing two hand cymbals together and cackling like a rabid hyena. It flew overhead in a flash of light, and Brophy took the opportunity to scope his surroundings, but there was no sign of Delaney. The monkey disappeared in a fading echo, and the American woman urged Brophy to enter the saloon bar up the flight of steps to his right.

A sharp pain shot from the palm of his left hand, and he realised his fists were clenched so tight, he was burrowing his nails into the soft skin. He cautiously eased himself up the steps, his eyes now adjusting to the darkness. The walls on all sides were adorned with black curtains that flapped in the meagre draught blowing through the place. He reached for the top of the steps where there was only one way to go. He stepped in through the wooden slatted saloon doors and was greeted by an animatronic barman, wearing a candy-striped waistcoat and round-rimmed glasses.

"Howdy, Stranger," came its tinny voice. "Haven't seen you round these parts in some time. Why don't you pull up one 'o them there stools and let old Earl tell you a story."

Brophy scanned every inch of the poky room as the barman spoke, poised for Delaney to jump out from any corner at any moment, and make a run for it, or try to tackle his pursuer. At the opposite end to where he stood by the swinging doors, a curtain flickered gently from bottom to top. Brophy edged slowly across the room. Old Earl began his story about the gold rush and its eventual decline.

"Hotels like this here one were built on the backs of gruelling work and gold flakes."

On reaching the curtain, Brophy extended his arm, attempting to keep his distance, if, in fact, Delaney was hidden behind there, and pulled it back slowly. He braced for impact. A shuffling of footsteps shuddered up the plywood floor. Feeling the sensation had arisen from behind him, he turned quickly and spotted an emergency exit opened at the end of the bar. Brophy rushed towards it and stepped through into a backstage type area with several active motors operating the hotel, a set of ladders being the only access to the ground and top floor. He looked down but saw no sign of movement. On looking up, however, he saw another curtain flapping as though someone had just gone through it.

He stepped onto the ladder next to him and began scaling it, conscious that a foot could come crashing out from behind the curtain and send him careening to the bottom. He'd undoubtedly bump into supporting scaffolding on the way down should such a scenario unfold. His eyes stung with the intrusion of sweat and dust, adding to the dread he felt.

Brophy reached the top without any other

sign of movement. Another exit door faced him, slightly ajar, flecks of purple and green light flashing through. He pushed it open and stepped into the grand presidential suite. A miniature four-poster bed was squeezed into the corner at the other end of the room. A chandelier overhead emitted a faint glow of yellow light whilst tube lights traced along the upper walls shining green and purple.

When his eyes focused, he saw a bulge under the white covers on the bed. He edged along the back wall to get a close look whilst keeping his distance should it be Delaney lying in wait under the covers.

"Step in and experience the delights that Madame DeBeauvoir has to offer," sounded out the southern woman's voice, but this time with added reverb to portray the atmosphere of an occult setting. "Move a little closer to Madame's bed, and we can have a closer look at you."

Brophy stayed where he was, searching for the customers' entrance to the room. He saw it on the other end, across from where he entered. He contemplated his next move, and a sudden shock stunned him to his very core. The figure under the bedsheets sat, bolt-upright, the white sheet whipped down, revealing blazing red eyes on a witch-like pale-skinned woman with black hair, streaks of grey striped through. With a deafening hiss, she bore bone-white luminous fangs, then turned to look in Brophy's direction.

"Come join the covenant of chosen ones. A world of instant gratification awaits you."

No sooner had she finished speaking than small spotlights clicked on on the wall beside the bed, shining down on five coffins, lighting up blood-gurgling miners in various states of decomposition. Ten arms shot out from the coffins, and the vampires groaned and gargled at their would-be recruit. The whole scene had sent a shiver down Brophy's body, and he was about to make his way for the entrance when he noticed the outline of a sixth coffin by the corner. He squinted to get a better look, but the white light from the five spotlights darkened the whole area around it.

He took a few steps forward, expecting another light to come on, and an even more insidious creature pop out and terrorise him. One of the miners' arms brushed off him as he passed, and he convinced himself that the sixth coffin must be empty. A quick flash of his childhood days, coming to this very amusement park, reminded him that half of the park's attractions hardly ever worked, and the ones that did always had something missing or malfunctioning. This was no different. He turned to head for the entrance and was about to make his way out, hope fading of catching Delaney.

A thud and a gasp stopped him in his tracks. He spun around, but it was too late to stop the onslaught of the bigger man, agitated that he'd blown his cover, dive out of the coffin and tackle the detective to the ground.

An immense struggle ensued. Brophy was on the ground on his side, with Delaney on top of him, struggling to get up to make his escape. Brophy grabbed onto his leg as he tried to flee.

"Leave me alone, you bollocks. I didn't do a thing."

Brophy began twisting Delaney's leg to trip him up, or at least put him off balance enough for him to get to his feet and fight toe to toe.

"If you didn't do anything, then stop struggling and let's talk."

Brophy managed to twist around and get onto his knees, giving himself more leverage to knock Delaney over. He grabbed hold of both legs now. Delaney's strength was formidable and Brophy felt well-defined muscles through his jeans. He managed to break one leg free and kneed Brophy in the side of his head. His brain rattled, and he almost blacked out. He let Delaney go to get to his feet. They were both shouting insults by then, Brophy threatening serious jail time for assaulting an officer.

After he released him, Delaney made a go for the door, and when he was just a couple of feet away, Brophy swung out his leg, expertly tripping him by making him tangle his legs around himself.

Delaney crashed down to the floor, hard. He let out an agonising scream. "Ah, me fucking arm."

"Who's in there? What are ye playing at? Come out, or I'm calling the guards," shouted a voice from outside the door. Whoever it was sounded nervous to enter with all the ruckus and shouting.

Brophy mounted Delaney's back and grabbed his arm, eliciting an indescribable yelp of pain.

"Ah, you broke me fucking arm, you bad bastard. This is police harassment. I didn't do a thing."

Brophy drove his knee into Delaney's back. "Don't you dare move an inch," he said through gritted teeth.

Delaney protested and squirmed in pain. A short, stout bald man, in his forties, stepped in. "What's going on in here?"

"I'm a detective from Waterford City Crime Unit. Call the gardaí and tell them to get here right now."

CHAPTER SEVENTEEN

"Detective Sergeant Brophy, come in and take a seat there, please," said Superintendent Russell, gesturing for Brophy to sit next to him at the long rectangular table of the meeting room on the third floor. The staff meeting room at Waterford Garda station was the nicest in the station besides Russell's office, which was next door. "Good work bringing Delaney in, Sergeant. You look like you have a bit of a limp," he said as Brophy approached the top of the table. "Nothing serious, I hope."

"No, sir. Just a little twist. It'll be back to normal in a couple of days."

He sat adjacent to Russell. Bennett was seated directly across from him and barely acknowledged his presence. Beside Bennett were two more men, the NBCI officers, he guessed. As was his habit, Russell waited until everyone was seated before he slowly lowered himself into his leather office chair. Russell was in his late fifties, had grey cropped hair on a substantial head, and looked like he hadn't walked a distance of more than the car park to his office in many years. He had a storied career on the force and was respected and revered up and down the country.

"This is Detective Leard," said Russell pointing his outstretched hand towards the man

141

closest to Bennett. Leard looked different to most detectives Brophy had come in contact with before. He looked more like an army ranger, a deathly look in his brown eyes, a glare like he was ready to pounce at any moment.

Brophy gave him a nod. "Detective." Leard didn't return the gesture.

"And this gentleman is Detective Inspector White," said Russell, moving his hand towards the other man.

The sound of his name caused Brophy to squint to restrain the surprise from his face. Detective Felix White was famous within the force. A smartly dressed man of about fifty, he took down some major gang figures in his early career and spent the last decade heading tactical teams that brought down the two biggest cartels in the country. Although he didn't get recognised publicly for his efforts, everyone on the force and in the underworld, knew what he was capable of. And now Brophy knew there was no other case in the country more important than this one at the present moment.

"It's nice to finally meet you, Sergeant Brophy," said White, smiling. "We know all about your work record and look forward to helping you on this one."

Bennett looked at Brophy, and the hate in his eyes was palpable.

"We've briefed the detectives on what we know so far, Detective Brophy. Before you go and question Delaney, they'd like to hear your take on things to this point."

Brophy was confused about the request and expected they'd rely on Bennett for such a summary of the case. He was the senior investigating officer, after all.

"Sir, it's early days yet, but judging by the sightings of Delaney near the crime scene, and now knowing that he's supplying meth to local dealers, I'd say there's a good chance he was either involved or knows something that can lead us to the culprits. He reacted to the sound of Clarence Veale's name and opened the door to us thinking I was Veale."

A subtle twitch of a frown passed over White's otherwise unreadable face. "What do you mean by that?" he said.

"We didn't want to announce ourselves lest he might do a runner before we got a chance to speak to him. So, I faked a Dublin accent and told the girlfriend, through the door, I was Veale and wanted to speak to Delaney."

"Why would you do that?" asked White, again giving away nothing.

"At the briefing last night, I heard there were several sightings of Clarence Veale in the area recently, so put two and two together and assumed, as Delaney was supplying the meth, he'd likely have had some contact with Veale."

"Good call, Sergeant. Your gamble paid off, it seems."

"Did you get anything out of him in the Mystery Hotel?" asked Bennett impatiently.

"I'm afraid not, Inspector. He was giving it loads about not having done a thing and police harassment."

"Did he deny having anything to do with the murders?" Bennett again.

"He didn't mention it, and I didn't want to bring it up in case it compromised our interview back here."

"Well, did you-" started Bennett until Russell shot him a patronising look that said 'be quiet and let the adults talk.' An attitude he wasn't unknown for when there were guests in his presence.

"Conal, what you're about to hear isn't to go beyond the walls of this room," said Russell in an almost fatherly tone. "Do you understand?"

"Of course, sir. I won't say a thing."

White said, "You know, we've made incredible inroads with our fight against the Quilty and Doyle cartels in the last couple of years. Most of the major players from each crew are locked up for a long time to come, and the rest are either in hiding overseas or have disappeared completely off the radar." White gave himself a self-congratulatory smile. "As I'm sure you realise, it was a massive operation that burnt up numerous resources and funding streams. Even Europol and Her Majesty's Crown Service have sent representatives over to us to learn about how we managed to pull it all off. This has given our forces an impeccable reputation in law enforcement, and this is why the top brass have been considering setting up regional headquarters with high levels of expertise all around the country."

This last statement made Bennett perk up.

White went on. "For an operation of this magnitude to have succeeded, we needed allies and informants on all sides."

A knot formed in Brophy's stomach.

"To be frank, we couldn't have done it without considerable help from the inside."

"Veale," said Brophy, more as a statement than a question.

"He's old-school, Detective Brophy," continued White. "Started out as a teenager with the post office heist crews in the late eighties. Back then, they had a code about killing. It rarely happened, and when it did, the guilty party was left hung out to dry, making it easy for our boys to catch up with him. Now. Jesus Christ, these savages will shoot someone down over a hundred euro debt then brag about it the next day on social media. It's a whole different animal we're dealing with. Most of the people we've taken down are under twenty-five years old, and some are even under twenty. So coked-up, they believed they were untouchable and acted accordingly. There was blood all over the streets of Dublin, and now the killings have stopped."

"Tell that to the Walters and Donahue families," said Brophy, trying to swallow the venom he tasted with the thought.

Russell seemed taken aback by his candour. "That's exactly the point, Sergeant Brophy," he said. "The last thing we want is for the remnants of this whole thing spilling onto our city. Waterford has never had anything like this before, and damned if it's going to start on my watch. That's why they've come down from Dublin. We need to put this to rest fast and make sure there's no follow-up."

"I'm confident we can work together to close this quickly," said White, looking from Bennett to Brophy. "Every media outlet in the country and many from overseas are watching this closely. If things are dealt with in a satisfactory manner, it'll be difficult not to make this station the headquarters of the entire South East."

"I'd just like to know one thing," said Brophy, the growing anger in him almost rising to the top.

"What's that, Detective?" asked White.

"Do you know if there's a connection between Veale and Jordan Walters?"

Brophy followed White's eye-line, moving from Russell to Leard. Leard shook his head slightly.

"I'm afraid I can't answer that at this time," said White.

"I think you just did," said Brophy.

"You'll be told only what you need to know for now," said Russell.

CHAPTER EIGHTEEN

Interview Room Two had the atmosphere and muskiness of a bar that had hosted a mass brawl just moments before. The light bulb overhead was slightly swaying somehow, even though there were no windows. The white walls absorbed the shadows like moonlight in a dense jungle. One would never believe it was the hottest recorded day of the year so far, outside the sun belting off and baking every surface in its grip.

Brophy and Leard took their seats on the opposite side to Delaney, whose left arm was in a sling and right wrist was cuffed to a custom-fitted looped bar on the square frame of the tabletop. He breathed heavily, almost growling at the two detectives across from him.

"I have to ask you, Mr Delaney, do you want your solicitor present before we start speaking?" asked Brophy in a tone reserved for such a situation, attempting to make it sound like it wouldn't make a difference if the solicitor was there or not.

"I don't need that clown here. I have nothing to hide, so let me go."

Brophy wondered if that was his intimidation voice he reserved for small-time dealers who owed him money.

"All in good time," said Leard. It was Brophy's first time hearing him speak, and he was surprised to hear his accent was so refined. Definitely in contradiction to his menacing appearance. "First, we're going to need to get a statement."

"What am I being charged with?" he hissed at his interrogator.

"Nothing yet. But so far, you've assaulted a guard, resisted arrest, and we've got evidence growing by the minute that you're supplying local dealers with methamphetamine. So, it would be in your best interest to tell us what we need to hear."

"I don't have to say a god-damn thing. I know my rights."

"Where were you between the hours of six and eight o'clock on Thursday evening?" asked Brophy.

"I was with me bird, wasn't I?"

"Which one?" asked Brophy.

Delaney sniggered. "The one you met today. Eva."

"And she'll clarify this, I presume," said Leard.

"Why wouldn't she? It's the truth." Delaney's smugness was growing.

Brophy said, "Why was your car spotted on CCTV several times in the Woodstown area that day?"

"How would I know? Me wheels were

stolen the other day. Probably some scanger trying to get some cash together for a fix."

"And I assume the police report will be able to prove this?" asked Brophy.

"Police report? As if I'd expect you coppers to assist me in getting my car back. No. I was planning to do my own police work on that."

"Where did you get the meth?" asked Leard.

"I don't know nothing about no meth," said Delaney, moving forward aggressively, then back slowly to an upright position. "I prefer a bit of Charlie myself. Columbia's finest. I'm not into the poisonous stuff. Rots your brain, so it does. Turns upstanding citizens into fucking zombies, as well."

"We have a dealer who says otherwise. He told us exactly where he gets it, for how much, and how often. Seems like a burgeoning business you've got there," said Leard, cold and unmoving.

"I'm sure whoever you have has made some kind of mistake and will see the error in his ways soon enough."

"As we speak, the baggies we nabbed from said dealer are being analysed for fingerprints and DNA. And the stuff is also being tested to see if it matches the kilos that were found in the house of a murdered family," said Brophy.

"I don't know anything about it."

"The evidence suggests differently," said Leard. "So far, we have multiple sightings of you near the crime scene at the time of the murders, a dealer who says you supply to him on a regular basis, and a senior detective who's going to be limping for a while after your brutal assault."

"What about me fucking arm?" he said, instinctively raising it and immediately wincing in pain at his mistake.

"You did that to yourself when you rugby tackled me in the boudoirs."

"I never touched your bleedin' boudoirs."

"God, you are thick as a plank," said Leard in the tone of an angry teacher scolding his worse student.

"Eh, easy now," said Delaney, genuinely surprised by the approach. "There's no need for that."

"What if I told you we tailed Frankie Doyle all the way from Naas to your front door?"

Brophy was stunned at this admission by Leard, and Delaney's face dropped.

"I never met that nutter in my life."

Frankie Doyle was the head of the rival cartel to Bobby Quilty's and was assumed by the media to be in hiding in Costa Del Sol since most of his charges were taken down. A much more ruthless operator than Quilty, he was widely believed to have started the murderous rivalry between the two gangs by killing Quilty's nephew with a tyre iron. The murder investigation pinned it firmly on Doyle, but a technicality in the proceedings caused the case to be thrown out of court and Doyle to walk free. A vicious cycle of revenge killings lasted for the next four years until new laws were passed, giving the gardaí more powers to arrest and charge suspected dealers and murderers and have them locked up whilst evidence was gathered in their cases. Brophy couldn't believe that Doyle would be stupid enough to still be in the country, involved in the drugs trade.

"Being a man so well versed in the law," said Leard, "I'm sure you know we can hold you until we gather enough evidence to pin the supply and murders on you. Portlaoise Prison is full to capacity, but I imagine we can find you a nice cell to share with one of Doyle's men."

"Or if they're not taking any guests, maybe one of Quilty's young bucks will take you in," said Brophy, still reeling at the direction the interview had taken, instinct kicking in, despite his annoyance.

Delaney eyed the two detectives, a bead of sweat rolling down his forehead. It was obvious he was thinking carefully about what to say next. He peered down at his arm and shook his head in a look of resignation. "It's not me ye need to be talking to about this."

"Is that right?" said Brophy. "Then, who should we be talking to?"

"You could start with that yuppie scientist, Barry Donahue."

"We're not interested in Donahue right

now," said Leard. "We already know what he's up to, and he's been taken care of. But I think you already know that, and you're attempting to throw us a bone." Leard began to rise from his seat. "I think we're done here, Detective Brophy."

Brophy followed along, got up, and limped towards the door, passing Leard as he went.

"Here, wait a minute, for fuck sake," called Delaney in a raised voice, not devoid of fear at that point.

Brophy opened the door and took a step out.

"Please, I'll tell ye what I know."

Brophy turned and was face to face with Leard. He was much more menacing looking in the fractured light breaking in the edges of the door. He gave Brophy a look to say, 'we have him now.' Brophy returned a hostile glare. He was reeling from not being filled in on the details before the interview began. He could only guess it was a way the NBCI boys used to show their authority over the locals. He was beginning to understand why Bennett felt the way he did about them. Leard retook his seat across from Delaney, and Brophy slowly followed suit.

"Let's hear it," said Leard. "And it better be what we need to hear."

"I want a guarantee that I won't go to jail," said Delaney, fighting back the tears.

"I'm sorry, but we can't do that," said Leard.

"Look, I didn't kill anyone. That's not my

style. I might nut a fella the odd time if he owes me, but I'm never in so deep that I'd need to off someone. Especially not some rich husband and wife."

"Why were you in the area then?" asked Brophy. "Were you picking up supply from them?"

"Fuck no. I never even heard of those people until I saw on the news that they were killed?"

"Why were you in Woodstown?" Brophy again.

"I was meant to meet Veale to get sorted for the month."

Leard remained silent, so Brophy continued.

"Where were you supposed to meet him?"

"In the car park of Woodstown beach."

"What time did you show up?"

"I arrived at about twenty to six. He was supposed to be there at quarter to. I waited for ages, so I did, but he never showed up. I took a spin around the neighbourhood and sent him a message asking what the hell he was playing at."

"Did you call him?" asked Brophy.

"No. That's strictly forbidden. I contact him on a messaging app, and he usually gets back within a few minutes. But this time, there was no sign of him. I drove back to the beach one last time, thinking maybe his battery had died on the trip down from Dublin."

"That's a highly unlikely thing to happen these days," said Leard. "Most cars have built-in chargers, and I assume you knew he drives a fairly new BMW. So, where did you really go after he didn't answer your message? And don't bullshit me, Delaney. I'm starting to lose my patience with you."

"I told you. I went back to the car park, smoked a spliff, and headed off by about half-six."

"Were there other people at the beach?"

"Course there was. We're havin' a tropical heatwave, aren't we? The place was teeming with families and foreigners."

"Did you talk to anyone at all, or is there anyone you're sure got a good look at you so we can place you there at that time?" asked Brophy.

"Let me think... There was one aul lad walking his dog who came right up to me window," he recalled with relief all over his face. "He gave me guff for smoking in a public place. I told him to piss off."

Brophy said, "What did this man look like?"

"He looked a little bit like Liam Neason. Lanky fella wearing a checkered shirt and jeans. Had a lovely looking collie that seemed as snobby as he was."

"Even if we track down this Liam Neason lookalike, it still doesn't prove you didn't pay a visit to the Walters' house and pulled the trigger."

"Ah, Jesus. Why would I want to kill those people?"

"Because they were supplying Veale," said Leard.

"Wouldn't you think I'd want them to stay alive then?"

Leard moved in close and came within a foot of Delaney's face. "Not unless you got a better offer, and one of the conditions of that offer was that you took care of your soon to be rivals."

"What are you on about, man?" said Delaney, straining to hide how intimidated he was by Leard.

"Allow me to run a scenario by you if you will," said Leard.

Brophy felt even more out of the loop by Leard's approach.

Leard went on, "You had a nice little number going with Veale. A highly addictive new drug on the streets, you were the only one in the city with access to. For the past six months, things had been going nicely. You'd found a few new saps to do your dealing for you, and plenty of people were getting addicted to the stuff. But you felt a little bit stiffed by Veale's extortionate prices. He was also holding back on the amount he'd give you at any one time, thinking he didn't want to flood the place with the stuff too soon and draw unwanted attention. You were pissed, but there was nothing you could ultimately do, just grin and bear it. But then you got a surprise call one day. A knock on Eva's door in Tramore. And you nearly shit your pants when you opened it to find none other than Frankie Doyle, standing before you with a big smile on his face and an offer of partnership. The big time, Delaney. What you'd always dreamed of."

Brophy was stunned by this detailed account, but not as stunned as Delaney.

"You're full of shit," he said in a high pitched voice. He looked as though his world had come crumbling down on top of him, and he was about to smother under the pressure.

Leard continued, "Doyle offered you a better price. But only on one condition. You had to take out the very people that were manufacturing for Veale to ensure you and Doyle were the only ones with a supply."

What happened next truly shocked Brophy. Delaney broke down in heaving sobs. "You're gonna get my whole family killed, you bastard," he said through up-curled lips. "I didn't want any of this shit." He sniffled and wiped his eyes with his right upper arm. "You boys started this whole meth thing by taking all the coke off the streets." He looked square at Brophy and momentarily composed himself. "You can lock up all the dealers, but you can't quell the demand that's out there." He looked down at the tabletop. "Say what ye want, but I didn't kill those people. I never even heard of them, and I'd no idea Veale was getting the stuff here in Waterford."

A knock came on the door. Leard looked at Brophy. "We're done here, Detective."

The two men got up and walked out, leaving Delaney distraught and mumbling to himself.

CHAPTER NINETEEN

Outside Interview Room Two, they were confronted with the sight of Felix White doing his due diligence in stalling an incredulous grey-haired solicitor in his early sixties, bemoaning the fact that he wasn't present for his client's statement.

On seeing Brophy and Leard appear down the hall, he said, "Not to worry, Mr Wilson, we'll get you a copy of Delaney's statement immediately."

Wilson turned as Brophy and Leard approached. "You two had no right to interview my client without my presence."

Leard swiftly sidled up to him. "We had every right. One could even argue, it's our job. He was well aware of his rights and offered to speak, all the same. You're welcome to go in and ask him."

Wilson barged past the two detectives, brushing shoulders with Brophy as he went, cursing under his breath.

"Detective Brophy. We'd like a word with you in here if that's all right," said White, signalling towards Interview Room One. Brophy didn't reply and headed into the room first. The two NBCI men followed him in, and White closed the door behind them.

"Can you tell me what the hell that was all about?" demanded Brophy with utter contempt. "I don't appreciate being strung along like that. I don't give a rat's arse who you two are and what power you think you have."

White glanced at Leard, who gave an affirmative nod in return. "Please accept my apologies for that, Detective. We did that intentionally to see how you'd react."

"Is that right?" said Brophy, his thread taut and ready to snap.

"We wanted to see for ourselves if what we'd heard about you was true," said Leard.

"Yeah? And what did you hear about me?"

White said, "That you've got top-notch instincts and are a very talented investigator."

Brophy calmed a little and was starting to feel confused.

White continued, "There's a new unit being set up in Dublin to investigate organised crime with international connections. It's very much on the QT right now, but suffice to say, we're going to need highly experienced and skilled detectives to work the unit."

Brophy looked to Leard, who was nodding his approval. "You're just the kind of man we need, Detective Brophy."

"So, what do you think?" asked White.

"Truth be told, I'm a bit surprised. But I'm gonna have to turn you down."

"This is a high-status position, Brophy.

You'd get to travel and work closely with organised crime divisions all over the world. After five, ten years, you'd walk into a senior position either here or up in Dublin. Anywhere you'd want, really. I know this is kind of springing it on you, in the middle of such a big investigation and all. But this is the pressure that comes with the job, is it not? At least tell us you'll think about it."

"I'm needed here once the upgrade happens. I've made assurances to Bennett and Russell."

White and Leard exchanged a wry look.

"The upgrade is going to happen, isn't it?" asked Brophy.

"Nothing is guaranteed," said White. "But there's a close eye being kept on how all this is handled."

"What else do you know about Veale and Doyle?" asked Brophy.

"Veale helped us out greatly in taking down the cartels," said Leard. "In exchange, we forgot about some of the cases we had on him."

"Did you know about this meth thing?"

"Fuck, no," said Leard, *not too convincingly*, thought Brophy. "If we had, we'd have closed it down immediately."

"Is he still in touch with Quilty?"

"Less and less so," answered White almost despondently. "Our endgame was that he'd eventually draw Quilty out for us."

"What went wrong?"

"We're not sure," said Leard. "He stopped answering Veale's calls. We can't be sure if he caught wind of the fact that Veale was working with us."

"And where's Veale now?"

Another look between the NBCI men, but this time, a look of resignation.

"We don't know," said White. "He went AWOL the day before the murders. Hasn't answered anything from our secured line."

"In the past five years, he never went more than an hour without answering us," said Leard. "That was part of the deal. Now it's been three days."

"He could be the shooter?"

"It's possible," said White.

"And he could be hiding out somewhere now, with Seán Walters?"

"That's what we need to find out." White continued. "I'm sure you can appreciate that this could blow back in our faces with very severe consequences. Public confidence in the gardaí is at an all-time high at the moment. Certain communities in the capital feel a lot safer to walk the streets at night and to let their kids hang around without the worry of being recruited by some of the scumbags we've locked up. But if this filthy meth gets onto the streets, that'll all evaporate, and we'll have a much bigger problem than the cocaine ever gave us."

"Jesus," said Brophy, the scale of the whole

thing just hitting him. "What about Doyle? Is he working for you too?"

"No," said Leard. "We think he may have caught wind of what Veale was up to and wanted to get in on it himself."

"So he teamed up with Barry Donahue?" said Brophy.

"We don't know."

"Don't bullshit me."

Leard said, "Honestly, we're not sure. We've traced a few calls between a house in Naas we believe Doyle has been hiding out in, and Donahue's mobile."

"I'm assuming the legality of procuring that information was questionable?"

"It doesn't make a difference," said White. "We'd need a lot more on them to make any kind of case, anyway. Up to the other day, we had nothing. Now we have two dead bodies and eight kilos of meth."

"And a missing ten-year-old boy."

"Of course," said White. "We also have to consider the possibility that they're all in on it together, with Quilty possibly calling the shots from Bahrain."

"It'd make sense. Given his friendship with Walters. But why kill them, and why take the boy? Surely they could have all gotten very rich from this."

"That's what we need to find out, and fast," said Leard.

Brophy said, "My priority right now is with finding that-" He was interrupted by a knock at the door. "Who is it?" he said gruffly.

The door opened about a foot, and Detective McCall popped her head in tentatively. "Everyone's needed in the Incident Room. Tech team are about to present their findings."

"Thank you, Sergeant," White said brusquely.

CHAPTER TWENTY

A large group had assembled in the incident room. Bennett was at the big desk by the display wall with Halpin, looking at an open file, pointing to its contents. Brophy was surprised but pleased to see Garda Sergeant Gough in attendance. He stood somewhat formally at attention, near the end of the table, looking a little taken aback by the hectic atmosphere of the packed to the gilt incident room.

Brophy took his position, standing beside McCall, in the middle of the crowd. He scanned the room, seeing many familiar faces, uniformed and plain-clothes, and noticed that White strolled towards the front of the room alone, with no sign of Leard. He shook hands with Gough as he passed, in a manner as old friends might do, then took a seat beside Bennett. Bennett acknowledged his presence with a curt nod and quickly turned his shoulder to him and continued his conversation with Halpin.

"What's going on?" McCall asked Brophy.

"I'll fill you in later, but this has gotten a lot more complex."

White tapped Bennett on the shoulder and gave him a serious, bordering on aggressive, look when Bennett turned to face him. He nodded to suggest getting things underway.

Bennett cleared his throat. "Attention everyone. Settle down, please." The murmur in the room faded to silence. "In a moment, Sergeant Halpin will present a number of findings Tech have already produced. As this kind of case is unprecedented for this station, and the media are swarming all over it, I'm under instruction to remind you all that whatever you hear in this meeting is for the sole purpose of our investigation and shall not go any further than this room. Is that clear?"

"Yes, Sir," rose a chorus of agreement.

"Firstly," he went on. "I should inform you that Detective Brophy brought Michael 'Budgie' Delaney in this afternoon as a possible suspect or witness to the incident on Thursday night. Due to insufficient evidence at this time, we've unfortunately had to let him loose without charge."

Brophy was perplexed at the revelation. He looked at White who remained expressionless at hearing the news.

"We have two squad cars on him, who'll keep tabs on him at all times until we gather enough evidence to bring him back in. Also, the boy Seán Walters still remains missing and is our number one priority at this point. His image has been well circulated around the country by now, and stations in every town and city are doing spot checks on the usual suspects in child cases. As of now, however, we have nothing to tell us where the boy is or if he was even taken. We're working on a few theories. One, that the shooter didn't know he was there until the parents were slain and panicked and took the boy, later killing him and disposing of the body elsewhere."

A chill passed down Brophy's body. His fingers trembled.

"This is unlikely, though, as the family were just finished dinner when the shooting happened, which would suggest the boy should have been present. It's understood the last sighting of him in public was at hurling camp at Saint Xavier's field. The head coach claimed he left early and got into a black Mercedes. The nearest CCTV, which is at the Waterford Crystal Leisure Centre, didn't pick up any black Mercedes at the time, unfortunately, so we haven't been able to confirm this. We're still working under the assumption that it was his father who picked him up but must consider the possibility that it was someone else. A jersey belonging to the boy was found in the wood near the house, which Sergeant Halpin will discuss with you shortly. We also have DI Felix White with us today, who'll brief you on his side of things after we hear from Halpin." He said the last part with disdain in his voice.

White stared straight at him, smirking.

Halpin shot to his feet and pushed in his chair. He had a no-nonsense get-to-the-point reputation, and if he had a problem with you, he'd never skirt around letting you know.

"Ladies and gentlemen, we have a few new findings that might assist in your enquiries moving forward. First, we can confirm that the jersey found was certainly belong to Seán Walters and had a significant amount of his blood across the front. Further tests found there to be no traces of gunshot residue, so if he was shot, it would have been from a distance."

Brophy held onto the irregularity of this possibility. If he was shot whilst running away from someone in the woods, the witness would have heard a separate gunshot, which was not reported, and either way, why would the killer discard evidence in the wood then take the boy anyway? It didn't make sense and made this whole thing that bit more baffling. Could Delaney have pulled the trigger on the parents, then got cold feet when he saw the boy and decided to hide him somewhere? It was possible. Or did Veale, with his record of abuse, have something much more sinister in mind for Seán Walters? There and then, he decided to visit the witness later that day and get a statement first-hand.

"The house has been searched, and there's no sign of the rest of the boy's kit from hurling camp that day. No boots, no bag, and no hurley. At that age, it's not unusual to wear the same clothes for the rest of the day, but that doesn't account for the lack of the gear bag and hurley."

Brophy gave McCall a look and thought, *Whoever picked up the boy must be looked into more.*

"We've also examined phone records from Mr and Mrs Walters mobiles, focusing on Thursday, but also looking back for any unusual activity over the last few weeks," said Halpin. "Jordan Walters made and received quite a few calls that day. Many were to and from board members and a couple of suppliers during working hours. Detectives will be given a copy of the log for further questioning of the higher-ups at Bioford Lab.

"He was also sent three text messages by his sister, all of which he replied to. One was early afternoon, saying she might be late for dinner because things were busy at work; another was to say she wouldn't make dinner, and to go ahead without her, she'd arrive a little later. One came shortly after that one saying she'd still take Seán shopping in Dublin on Friday morning for clothes for the concert. Then we have a couple of calls that we haven't yet been able to trace."

"And why is that, Sergeant Halpin?" asked White.

"They're coming up as unknown numbers, and even the phone company has been unable to get an accurate reading and location on them."

"Scramblers," said White, as if it was the most obvious thing in the world. "Many of those involved in the drugs trade use them. They download an app on their phones, and the signal bounces all over the place with high frequency. It's a waste of time spending any more man-hours on it, Sergeant. They're untraceable." White faced the crowd and raised his voice a decibel. "But I think it's safe to assume those calls had something to do with the murders and what was found in the garage."

"Shall I go on?" asked Halpin, his forehead creased, obviously perturbed by the interruption. White gave him a slight nod. "Mrs Walters' phone was far less active on Thursday. There were three calls to her uncle, Barry Donahue."

This information raised an eyebrow with Brophy, and McCall's expression showed a similar confusion. Donahue claimed not to have spoken to his niece since she had dinner at his home, two nights before the shooting.

"The unusual thing about her calls is that there was a series of messages from another unknown person that were all deleted. We're having difficulty tracing those too but hope to get a clearer picture on them in the next couple of days." Halpin gave Bennett a look to say that was all he had for now and sat back down.

"Thanks for that, Sergeant Halpin. That gives the team a lot to look into over the next couple of days."

White tutted audibly, with a slight shake of his head. Bennett cut him a look that didn't take an expert in body language to read. He'd have liked to lay him flat with a punch there and then.

"We'll try not to keep you too much longer, ladies and gentlemen," said Bennett, not taking his eyes off White. "But before you go, Mr White here would like to bestow some pearls of wisdom on you all. So please bear with him a moment."

"Thank you, DI Bennett," said White with a smugness that made him appear beady-eyed and sinister.

Brophy was beginning to wonder if something in the men's past had created such searing loathing between them. Both had certainly made their share of enemies in the force over the years.

"I'll try not to keep your team too long," said White. "As you're all aware, Michael Delaney is our chief suspect at this time, and as far as I'm concerned, the bulk of our efforts should be put into gathering evidence to prove this. Delaney was supplying meth to local dealers, and we fully expect the sample taken from one of his dealers to match what was found in the Walters' garage. This naturally leads us to believe Jordan Walters was manufacturing the drug in his laboratory and providing it to Delaney in large quantities. We're currently working under the assumption that Walters was in some way working with Bobby Quilty. As you know, the two have been friends for years, and I'd bet my house that the unknown numbers on his phone would, if possible, be traced back to Bahrain, where Quilty is known to be hiding out. This particular line of inquiry has thus far been kept from the public." He gazed slowly across the assembled officers and took on a more serious note. "We're sincerely hoping it will be kept that way, at least until we find the boy and bring in the killer if it is Delaney or somebody else."

Brophy wondered if there'd be any mention of Veale, then chastised himself for even considering it an option. If Veale was involved in the murders, it would be up to the NBCI or him and McCall to bring him in. No one else would get a look in.

"The clock is ticking, everyone. I suggest we round up anyone who has even heard about meth being on the streets of Waterford and find out what they know. If this stuff gets a foothold, it'll make the cocaine problem look like a trip to Disneyland. I've been to several cities in America to see how they deal with the epidemic over there, and I can assure you all, it's not a pretty sight. People strung out on this stuff are liable to do anything, and they leave a path of destruction in their wake. Let's put a lid on this, everyone, and fast."

CHAPTER TWENTY-ONE

On the way out to Woodstown in McCall's Audi, Brophy filled her in on everything he'd learnt about Veale and Doyle. She didn't seem too surprised by any of it but was her usual sullen self for being left out of the loop. As always, she blamed Bennett.

"What do you think is going on between Bennett and White?" asked Brophy.

"Who knows? Probably your typical case of mono e mono. Two massive egos who can't accept that someone else might be able to do as good a job as them."

"I don't know," said Brophy, clutching the side of the passenger seat as she raced around a bend on the N25 leading to Woodstown. "I think there's more to it than that. Something happened in the past that made them despise each other."

"Maybe Bennett is worried that if he doesn't get to lead on this case and bring down the killer, his promotion when Russell retires will be under threat."

"Could be."

"Do you think it was Delaney?"

"I don't know. I would have never thought he was capable of such brutality, but the longer you're on this job, the less I put anything past anyone. I mean, he was in the area at the time, he deals in meth, and he got a house visit from Harry Doyle. The makings of a motive are there, but I still need to know more."

"The kid?"

"It doesn't make sense. Why would they take him? What could the endgame possibly be? Leard alluded to something in the interview that we need to find out more about. He said they knew all about Donahue and Doyle. Maybe they were planning to go into competition with Quilty and Walters and needed to win Delaney over to get a foothold in the local market."

"Seems plausible. You think Donahue's capable of murder? Of his own niece?"

"He doesn't seem the type, but when people are up against it, you never know what they'll do to save themselves."

"If he was involved, he might have arranged to have the child taken and has him safe somewhere."

"Let's hope so," said Brophy after a pained sigh. "The alternative is that this is all Veale, and he had his way with the child before disposing of him somewhere he'll never be found."

Brophy had a brief flash of the missing person picture of Mel Fanning that went up around the country. A slightly blurry image of a young girl, seventeen years old, with a big smile, half-obscured by her wavy brown hair. The photo was taken the last night she was seen alive, on a digital camera found in her then boyfriend's house and taken as evidence that they were together on that fateful night. A fact he and his friends initially denied, but later admitted, never giving a clear explanation for their false accounts or change of story.

"We need to stay focused, though, Brophy," said McCall, bringing him back out of his trance. "I know this is a tough one, but we still have a chance to find him, so let's keep our eye on the ball."

A few minutes later, after a period of reflective silence, they passed the pub-cum-shop where the CCTV of Delaney's car was captured.

"Slow down a bit so I can see how long an average journey of a non-rally-driving person would take to the beach."

McCall eased off the accelerator, and Brophy kept a close eye on his phone's stopwatch. They arrived at the beach about four minutes later, having decided to have a look before calling to the witness's house.

The car park, as expected, was full, and the beach was packed with people, mostly families, enjoying the last couple of hours of sunshine on a Saturday evening. Brophy asked McCall to double-park near the far end. He got out of the car and walked towards the white sand, taking in as much of his surroundings as he could. The tide was almost fully in, inhibiting the space people had on the thin stretch of a strand. He looked down towards the end of the beach and saw an outcropping of rocks that had to be scrambled across to continue on down the shore in the direction of the Walters' house. About five hundred metres away, the land came out to a crook, and he guessed after a sharp bend, the next length of beach would lead to the back of their property. The distance and the bend might account for why no one else on the beach that day heard the gunshots. Now he had a better bearing of the layout he was ready to talk to the witness about his movements that day.

Five minutes later, after taking a couple of wrong turns, they finally arrived at a small cottage nestled in a grove of native trees that should have stood out in the middle of all the Sitka spruce trees but was well hidden down an obscure grass-covered boreen. They got out of the car and had a quick look around, taking in the unkempt garden Brophy imagined was probably pristine in its day. The kind of garden and cottage country-style magazines came to photograph and feature in their publications.

As soon as they started walking towards the blue front door of the house, a low-pitched barking emerged from around the side. Brophy braced himself for confrontation but was soon greeted by an amorous collie who jumped all over him and McCall. It finally rested on McCall, who was much more experienced with dogs than Brophy. It immediately clicked with him, and no doubt McCall, that the witness was also the Liam

Neason lookalike Delaney claimed had given him grief for smoking cannabis on a crowded beach.

"Just our luck, eh?" said McCall at the realisation.

Brophy didn't reply and proceeded to the front door, wincing in pain, having momentarily forgotten about his sore ankle. He gave a solid knock and took a step back. McCall was still petting the dog a few metres behind. He waited a good fifteen seconds before giving another knock and calling out for anyone to answer.

Suddenly, the collie scampered back around the side of the house. The two detectives stood at alert and waited for someone to appear at any moment. The house owner emerged, and the first thing Brophy noticed was how tall he was. At least six-six, slim and, despite the untended state of the house, clearly took good care of himself. He wore a brown peaked cap, red and grey checkered shirt, and had an air rifle slung over his shoulder. The resemblance to Liam Neason was all too apparent.

"Detectives. I've been expecting you," he said in a clipped accent that almost made him sound upper-class English.

"Mr Harrington," said Brophy, extending his hand. Sam Harrington gave it a firm shake. "Thanks for taking the time to see us. I know you've been through this several times already."

"Don't mention it, Detective...?"

"Conal Brophy."

"Well, well. The hurling star. I'm honoured," he said but already had his eyes on Brophy's blonde partner by the time he finished the compliment. "And this is?"

McCall had gone back to petting the collie who'd swung around the house, tail wagging fervently, after its owner. She approached Harrington. "I'm Detective Sergeant McCall," she said, attempting but failing to hide the charming effect Harrington seemed to have on her.

"What do you shoot out here?" asked Brophy.

"Oh, nothing much. Mostly just target practice. Keep the eyes sharp for hunting season. We get the occasional pheasant, but mostly they keep away from these horrid spruce trees."

"Can you get to the Walters' house through the trees walking from here?" asked McCall, raising an eyebrow of Harrington.

"Yes, you could. There's a stream and a rather brambly ditch, but you can make it there in about ten minutes," he said, never moving his eyes from McCall. Brophy was shocked to see her almost blush. "If you were in a rush, I'm sure you could do it in less. Young Seán cut through the odd time, to come and play with Meave here," he said, looking down at the collie, the sullenness causing a momentary tremble in his otherwise astute charm. "I do hope you're making good headway in finding him. What an ordeal; to lose one's parents in such a violent manner."

"We're working on a few promising leads," said Brophy, surprised at his own candour. "But we'd like to get a few things straight before we proceed."

"Of course, Detective. Anything I can do to help. Shall we go inside and take a weight off?"

Harrington led them in through the hall, and Brophy was confronted with what he'd expected, judging from the state of the outside. Things were scattered all around the place, but it wasn't the kind of mess that had rubbish and mouldy food containers lying around. Old books, half-made models of sailboats, and various ornaments and wooden boxes gave a view into Harrington's varied interests. Several guns hung on the walls of the cosy cluttered living room he ushered them into.

"This is a nice place you've got here," said McCall. "How old is it?"

"Oh, let me see. Over a hundred and twenty years, at this point."

"Did you grow up here?" asked Brophy.

"No, no. I spent most of my early years in England. My mother grew up here, and we spent many a fine summer holiday with my grandparents. This whole area was my back garden, the beach included. I used to ride horses all over the place on days like these. But now it gets a little crowded for that. Please, sit," he said, gesturing to the maroon Chesterfield sofa.

They sat down, and Harrington went to a drinks cabinet in the corner of the room and pulled out a bottle and three glasses. He then sat in an armchair across from the detectives and proceeded to pour three hefty measures of brandy. "I'm sure you've had a very trying few days," he said. "No harm in having a little soother to take the edge off."

Both Brophy and McCall picked up their tumblers and took a sip.

"Did you know the Walters well?" asked Brophy after placing his glass back on the table.

"Well enough as neighbours, I suppose. We didn't socialise or anything like that. Mrs Walters was extremely friendly and would always stop for a chat if we met in the village. Jordan was pleasant enough too. Always seemed rather preoccupied, though. Like he had the weight of the world on his shoulders."

"Did you, by any chance, have an encounter with a rough-looking character from the city in the car park on Thursday evening?" said Brophy.

Harrington's brow folded in towards his eyes. He seemed surprised that Brophy knew about this detail. "As it happens, I did. Ruffian in a Ford Fiesta, smoking a joint. Not an uncommon incident in these parts, but annoyed me deeply, his guile doing it in the presence of so many kids who were only feet away on the beach. Who is he?"

"Is that the same time you were out walking

and heard the gunshots?" asked McCall.

"Yes, it is. I took my usual route around the rocks and across the Gallopers' Spit."

McCall gave him an inquisitive look.

"That's what we called the stretch of beach when we were young. We used to race the horses up and down it. I reached the vicinity of the house about fifteen minutes after my encounter with the pothead, then heard the gunshots."

"We're a little unclear as to how many shots you heard, Mr Harrington," said Brophy. "Gough said you told him four or five. Can you remember which it was?"

"At the time, I was quite certain it was five, two of which were in such close proximity, they almost sounded like one shot to the untrained ear. But I've been second-guessing that in the last couple of days. Now, I'm thinking the first shot was so loud it may have caused a minor case of diplacusis."

"Diplacusis? What's that?" asked McCall. Brophy already knew the answer.

"You see, Detective McCall," he said, staring straight at her, a hint of a smile never too far from growing to a full-on grin, "I've been shooting guns from a very young age and in days gone by, health and safety wasn't what it is today. I've fired off thousands of shotgun cartridges without wearing ear protection. And now, at the tender age of fifty-seven, my hearing isn't what it could be. And several times in the last few years, I've heard double sounds that seemed quite unlikely or downright impossible. Like the local church bell gonging twice within a fraction of a second. This is what's known as diplacusis."

"What did you do immediately after hearing the shots?" asked Brophy.

"My initial reaction was to head towards the house and see if everything was all right. Then I stopped and thought about the sound of the shots. Initially, I thought maybe some hunters got too close to the house, but then it dawned on me that they were not the sounds of air rifle rounds or shotgun blasts. My heart sank, and I feared something untoward may be afoot.

"I took out my phone and called Sergeant Gough and told him what I'd heard. He told me to stay put and not to go near the house. If it were an intruder, they would likely be still in the house. He said I should head back the way I'd come and wait for him to call back with news."

"And he was at the station when you called him?"

"I'm not sure, but I presume so. As I understand, it took him less than ten minutes to arrive on the scene. That would certainly be conducive with him being in the station at the time."

"What did you do next?" Brophy asked.

"I did as he said. I doubled back down the beach at a much faster pace than at first and reached here about twenty-five minutes later. By then, I could already hear the sirens, and I knew something awful must have happened." He took a long sip of his drink. "Sergeant Gough never called back, understandably so, and I heard a report on the news later that a family had been murdered in Woodstown, County Waterford. It's unbelievable, really."

Harrington looked on the verge of tears, but Brophy wasn't buying the pained sincerity. He pegged Harrington as an emotionless relic of the landed gentry, bitter and likely hiding from something.

McCall took the bait. She spoke in a commiserate tone. "I'm very sorry, Mr Harrington, we just have a couple of more questions for you."

Brophy drank from his glass and tried to hide that he could see the twinkle reappear in Harrington's eyes as McCall spoke.

She went on, "Do you think the man in the Fiesta could have made it to the Walters' house in the time after you saw him and before you heard the gunshots?"

Harrington looked aghast. *Fake.* "Are you saying..? Yes, I'm sure he could have made it in that time. It's a five-minute drive, and I heard the shots about fifteen minutes after our altercation. So, yes."

"Have you ever seen any other suspicious characters in the area that you think weren't going to the beach?" asked McCall.

"Not that I can think of. I've been wracking my brain the last couple of days to try to remember any such a thing, but I'm afraid there's nothing unusual I can recollect."

"How about Dublin reg black Mercedes or BMWs?

"Certainly none that I can recall. Sorry."

"That's fine then," said McCall. "Thanks for your time Mr-"

"It's my understanding that the Walters applied for planning permission to build a small jetty on the beach in front of their property." Harrington's eyes turned a beady black, darting right at Brophy. "A local property owner objected both times they made the application, and they've been waiting a couple of years to reapply. Do you know anything about that?"

Harrington's chest heaved forth, shoulders drew back, and a blast of air expelled from his flaring nostrils. "I'm not quite sure I like what I'm inferring from that line of questioning, Detective Brophy."

Brophy quickly gave the impression of apologising, offering just enough regret in his tone to do so. "I don't mean to come across as accusing anyone unduly, Mr Harrington, but we need to rule everything out. Part of that is ensuring they have no enemies in the area."

Harrington forced a smile that was far too broad for the agitation his body language exuded. "I could never allow them to go through with that project, Detective. And I told them so, face to face on both occasions, even though I was under no obligation to do so, that it was I who formally objected to their application. Building a jetty as they'd proposed would completely destroy the environment on the beach. And god knows what kind of jet skies and motorboats they'd have sailed from there. I believe they realised this after the second application and gave up on the idea. That's why such a long period has elapsed since their previous attempt."

"Of course," said Brophy. "Thanks for clearing that up." He rose from his seat, as did McCall. Her displeasure at his typically maverick approach was like a dagger in his side. He knew he'd get a rollicking in the car. Harrington stood and shook Brophy's hand, the grip much tighter than in front of the house.

"Thank you, Detectives," he said whilst shaking hands with McCall. "And like I said, anything I can do to help, you know where to find me." He sat back down and picked up his glass, a move that suggested they show themselves out.

CHAPTER TWENTY-TWO

"Do you want to tell me what the hell that was about yesterday evening, steamrolling Harrington like that, not making me aware of the situation first?" said McCall, slamming the door shut behind her after getting into Brophy's car at the station car park the next morning.

She said nothing in the car on the way back to the station the previous night, instead biting her lower lip, a habit she had when she was holding back saying something that revealed her sensitivity. Brophy had observed it every time in his presence for weeks after their one night together. On that occasion, she eventually stopped doing it, leaving her lip chapped and raw in places and said nothing more about it. This time was different.

"I'm sorry. I wasn't planning to come out with it, I promise. I came across the failed application bid in the file Kenneally posted the other night," said Brophy.

"So did I? That doesn't mean I was going to accuse one of our only witnesses in the case."

"I wasn't accusing him."

"Then why did you say it?"

"I get a bad feeling about him, is all?"

Her sigh bordered on an angry grunt. "How do you mean, 'a bad feeling'? Harrington was

186

nothing but polite and forthcoming."

"I know that, but I just had to see for myself."

"See what?"

"His reaction when I said it."

"What did your instincts tell you then? Do we have our killer?"

"No. I don't think he cared a toss about Jordan Walters, but his fondness for the wife and son seemed apparent."

"Jesus, Brophy, I don't know what goes through your mind sometimes. Keep me informed next time, all right?"

"All right. I'm sorry."

He put the car into gear and headed out of the station car park. The instruction had come from Bennett, early that morning to go to Barry Donahue's house again and try to get information regarding a possible connection to Veale, Delaney, or Doyle. From the way he'd asked Brophy, Brophy deduced that Bennett wanted it done without the foreknowledge of the two NBCI officers.

They made the journey across the deserted Sunday morning city centre, a word hardly exchanged between them. The heat and sheen from the sun only served to worsen Brophy's sleep-deprived headache.

They arrived outside Donahue's house just after nine-thirty. The Mercedes wasn't parked in the driveway. In its place was a blue Peugeot

SUV. As McCall reached out to press the intercom button on the front gate pillar, she was interrupted by the sound of screeching tyres coming around the corner at the end of the leafy road. A black 'D' registration Volkswagen sped towards them and stopped just shy of Brophy's position a few feet back from McCall. Leard and White sprung out of the car. Leard's demeanour was instantly recognisable; grouchy that they'd attempted to leave him out of the interview.

White played a cooler hand. "Morning, Detectives. Thanks for waiting for us before you went in," he said.

There was little Brophy, and McCall could do but follow White's lead. He was the senior officer on the case after all.

"Sergeant McCall, you can wait outside. Make sure no suspicious characters are hanging about," said White.

She squinted in suppressing the rage she must have felt at yet another dismissive exclusion by a superior.

Leard brushed past and pressed the buzzer. Within seconds, the reply came. "Please come in, Officers." Brophy recognised the voice as Donahue's. "We've been waiting for you."

The gate began opening with a judder as the motor kicked in, then smoothly opened inward on both sides. Leard and White led the way, leaving Brophy behind, giving an apologetic look to his partner. She irritably signalled him on with a curt nod.

He reached the front door just as Barry Donahue opened it. Donahue looked as though he'd aged in the two days since they left him crying hysterically in his study.

"I'm Detective Inspector Felix White. And I believe you've already met Detective Brophy," he said, ignoring the presence of the third detective.

"Yes, welcome back, Sergeant Brophy. Thank you for your patience the other day. Everything is still very raw, as you can imagine."

"Don't worry about it," said Brophy. "You were very helpful."

"Has there been any word on Seán?" he managed through a cracked voice.

"We're working on some very credible leads," said White, cutting off Brophy's chance to answer the question directed at him. "May we come in, Mr Donahue? There's a few things we'd like to go over with you."

Donahue didn't say anything but opened the door widely and started across the hallway, slouch-shouldered. A few moments later, the four men were sitting at the kitchen table, positioned next to a full-length corner window. The heat was almost unbearable for Brophy, but none of the others seemed to mind, as far as he could tell. Donahue didn't offer them a drink.

"Your family not in?" asked Brophy.

"No. My wife has gone to Dublin with the children for a few days, until the funeral." It looked as though fresh but well-worn lines appeared on his ashen face by the second. His hair looked greyer than a few days before.

"Mr Donahue," said White, "My colleague and I are from the organised crime division of the National Bureau of Criminal Investigations." Donahue didn't seem in any way perturbed by the fact that detectives of that importance were on the case. "We'd like to be transparent with you in as much as we are permitted at this time. So, I'd like to inform you that a substantial amount of narcotics were found in your niece's house, with a probable street value of a few hundred thousand."

Donahue brought his forehead to meet the palm of his hand and rubbed it several times.

"Is there anything you can tell us about that?" White said in a monotone.

Donahue looked up at him like he'd seen the deaths of all his family flash before him.

"Were you ever suspicious that Jordan might have been manufacturing drugs in his lab?" asked Brophy.

"Oh, dear God, how could this have happened?" said Donahue. "We were all supposed to go on a family holiday in September, and now she's dead, and Seán is nowhere to be found." He broke down in sobs but tried his best to fight them back with his fist clenched over his mouth.

With an air of aggression in his tone, Leard

said, "Was Jordan going on the holiday with you?"

Donahue's expression changed to one of utter hatred. "That prick has never been welcome here or anywhere near my family. It destroyed me that Maura wanted to marry him. Arrogant shit, always thought he was untouchable."

"So, I'm taking it you knew about his indiscretions?" said Leard.

"What if I did? Would it have saved them?" he answered with a snarl.

"Probably not," said Leard coldly. "We also believe you've had some contact with Frankie Doyle?"

A minute but furtive flicker of the eyes, and Donahue said, "He was in touch. But I refused. There's no way I'd ever get involved in that racket. I have my principles."

"What about your son, Aidan?" The guilt was writ large on him now, and he bowed his head. "It's my understanding he has some sizable gambling debts to some dangerous people."

"I guess there's nothing you people don't know, is there?"

"And, we also know you agreed to make him two kilos of methamphetamine," said Leard.

"Mr Donahue, we need you to set up a meeting with Doyle to deliver the drugs," said White.

"I don't know the first thing about making that stuff."

"But your niece did," said Leard. "And she was willing to help to keep your son, and you, out of trouble."

"You don't think Doyle was involved with what happened, do you?" said Donahue, the realisation pouring over him. "Why would he want to hurt them? They had nothing to do with our arrangement."

"But if they were working for Bobby Quilty, then he had every reason in his fucked-up world to do what happened," said Leard. "These people don't mess around. They've more blood on their hands than you can possibly imagine, and if you think you and your family are going to be square with Doyle after you produce the two kilos, you've another thing coming."

"I didn't want any of this," said Donahue, panting heavily, as though he was about to lose it.

"Look, Mr Donahue, we can help get you out of this and keep the rest of your family safe if you go along with us. But you need to trust us," said Brophy with as much compassion as he could muster. "Whether Doyle is directly responsible for the murders or not, what is for certain is that he needs to be stopped before more innocent people are destroyed by this whole thing."

"Who's innocent?" said Leard.

Brophy felt like punching him straight in the mouth for that remark. "Seán Walters is innocent.

As are Mr Donahue's wife and children."

White interjected, "We really need you to cooperate on this, Mr Donahue. If you do everything right, I think we can manage to keep you out of prison."

"Prison? But I haven't done anything wrong."

If we brought a team in here to search your house from top to bottom, would we find anything to prove otherwise?" said White.

Donahue perked up and confidently said, "Go right ahead. You won't find a thing."

"How about if we search your lab?" said Leard.

Try as he may, Donahue was unable to hide the answer from his face.

"Thought as much," said Leard. "We can do this one of two ways; we search the lab and find the drugs, and you do at least ten years for your involvement, or you help us rein in Doyle, and you get to keep your freedom, for what that'll be worth."

Donahue went a paler shade of white and looked to Brophy for reassurance.

"It's best to go along with this," said Brophy. "If we bring Doyle in, and he has something to do with what happened in Woodstown, we can possibly find Seán faster, hopefully, safe and sound." Donahue nodded. "But we need to move quickly. Every hour Seán is held captive, he's in far more danger. If he's being held by some of

Doyle's associates, they might see the net is closing in on them and do something drastic if they feel nervous."

"Okay, Detective Brophy. I'll do whatever you say. I trust you'll do the right thing by Seán."

"What about us?" said Leard. "Don't you trust we'll do the right thing about Seán?"

Donahue straightened up and assumed a modicum of the high society gentleman he was before all this started, and said, "One look at you and your partner, and I can see you don't give a damn about my nephew or his parents."

"Oh, that hurts," said Leard in a mocking tone. "We value the lives of every citizen-"

"That's enough," said White briskly. "I'm only going to ask you once; are you with us on this, Donahue?"

"I'll do whatever it takes to get Seán back."

At that moment, Brophy knew for certain Barry Donahue wasn't involved in his nephew's disappearance.

"But do you think he'll agree to meet me with all of this going on? Surely he knows the place is crawling with detectives."

"Don't worry about that," said White. "This is the only world he knows. If he thinks he can get the edge over his rivals with this, he'll come out like a rat sniffing a pound of cheddar."

CHAPTER TWENTY-THREE

Donahue left the house with White and Leard, the NBCI men having told Brophy they'd inform him when he was needed again to assist with the sting operation. Brophy suspected they'd go it alone and not want any of the local officers to get too much information on how they dealt with the big hitters in the cartels. Knowledge is power, and they were notorious for keeping that knowledge to themselves and not sharing it with stations that might be affected by the drug wars. He didn't much care. He only wanted to know if Doyle had anything to do with the kidnapping of the boy; how they got that information didn't concern him.

McCall, on the other hand, was eager to see how they operated and again expressed her displeasure in being left out with an expletive-laden rant. She barely let up on the ten-minute journey to the fishing village of Dunmore East.

"Does it really not bother you?" she asked, after taking a respite from her tirade.

"I'm over it, Christine. They're gonna do what they're gonna do. It's always been the way. I just want to find out what happened to the boy."

"I know. That's my priority, too," she said unconvincingly.

Brophy realised the thrill of the chase against the country's biggest gangsters was a major enticement for many of the officers on the local force. It would unwittingly take precedence over finding the boy. That was only natural. It was why half of them joined up in the first place. The thrill, the hunt, the confrontation.

"Where's the house?" he asked as he turned onto Curraghmore Terrace after circling a round-a-bout.

"I think it's the third house on the right, just up ahead."

Brophy pulled up beside a row of newly built terraced houses, uniformly painted yellow, a different colour front door the only thing telling them apart. Despite their small size, Brophy guessed they must cost at least half a million, being only a stone's throw from Lawlor's Beach and the centre of the tourist village, with its popular pubs and cafes.

They got out, and McCall led the way into the third house and knocked. Within seconds, the door swung open. Brophy was taken aback by her beauty and soon became self-conscious that he was staring as McCall shook hands with Ciara Walters. She was dressed in blue jeans and a white blouse, her blonde hair hanging loose.

"Thanks for making the journey, Detectives," she said. Her eyes were bloodshot but not as much as the night in the station. "I couldn't face driving to the city right now."

"We're happy to come," said McCall.

"I don't suppose there's anything new on my Seány?"

"I'm afraid not at this time," said McCall.

Her chest heaved to hold back the crying. "Please, come in. I've just brewed some coffee."

The inside of the house was much more modern than the fake fishing village chic of the exterior. They sat at a tiled island counter in the kitchen. The smell of baking and freshly brewed coffee made Brophy want to curl up on the sofa and sleep. She poured them a cup and put milk and sugar on the counter in front of them.

"What are you baking?" asked McCall.

"Oh, they're chocolate chip cookies for some of the neighbour kids. They've all been so wonderful the last couple of days. Some of them go to school with Seán. I wanted to give them a little something. Anything to keep myself occupied." She brought her own coffee to the island and sat on a stool adjacent to Brophy.

"This house is beautiful," said McCall. "Is it yours?"

"It's the family's. Dad bought it before it was built. Unfortunately, he never got to see it finished."

"The other night, you mentioned to us about your brother's friendship with Bobby Quilty?" said Brophy. Her eyes showed resignation, if not surprise. "Do you know if they've remained friends over the years?"

The bell of the oven timer gonged. "I've always suspected that, yes, they remained close, but never wanted to ask. I know my father would have huge blowouts with him over it. Especially around the time the murder of Quilty's enemies started. It seemed like there was a new one on the news every day. My father was afraid Jordan might somehow get targeted, seeing how Quilty's gang did the same to friends of his rivals who had nothing to do with criminal activities. I don't think my dad ever believed him that they weren't friends anymore."

"Have you ever met him?" asked McCall.

"Quilty? Of course. He used to come and stay with us the odd time when they were at school. I don't think he was involved in the drugs trade then, but who knows?" she said with a deep sigh.

"Would you be surprised if we told you there was a large amount of drugs found in your brother's garage?"

She looked surprised yet ready to hear it at the same time. "Not terribly. And it would make more sense out of what's happened to know he had finally entered that world. Truth be told, I think he always wanted to be part of Quilty's empire. My brother loved the feeling of power over people. He used to go into the lab with my father as a teenager and boss people around. He bothered Dad endlessly about wanting to tell someone they were fired. I think Dad felt a bit ashamed of him at times."

"Yet he left him the family business?" said McCall.

"He left it to both of us. I'm a biomedical engineer too. But I chose not to work there, after Dad passed away."

"Why is that?" asked Brophy.

"I won't lie to you, Detective Brophy," she said, gazing through troubled eyes at him. "We didn't have the best relationship in recent years. I didn't agree with how he runs the company. He takes far too many big risks with finance. Always trying to outbid rivals. Sourcing less than high-quality materials from China. Let's just say, we get along better when we're not working together."

"What happens with regards ownership of the business now?" asked Brophy.

"I guess it goes to me, but there's also a small board of investors, so we'll have to sort out a way forward when this has been dealt with." A tear escaped her right eye and rolled down her cheek. "Oh, but I don't care about any of that, Detectives. I just want Seán back. Then I'll happily give up the business to whoever wants it. You have to understand, he's like a son to me. I come down from Dublin as much as I can to see him, and he often comes to stay with me, either here or in Dublin. The thought of him out there somewhere, afraid and alone, destroys me."

"You mentioned that you were supposed to

have dinner with them on Thursday evening but you couldn't make it?" asked Brophy.

"That's right. I had to work a little later than expected at the lab."

"What time did you contact your brother about not coming?"

"I sent him a few messages during the day telling him I wasn't sure if I was going to make it or not. I was meant to get down early and take Seán to buy some clothes for the concert."

"Did your brother mention who would pick him up from hurling camp?" asked McCall.

"I don't think so. I assumed he would do it. I think he usually does, then takes him back to the lab and waits for Maura to come a take him home. She has Pilates class in the city until two."

"Would Jordan have brought him home and left him by himself until she got back?" Brophy again.

"Of course, not. He's ten years old. Why do you ask?"

Ordinarily, Brophy would have deflected the question with one of his own, but on this occasion, he felt compelled by reasons of compassion to answer. "We're not sure who collected Seán from camp. We don't have CCTV of Jordan on his way home at that time, so we don't know if Seán was with him or not." He sensed a dagger stare from McCall, shocked at his submissiveness.

"How was your relationship with your

sister-in-law?" asked McCall, Brophy thought, trying to avert him from giving away any more evidence.

"We get along well. I've always liked her, even when we were in school together. But I wouldn't say we were close friends. She was a great mother to Seán. She'd never let anything happen to him if she could avoid it. If Jordan was involved with Quilty, I seriously doubt she knew about it. She'd flip out if he brought that kind of danger around Seán."

"Thank you, Ms Walters," said McCall. "You've been very helpful. As soon as we know any more, we'll let you know."

"Thank you, Detectives. I trust you'll do everything you can to find Seán, but please do more than that. Whatever you need from me, I'm here." She wiped tears from each cheek with the butt of her wrists.

Brophy and McCall got up to leave.

"Thanks for the coffee," said Brophy and gave her a half-smile.

"Your welcome. Let me see you out."

They walked across the narrow hall to the front door. McCall went out first, followed by Brophy. Just as Ciara Walters was about to close the door behind them, Brophy called out. "One more question, if you don't mind?"

"Not at all. What is it?"

"Do you know if anyone else was supposed to have dinner at your brother's house that evening?"

"Well, yes. I thought you would have known that already. Barry Donahue and his son, Aidan, were due to join us but apparently, they also had to cancel."

"Okay," said Brophy. "I just wanted to double-check. Thanks for your time."

CHAPTER TWENTY-FOUR

"Do you think we should tell them?" asked McCall when they got back into Brophy's car.

He pulled away from the curb and drove towards the beach and the village. "Tell who, what?"

"That clown White and his lapdog, Leard. Should we tell them that Donahue is still not being straight with us?"

"Why wouldn't we tell them, Christine? It's their investigation. If we don't tell them, it could obstruct them finding the boy."

"I think their not sharing all the intelligence they have is already compromising finding the boy. Why don't we have a shot at Donahue first?"

"I don't know. I think it's better to be transparent."

She gave him a look she only pulled out in desperate times, usually when she wanted him to cover for her if she wanted to head off early; sometimes to allow her lead on a case in which she has a particular disliking for the one under investigation. Her head slightly tilted, one eyebrow raised, and her lips almost at a pout.

We'll see if we can set up an interview with Donahue when we get back. But they'll definitely be listening in, so you better make it good."

The car rolled by the pier, and Brophy looked out at all the fishing boats of various shapes and colours. A mixture of fishermen and tourists jostled for space along the wooden jetties.

"You fancy her, don't you?"

"What are you on about now? She's a bereaved aunt of a missing child with a murdered brother."

"Quite the beauty, though, don't you think?"

"I'm not gonna do this with you now. This case is serious. I don't need any distractions."

The chat was lighter than it had been the last few days on the journey back to the city. McCall was excited about the Munster rally championship coming up in three weeks. She qualified easily in the heats and was dead set on winning the race outright and become the first female to do so. She begged Brophy to come and see her. He never had before, and he promised her he'd think about it, which in Brophy talk was a 'definitely not.'

As they were cutting through the city, making the final approach to headquarters, Brophy's phone lit up in its holder on the dashboard. Detective Dunford's name flashed up. He pressed the green button then a button with the Bluetooth symbol.

"Dunford. What's the craic?" said Brophy.

"Not much. We followed up on a few pointless leads this morning. I'm hoping to interview a couple of the board members later if they don't object to having their Sunday afternoon disturbed by lowly police business."

McCall sniggered at Dunford's remark.

"Good work," said Brophy. "How is Garda Mallon getting along with you?"

"She's great, Sergeant. A real natural if ever I met one."

"Good to hear. Was there something else you couldn't wait to discuss? We'll be at HQ in five."

"Actually, there is, yeah." He paused for a few beats. "My buddy in the Kilkenny station gave me a call a while ago."

Brophy instantly tensed up. McCall cleared her throat so Dunford would know Brophy had company.

"He said that Maurice Scully was taken into Kilkenny General early this morning after taking an overdose. He's in an induced coma. They're not sure if he's going to make it. Just thought you should know."

Brophy didn't say anything for a few long seconds and stared intently at the city street in front of him. "Thanks, Detective." He pressed the button to ring off.

"Red light, Brophy," shouted McCall.

He slammed on the brakes, sending the two of them jerking forward.

"Jesus, man. Take it easy." He didn't reply. "Look, forget about him. He's stonewalled you for years. I don't think he's the type to suddenly become remorseful on his deathbed."

"You don't know that," he said quietly.

They were at the station within a couple of minutes. Brophy pulled up to the front door and gazed straight ahead, an obvious signal for McCall to get out of the car.

"I know I can't stop you from going there, Conal, but please don't get your hopes up again." She laid her right hand over his on the steering wheel. "I know what that case has done to you. Don't-"

"Thanks, Detective. I'll see you later."

She got out, and Brophy sped away.

On the forty-minute drive, a million thoughts went through his mind. He'd always blamed himself for the failure to close the case and find Mel Fanning's body. To him, and many others, it was evident her boyfriend and two of his friends were responsible and hid the body, sworn to each other to take their secret to their graves. One of the three, Rob Dalton, died by suicide six years earlier, and Scully's drug addiction had gone from bad to worse in the proceeding years. Dalton had called to arrange a meeting with Brophy two days before his death but never showed up. This time he was prepared to try anything to get a confession out of Scully, even though he'd been the most belligerent of the three during the initial investigation.

After crawling along the heavy traffic on the

outskirts of Kilkenny City, he reached the hospital. He assumed the fullness of the sprawling car park was due to it being Sunday afternoon, peak visiting hours. Either that or people were still refusing to accept expert advice and stay out of the sun's direct heat as much as possible. Judging by what he'd seen at beaches the last few days, it was probably a mix of both.

A brief exchange ensued with the nurse at reception about whether a non-family member should be allowed to visit Scully at that critical time, but an astute flash of his warrant card gave rise to second thoughts. She didn't page her superior and directed Brophy to the ICU on the third floor.

On reaching the third floor, he found the calmness, compared to the hectic to-ing and fro-ing of the ground floor, to be slightly eerie. Only a few nurses were to be seen in the ward-rooms, wearing protective gear and leaning over still patients. A woman in her sixties was the lone visitor, sitting on a blue plastic chair at the opposite end to the lift. She had a tissue in her hand, bringing it to her nose and sniffling on a couple of occasions. She wore grey sweat pants and a green cardigan that hung on her skeletal frame, only the points of her shoulder making it look like it's not laying flat on itself. Recognising her immediately, Brophy braced himself for an awkward encounter.

"Mrs Scully, how is he?" he said, portraying

as much remorse as he could rouse in himself.

"Oh, there's no change, Doctor." She said, looking up through heavily bloodshot eyes. He suddenly remembered that she'd had her son when she was a teenager, so couldn't be more than in her late forties. "Shouldn't I be the one asking you that, anyway, Doctor?"

"I'm terribly sorry for all your trouble, Mrs Scully, but do you think it would be okay if I try to ask Maurice a few questions?"

Her wavering presence became stunted by a flash of recognition in her eyes, but it seemed as though she couldn't quite make out who he was. "What a strange request?"

"I know it couldn't possibly come at a worse time, but-"

"Wait a second. It's you," she said, a flash of hatred making her more alert now. "That Waterford hurler cop, that tormented those boys over that slag, Mel Fanning. You have a nerve showing up here." She was breathing heavily now and looked down the corridor to see if anyone was there to back her up. "Get out of here, or I'll call the guards."

"I am the guards, Mrs Scully."

"Don't you 'Mrs Scully' me. My marriage broke down after your investigation. We couldn't find jobs. My husband was attacked in pubs. We couldn't go outside the door without being reminded about the tramp. He took off to England, and we've barely heard from him. And my boy, Maurice, hardly sober a day since."

"I'm sorry for how things have worked out for you and your family but think of Mel Fanning's family. They've been suffering every day since, too. Through no fault of their own, and they still have to live with the heartbreak of not knowing what happened. Now, I know those boys knew something. I'm not saying they're responsible, but I know they have information that can help us find her."

"Get the fuck out of here, you pig," she shouted shakily at the top of her voice.

A nurse came running out of one of the rooms and made his way to where she sat. Brophy glanced in the glass partition to Scully's room. He saw him lying there unconscious, various tubes leading out of his hands and nose. Before the nurse reached them, Brophy took out his warrant card and stepped towards the young man in scrubs.

"What's going on here?" he said with authority larger than his size.

"I'm a detective from Waterford City Station." The nurse looked closely at the card. "I wanted to see if Mr Scully was awake so I could ask him some questions about an ongoing missing person case."

"Well, I think it's obvious he's not awake," said the nurse, gesturing with his head. Brophy followed his head movement and winding up to turn away and say something to the nurse; Scully raised his head from the pillow a few inches.

Brophy did a double-take. "He's awake. Just one minute, that's all I ask," he said and brushed past the nurse. He opened the door and entered with speed and agility enough to give himself a few seconds, then locked it after him. He heard Scully's mother cry her protests outside but dared not look back might he have a change of heart.

"Maurice, hello. How are you feeling?" he said on reaching the side of his bed.

The nurse was banging on the door now, shouting at him. Scully, clearly confused by the ruckus and appearance of a stranger at his bedside, blinked rapidly as if it might help him make sense of things. His eyes were sunk deep like lugworm holes on wet sand, his skin a sickly greenish-blue. Every strained breath revealed the contours of his trachea. His hair, a deep black, looked as though it merely rested on his head, ready to blow away at any moment. Brophy couldn't figure out if it was from the overdose or years of addiction. Likely both, he conceded.

"Who are you?" he said in a raspy half-whisper.

Brophy leaned over, revealing himself more directly to Scully. "Don't you remember me, Maurice? You said you admired my side-line-ball strikes in your playing days."

His eyes focused more on Brophy, and recognition flickered. "What do you want?"

"I want to give you one last chance to do the right thing. I met Mrs Fanning recently. She used to be good friends with your mother, didn't she? Childhood friends, I believe. You should see her now, Maurice. Lost all hope of ever knowing what happened to her seventeen-year-old daughter, her only child. She's a shell of a woman."

Scully sniggered, a ragged wheeze of a laugh. "I told you-," he paused to take a laboured breath. "That I have no idea what happened to that girl." He smirked and turned his head to look out the partition window. His mother was banging on the glass, attempting to clear Brophy out of her son's room.

"What about my ma? Look what this has done to her?"

"I know, Maurice. Nobody wins in a situation like this. But Foylan seems to have done well enough for himself."

Scully turned back to Brophy, and his anger was palpable. "Surprised any of us come out the other side with what you and your crew done to us. Didn't show myself outside the door for two years, you bastard," he spat at him.

"That's because people know what happened, and they're disgusted. There's still a chance to set things straight. Release everyone from this, your mother included. Isn't that what you're trying to do with this overdose, anyway? Why not give that chance to a dozen others too?"

Scully's rage was beginning to soften, and Brophy thought his eyes were tearing up. He went with it. "You know, Rob called me a couple of days before he passed away? He wanted to meet up and talk to me."

"I know," he said, the tears and grief now pouring down his face. "And he couldn't even get that right. Left me here all by myself, that coward."

"You can change it all. Just tell me where she is." Brophy didn't notice the large security guard jostling with his set of keys in the lock. He barged in with a whoosh and a crack.

"What the hell are you doing in here with that man? He's in a critical condition," shouted the guard in a cockney accent.

Brophy paid no attention and tried again. "Where is she, Maurice?"

The guard grabbed his upper arm, but Brophy pulled back to await Scully's answer. He was positioning to say something. Twenty years in the job and Brophy knew that look.

"Fuck off, you pig. I don't know a thing."

By now, the guard had his two hands on Brophy, and he angrily shook free and shouted that he was a cop. He fumbled and pulled out his warrant card. "Here. See. Look," he said, his heart rate fluttering.

"I'm gonna have to ask that you leave, Sergeant Brophy. He's a sick man. He can't have any more stress right now."

Scully's mother was shouting blue murder at Brophy, the nurse trying to calm her down.

"Okay, I'm leaving."

Scully started screaming at the top of his lungs, and after a few seconds, Brophy realised he was laughing.

CHAPTER TWENTY-FIVE

Monday morning brought no relief from the heat, and humidity levels were at a point Brophy had only experienced once, on a trip to Thailand, courtesy of the county board for winning the Munster Final in '01. Mixed with his displeasure was the fact that he'd barely managed three hours sleep the night before, the chaos of the last few days playing hard on his mind. He wore a black polo-neck to offset the brightness of the beige linen pants he put on, the lightest item of clothing in his possession.

He arrived at Glencairn Industrial Estate at a little after nine. The car park of the one-storey flat-roofed white building was all but full. Business as usual. McCall had called him a while earlier to say she'd be running late and pleaded with him to wait until she arrived to question the employees. In his foul mood, he begrudgingly agreed to hold off on the second interview with the board member, David Hughes. But first, he'd interview the receptionist by himself.

The lobby was more like that of a hospital; one of the very expensive private ones like where he was taken if he had an injury during the inter-county championship. The walls were white and adorned in places with white PVC panelling, the name of the company spattered here and there in blue letters. At first, he thought there was no one at the reception desk but as he drew closer, heard sniffling coming from behind it. He leaned over and saw a young lady with her head rested on her crossed arms on the desk.

"Am, excuse me? Are you Clíodhna Devlin?"

She raised her head from her arms, and her face was all puffy and streaked with make-up infused tears like she'd been crying for days. "Yes," she said in a trembling voice. "Who are you?"

"I'm Detective Brophy. I'm investigating the death of your boss, Jordan Walters." Her face quivered, and he anticipated an explosion of grief. However, she managed to hold it together.

"Oh, yes. I was expecting someone at some stage today. I just thought it'd be more than one person, and they'd be wearing uniforms, is all." She dabbed at the tears with a red hankie, and for a brief second, he saw what Walters must have been attracted to. Although not conventionally beautiful, her big blue eyes and doll-like face gave her a hidden magnetism most men would find difficult to deflect.

"Do you think we'd be able to go somewhere to have a chat, Ms Devlin?"

"Of course," she said, braving an attempt at a smile, revealing yet more of her strange allure. "We can go to the waiting lounge across the hall there." She got up and walked around the desk, and in a business-like manner, ushered him across the lobby to a room beside the security doors, leading into the labs. Brophy sat on a two-seater sofa facing the door, and she sat on a swivel chair across from him.

"Firstly, I'm very sorry for your loss. How well did you know Jordan Walters?"

"Oh, not that well," she said, not making eye contact as she spoke. "But he was a very good boss. Took good care of all the staff." She trembled again.

"Have you ever seen anyone here with Jordan who wasn't connected to the company?"

"Let me see?" she said, overemphasising her attempts at recollection with head tilts and 'Em's.' "No, not that I can think of now."

"We will be able to find any irregularities on the sign-in ledger we took as evidence, you know?"

"Really? Oh. The only person I've ever signed in that wasn't here on business was that Barry Donahue man. Bloody creep, he is."

"Why do you say that?"

"He tried to hit on me every time he was leaving."

"That must be frustrating, especially given that he's a married man."

She forced an awkward smile. "Except that one time, a few weeks ago. He left in a bit of a tear."

"Any idea why?"

"Jordan said he was trying to get out of a deal." The guilt flushed down her face. She knew she'd slipped up.

"You seem closer to him than a receptionist usually would be unless there's some kind of personal relationship you're withholding from us."

"Withholding?" she said, clutching the red hankie with two hands now. "That sounds very serious."

Brophy put on his best concerned-friend voice. "But if you have no connection with the crime itself, there'd likely be no need to have your name brought into any potential future court case."

"Oh, my god! My mother will kill me. She thought this job was the best thing for me, getting away from Limerick for a while. If she found out I was involved with my boss, and now he's been murdered along with his wife... Oh, for cryin' out loud, what's happening?" She broke down again. "It's not like that, Detective. We were very close. I never meant for it to happen, but he was so charming and good looking. We fell for each other. That's all. I'm sorry," she said and wiped her eyes.

"It's okay. It's not your fault."

"He had a very unhappy marriage. I think he wanted to leave her."

"Did he tell you that?"

"Not exactly. But he often talked about

selling up shop and taking me to Bahrain to live the high life. One of the things I found so cute about him was that he thought he was some kind of big-shot gangster or something the way he talked sometimes."

"What do you mean by that? What would he say?"

"Oh, just silly things, like if he'd an argument with a client or supplier, he'd tell me in private later that he could have the person and his family wiped out if he wan-" Her face turned to one of shock realisation. "And that's what happened to him, isn't it? Someone came after him and his family."

"On Thursday, he left at eleven-thirty to pick up his son from hurling camp." Her eyes shot to the side. "Are you sure he didn't bring the boy back here?"

"I'm certain."

"He was gone for almost two hours. Have you any idea at all where he might have gone?"

She didn't say anything, just gazed ahead, doughy-eyed.

"What is it, Clíodhna?"

"He didn't pick up his son that day."

"What? How do you know?"

"Because he was with me the whole time. We went to a Hotel 6 on Cork Road. I left with him and returned with him. We were never out of each other's sight."

"Why didn't you tell the officers who

questioned you on Friday?"

"They never mentioned him picking up his son. They just asked me what time he left and returned, so I told them."

"Okay. That's fair enough. But you might need to make an official statement to that effect at some stage."

"You said you'd keep my name out of it."

"I said I'd try my best, and I will. I don't think there'll be any need to make this public."

"I can't believe he's actually dead," she said and broke down crying again.

Ten minutes later, Brophy met a leaden-faced McCall out in the car park. She was smoking a cigarette and wearing a black skirt and white blouse, making her look quite business-like.

"What did the receptionist have to say for herself?" she said and took a deep draw from her smoke.

Brophy edged in close as if someone might be listening in. "He didn't pick up the boy at hurling camp."

"You serious? How do you know?"

"As expected, they were having an affair. She said he was with her at lunchtime on Thursday. They went to a cheap motel for a bit of a mid-afternoon roll."

"Jesus. So who?"

"Send a message to everyone on the team.

Let them know we still need an I.D. on the car that picked him up."

McCall rested the cigarette between her lips and began pounding on her touch screen with a speed that dismayed Brophy. "And tell someone to call the Motel 6 on Cork Road to verify their presence."

She finished the two messages and took another couple of drags, then threw the butt at Brophy's feet.

"Hey! What did I tell you about that?" he said with a wry smile. "Let's go in to talk to this Hughes character, see what he has to say.

They entered the lobby and were greeted with a big smile from Clíodhna Devlin. Good morning, how may-" she said before becoming self-conscious, discovering it was Brophy returning. The sunny disposition drained from her face. "Detective. Mr Hughes will be waiting for you. Third door on the left."

She buzzed them through, and McCall gave her a sarcastic smile as she passed.

Brophy stopped outside the office door and looked down the empty, silent hall. The left side looked to be taken up by offices, and meeting rooms, whilst along the right were secured, tightly shut lab doors. Music played over unseen speakers giving the place a new-age vibe. He gave a nod to McCall and she knocked three times on the black door.

"Come in," came a muffled voice from

inside.

McCall entered, followed by Brophy.

The room was larger and brighter than Brophy had expected, the back wall an expansive patio window with a door that led out to a quad garden, ornately laid out with Japanese style plants and wooden furniture. Hughes sat in a black leather chair. His hair was light brown and coiffed, and he wore a brown pinstripe suit with a blue shirt and red tie. Attempting to maintain an air of cool, he glared at the detectives as they entered, sitting cross-legged, his elbows resting on the sides of his over-sized chair, fingers tented in front of his chest. Brophy saw right through the calm guy act.

"Take a seat there, please," he said without moving from his position.

The office didn't have much in the way of filing cabinets or shelves, but Brophy assumed maybe those things were now obsolete in the corporate world. Unlike the station, where everything they had seemed to be stuffed into a filing cabinet somewhere. They sat on the two chairs facing Hughes.

"I'm Detective Sergeant McCall and this is Detective Sergeant Brophy."

"Terrible thing, what happened to Jordan and Maura." His eyes showed a deep sadness. "We've all known each other for many years, you know?"

"Yes, we know. And we're very sorry for

your loss. It must have been difficult to come into work today," said McCall.

"Truth be told, I didn't want to come near the place for a while, but the other board members pleaded with me. They thought, because of our closeness in age, I'd be more of a comfort to the technical staff. A show of solidarity, if you know what I mean?" He hardly took his eyes off McCall as he spoke.

"And did it work?"

"Did what work?"

"Were you a comfort to the employees?"

He puffed out his cheeks, and regret was plain in his features. "To be perfectly honest with you, I don't think they care all that much. The few of them who said anything showed more concern for their jobs than anything else."

"I take it Jordan didn't have the greatest rapport with his staff," said Brophy.

"You could say that."

"How about you and he?" said McCall. "Did you have a good working relationship?"

"As I said, we've been close friends for years."

"That's not what she's asking," said Brophy. "She means did you work well together? Always on the same page and things like that?"

He looked a little stumped by the question. "It's a high-pressure industry. We need to be very precise with things. Deadlines can be quite intense, and tempers definitely flare up at times.

Mostly Jordan and I worked very well together."

"You're the accounts manager as well as being on the board, is that right?" asked McCall.

"That's right."

"How is the financial state of the company?"

He smiled, proud of himself. "It's excellent. We're one of the most profitable homegrown companies in Waterford. We've won numerous awards from the Chamber of Commerce."

"Can we have a list of your investors?"

"I'm afraid that's confidential. We couldn't possibly give out that information."

"We can have a summons within forty-eight hours, so it's better to hand it over now," said Brophy.

"If you don't mind, I think I'll wait to see that summons."

"Fair enough." Brophy looked around the office again, thinking about how relaxing it would be to work in a space like that. "Did you go to school together?" he asked, focusing on making eye contact with Hughes again.

"Yes. Secondary school and university," he said with slight irritation.

"Then I take it you're also pals with Bobby Quilty?"

The strain of faking a smouldering resting face, drained from his features. His lower lip quivered. "I-I came across him from time to time. Never cared much for him though. Even in secondary school, he had notions of big-time crime."

"When we check the financial records of the company," cut in McCall, "I assume we'll be able to account for all the great profits that come your way?"

"Of course. Why wouldn't you?"

"What about the offshore accounts?" said Brophy firmly.

Hughes's face reddened. No way could he hide his fear now. "Please. I had nothing to do with anything. I just did what I was told. Every account I cleared had the proper paperwork and invoices."

"What are you so afraid of then?" asked McCall.

"Are you fucking serious? I have a family. A wife and two daughters. That's what I'm afraid of."

"There was a large amount of drugs found in Jordan's garage," said Brophy. "And if you want us to protect you, no bullshitting. From now on, if we think you're not giving us a straight answer, we walk out."

Despite Hughes's questionable tan, he went truly pale. "I had nothing to do with it, I swear to God."

"But you knew it was going on?" asked McCall.

"Not before I took the job. I always knew Jordan and Quilty had a very close relationship. But I never imagined he'd get involved with that business."

"How long has he been making meth in these labs?" said Brophy.

"Meth? I don't know anything about any meth. I always thought they were only involved in cocaine."

"We suspect he may have begun manufacturing methamphetamine in this lab," said McCall. "What makes you think he was into coke?"

Hughes's head bobbed lightly over and back, and he loosened his tie and opened his top shirt button with shaky hands. He whipped out his handkerchief and wiped his dripping brow. "I think maybe I should see a solicitor."

"You have every right to do that, David, but you're not under arrest or being charged with anything. Or we can end this interview, if that's what you want and we'll come back with an official order. But you should know, if a solicitor gets involved now and certain people find out, you might put yourself in danger," said McCall.

"We know how these people operate," said Brophy, "And if you truly had no part in criminal activity, we can keep you out of it and protect you. But you have to tell us what we need to know."

Hughes twisted and squirmed in his seat. He crouched down all of a sudden and vomited into a bin under his desk. McCall grimaced, and Brophy went on. "How long has Jordan been working with Quilty?"

"Years for all that I can tell," he replied after wiping his mouth with tissues taken from a box on his desk. "Small amounts used to come in with lab supplies from overseas. At the same time, money was being pumped out through the company accounts. I didn't know what was going on at first. I foolishly thought we were that profitable. Then I began to look into things more. I wanted to leave the company as soon as I discovered what they were up to. Jordan basically threatened me that if I left, Quilty might get nervous and do something. I've been living with this shit for eight years," he said, close to blubbering. "But then it all but stopped a year ago when that police operation put a bunch of these guys away. I never knew anything about any meth, and that's the truth."

"Can any of the paper-trail be traced back to Quilty?" asked Brophy.

"Not a chance. He's way too careful. My guess is most of the investors are false identities. I doubt the people exist, at all."

"Was Maura part of it?" asked McCall.

His lips clenched, and his eyes gave McCall the impression of someone defending a loved one who's been attacked. "Not a chance. Jesus, poor Maura was an angel. All she cared about was her fundraisers and making sure Seán had the right friends. There's no way she would have tolerated any of this. That's what makes it all the more difficult. She had to pay the ultimate sacrifice for that asshole."

"What do you know about her uncle, Barry Donahue?" asked Brophy.

Hughes took a pause, his chest heaving with restrained rage. "He's a fool. After Mr Walters passed away, he tried everything in his power to try to take over this company, buy Jordan out, and merge it with his. He always used Maura as leverage to get to Jordan."

Brophy cursed in his mind at his phone, vibrating in his pants pocket. He always told himself he'd turn it off when interviewing someone but mostly forgot to do so. He fished it out as McCall asked another question and jabbed his finger towards the red circle on the screen before seeing it was Felix White. Brophy excused himself and rushed out the door to answer.

"What can I do for you?" he said abruptly.

"Where are you, Brophy?" returned White's voice with more than a hint of anger.

"We're at Bioford Laboratory interviewing some employees."

"Who are you with now?"

"David Hughes. Why?"

"I need you to cease your interview and get out of there at once, is that understood?"

"What are you talking about? We have an investigation to carry out."

"My investigation, Brophy. And as your senior officer, I'm giving you a direct order to step down. We have a team on the way. I want you gone by the time they arrive." With that, White rang off.

A fury churned in Brophy's head. The dark walls began to close in on his vision, and he felt faint for a few seconds. He took two deep breaths to compose himself and stepped back into the office. "McCall? We need to go."

She turned in her swivel chair to face him, confusion in her furled-up forehead. "What do you mean? I still have a few more questions for Mr Hughes." She screwed up her face to suggest she was getting somewhere with Hughes, and she needed to go on.

"Thanks for your time, Mr Hughes. You'll be hearing from us again soon."

Hughes also looked flummoxed at this point, his body language indicating he was ready to pour out his soul like the information had been held at ransom for years and was now offering him relief to be finally getting out.

McCall turned back to Hughes and said, "Thanks for the information, David. And like my partner said, we'll do everything we can to prot-"

"Now, McCall."

She shot to her feet and walked out without looking at Brophy.

At the security door, waiting to be buzzed out, she said, "What in the name of God was that all about? You've never done that before."

"That was White on the phone, ordering us

to leave. Sounds like the place is going to be raided by his crew."

"For fuck sake, the media will be all over it."

The door buzzed, and Brophy said, "I know," before stepping into the lobby and heading for the front door without a hint of acknowledgement to Clíodhna Devlin.

CHAPTER TWENTY-SIX

McCall gunned the engine and shot out of the car park before Brophy even had time to ease his Saab out of its tight parking space. The Monday morning traffic was worse than its usual race to the next set of traffic lights. The sun still sweltering, many cars on the road had packed roof-racks, and he also passed an oversized caravan crawling along Cork Road. Luckily they could avoid the centre of the city to get to Donahue's lab. In all, the industrial park was only two kilometres away from the station.

When Brophy skidded onto the final stretch of road, he spotted McCall standing at her car, her arm resting on the open door, gazing at the commotion across the road. A crowd of workers from other businesses on the street were gathered in small groups observing the Special Branch executing their order to raid the premises. At least eight squad cars and three Tech Bureau vans sat facing inwards at the front of the building, an old grey-stone warehouse converted into a state of the art space, like several other premises in the area. McCall gave a nod of annoyed acceptance when she caught sight of him walking towards her.

"Great to be in the know, isn't it?" she said and took a box of cigarettes from the dashboard.

She took one out and lit it, raising a mocking eyebrow to Brophy's disapproval.

"They made out yesterday they were going to protect him if he complies. What have they found out since?"

"Maybe you can ask your new pal over there," she said, blowing out a sharp spear of smoke in the direction of Leard, marching out the glass door entrance to the lab.

"C'mon. Let's see what he has to say for himself."

"Are you sure I'm welcome in your inner circle," she said, cocking her head to the side.

"I think Leard is the kind of man who's severely weakened in front of a strong woman, so let's go," he said with a gotcha-grin.

They walked across to where Leard was issuing instructions to a few plainclothes and uniformed guards. Within seconds, having received their directives, the officers scattered.

"What's going on here?" asked Brophy.

"What does it look like? We're searching a lab where methamphetamine is being produced," answered Leard. He looked at McCall with something bordering on disgust when she took a pull of her smoke and blew it in his general direction.

"It would be useful for us to know these things are happening so we can plan accordingly," said McCall. "How are we gonna find this boy if we don't know how the investigation is being carried out?"

"You'll know what you need to know when you need to know it," replied Leard. Sweat rolled down his forehead.

"We've proved that it wasn't Jordan Walters who picked up his son," said Brophy, attempting to steer the exchange in another direction.

"Proved? You haven't proved a damn thing. All we have is the receptionist's word. How do we know she wasn't involved?"

"This isn't the way to find him. Making all this noise will only scare people away. How do you expect Doyle to come out of the woodwork if you're raiding the lab where his stuff is being made?"

As Leard was about to answer, White and two uniformed gardaí emerged from the building, escorting a tearful, distraught Donahue in handcuffs.

"We took Doyle in this morning. Gave a knock on his Naas door just before six," said Leard.

"And?" said Brophy expectantly.

Leard rounded pointedly on him. "And he'll be questioned later. No sign of the kid, if that's what you're getting at."

At that moment, Donahue passed them. He pleaded, "Why are you doing this to me? I thought you were going to help me."

"Get him out of here," said White, stopping beside Leard.

The two gardaí dragged him away. Brophy looked beyond the paddy-wagon and saw a couple of reporters had already arrived and were snapping shots of the arrest.

"Detectives. From what I understand, you got information from the receptionist about the whereabouts of Walters last Thursday at lunchtime?"

"We're quite certain it wasn't him," said Brophy.

"We have a team over at his house now, searching for the boy," said White as though the information would appease Brophy's dread.

"What about Veale? Any sign of him?"

White glanced at McCall as if he was offended she was in the know about Veale.

"I've told her everything. She's my partner," said Brophy. He saw McCall tighten her lips to hold back a smile.

"The details of Veale were supposed to be confidential," said White.

"They are confidential. That's why I told her."

"We still have no idea where he is."

McCall received a call and broke away from the group.

"Is that why Delaney was cut loose? To draw him out?" asked Brophy.

"You could say that," said White, lowering his head in a rare show of self-consciousness. "But unfortunately, that hasn't worked out very well."

"What's that supposed to mean?

"Delaney shook his escorts off in the middle of the wee hours. We have no idea where he is now. We've checked his home and the place in Tramore. He's nowhere to be found."

McCall returned and grabbed Brophy by the elbow. "C'mon. We need to get going. Pleasure as always, Detectives."

CHAPTER TWENTY-SEVEN

The village of Portlaw was a twenty-kilometre drive from the city, half of the journey snaking along winding country roads. The district of Cuilbeag was easy to identify once reached on the outskirts of Portlaw. It had a narrow two-lane road, scattered with potholes and discarded pieces of fresh timber, canopied on either side by a dense forest of logging pine trees.

Brophy's heart raced, almost keeping pace with McCall's erratic driving. The call she received had come from a local station sergeant she was friendly with, and due to the two sizable raids happening in the city at the time, no other units were available to intercept with them. The Tech team would be busy for hours to come.

Sergeant Costigan informed her a logger had arrived to work an hour early, and when he got to the logging yard, he noticed a Ford Fiesta parked down along one of the numerous dirt tracks that spread in all directions from the central yard. The tracks had just enough room for the logging trucks to ease down, load up, and reverse back to the yard to treat the felled trees. The worker took a closer look and saw a tall man wearing a tracksuit, in the middle of the wood, digging a hole and burying a gym bag. Wary of the stranger's intent, he decided to take refuge in the small prefab staffroom and call his friend, Costigan. Alarm bells went off in Costigan's head, having been on alert the last few days for any sighting of a Ford Fiesta that may have been of interest to the investigation in the city. Before Costigan arrived at the logging yard, the culprit had already left in the Fiesta.

When Brophy pulled into the yard, he saw McCall and a uniformed garda arguing with eight angry loggers. He parked beside a blue corrugated iron shed and walked over to the crowd.

"What's going on here," he said loud and aggressive enough for everyone to instantly know he was in charge.

A chorus of angry voices was directed his way, and he could make out the conflict was because they were not being allowed to start work until the area was properly searched.

"Who's the foreman here?" he shouted.

The commotion settled to a murmur, and a short, stout man in his thirties, with a prematurely greying beard, stepped forward.

"I am. And we've almost lost an hour and a half of work time because of this guard. Someone needs to tell me what in the name of Christ this is all about. This is private property, you know?"

Brophy turned to Sergeant Costigan, a tall, broad-shouldered man in his early fifties. "Where was the person seen?"

Costigan pointed straight past Brophy's

shoulder. "The car was parked down that trail and he was seen in the middle of that section of woodland, between the two tracks." He said the last part after raising his other hand in the direction of another track.

"Tell your man to grab a shovel, and let's have a look," said Brophy.

The logger who called Costigan ran off to one of the sheds and quickly returned with a spade.

"I'll allow ye to go back to work after we check out the area, but stay back here until we're done," Brophy directed the remaining workers.

His walking pace was almost a jog, and the three officers tailed the logger a hundred metres along the path. Then he took a sharp turn to his left, heading in through the trees. Shafts of sunlight squeezed around the trunks, leaving the forest floor looking like a melted chessboard dripping off the face of the earth. Brophy's clothes were soaked with sweat and McCall was panting with the effort and the fast pace.

"Those smokes are catching up with you," he said to her.

"Ah, shut up, will you? I could outrun you any day, former All-star or not."

"Touché."

The logger stopped just in front of a densely packed cluster of trees. He pointed into the relative darkness of the section. "Right over there," he said. "See? You can see where the soil is unsettled."

Brophy squinted to locate the area he was pointing out. He quickly honed in on it, and the first thing he asked himself was whether a child could fit under a patch that size. He concluded that one could.

He reached out without uttering a word, and the logger placed the shovel in his hand. Brophy trudged over the mostly dried pine needle foliage. On reaching the spot, he deduced whoever it was had made an effort to cover the area over with the detritus of the forest floor, and from this close-up position, probably believed he'd done a good enough job. Only from a distance was the patch so distinct.

His throat tensed up as McCall reached his side. He placed the point of the arrow-shaped shovel at the edge of the area and pressed down on the upper rim with the sole of his brown shoe. He eased it down with his eyes half-closed, waiting to feel the sensation of coming into contact with soft flesh. A harrowing thought flickered in his mind; at least it would be better to find the boy dead than to never know, like the Fanning family in Kilkenny.

The shovel went down unimpeded. Brophy flicked a lump of soil to his left and stuck it into the dry earth again. After a few more digs and nothing found, the ground started to feel looser. The hole now about two-feet squared around the perimeter and a foot deep, he struck something soft. He looked up at McCall and found she was entranced by what he was doing. He flicked away the topsoil and revealed part of a zip and strap of a sports bag. Lowering himself to one knee, he pulled gently at the strap. It was in tight at first, then gave way, raising the fresh soil as it emerged. Brophy pulled the bag fully out and laid it gingerly on the loose soil beside the hole. The contents of the bag clanked as it touched the ground.

"What do you think it is?" asked McCall.

Brophy shrugged but was unable to disguise the worry from his face. He eased the zip open slowly. Once fully across, he parted the sides. Several handguns looked up at him.

"Guns!" said McCall.

"Five or six and a bunch of cash." He pushed the guns to the side to get a better look at the money. "Tens of thousands, I'd say."

"Step back from it. I'll give Tech a call. But we might have to wait here quite a while and stand guard."

Shortly afterwards, after some heated debate, the logging crew went back to work at the opposite end of the forest. The noise of heavy machinery, along with the piping heat, drove Brophy half-insane in the three hours they had to wait for a small tech crew to arrive from the city.

CHAPTER TWENTY-EIGHT

The rest of the afternoon was spent in the incident room, writing up reports from the last few days and updating the PULSE system with any relevant information. Both Brophy and McCall were denied access to the interviews with Donahue and Hughes, it becoming increasingly clear White and Leard wanted to play the close game from there on out.

The pulsating pain in Brophy's ankle felt like a ticking clock, counting down the seconds the case painstakingly drifted away from them, counting down the minutes Seán Walters was still unaccounted for.

"Stop tapping your foot," he said to McCall seated at another desk across from him. A habit of hers he thought had gotten worse over the years they'd worked together, an involuntary reaction to frustration when something wasn't going her way.

She doubled down and tapped even harder whilst giving him a death stare.

"What did I do?" said Brophy.

"Why is it we have all this setup?" she said, waving her arm around to take in the packed incident room full of files and officers. "Yet we're blocked from doing our jobs the way we were trained to."

"It's a travesty. Anyway, don't worry. Halpin is on our side. He'll make sure we get files on whatever they come up with. But I don't like how they're going for Hughes and Donahue. It sounds like they were both coerced into doing what they did. Let's just hope their names don't get splashed all over the papers."

"If they find Delaney's prints on one of the guns that's found to be the murder weapon, this could all be over very soon."

"Not until the boy is found."

"What do you really think of the aunt? Do you suspect she has anything to do with all of this?"

"It's hard to tell. God, some of these upper-class folk can be hard to read. So cold and calculated, if you know what I mean?"

"I know. I got a feeling she was holding something back from us, though. You might have missed it; you were so smitten with her."

"I wasn't smitten with her."

"I don't know about that," she said mockingly. "I know you have a thing for blondes."

"You're a blonde, aren't you?" He realised his mistake half-way through what he said, feeling the complexity and awkwardness of it trail up from his stomach to his chest. He thought he could register a slight quiver of the lip and a reddening of the cheeks on McCall, something he knew drove her demented, allowing others to see such vulnerability in her.

"I wasn't aware you noticed," she said by way of a comeback that fell somewhat flat.

"Sometimes my detective skills come to the fore at the worst of times," he said as a roundabout way of saying 'sorry, I fucked up.'

Before she had a chance to come up with an equally dismissive retort, Brophy's mobile started to slide across his desk with the vibrations of an incoming call. He saw Garda Desmond's name pop up on the lighted screen and picked it up and answered.

"Noreen? What can I do for you?"

"I'm on the road today, and Bennett asked me to drive by Barry Donahue's house every so often to see if any of the family show up."

"And?"

"Passed there a while ago and saw a black Mercedes in the driveway that wasn't there an hour ago. Bennett told me to let you know."

"Okay. Thanks for that, Noreen. I owe you a pint."

"You owe me more than that," she said with a husky laugh and rang off.

Brophy edged in over his desk to get closer to McCall. "Looks like someone from the Donahue household has come back from Dublin."

"Could be the son, Aidan," said McCall.

"How about we go check it out? I'm sick of sitting around doing nothing."

Within a couple of minutes, they were in McCall's car, heading across the city. A small argument ensued about turning on the air conditioner and closing the windows, but McCall was having none of it.

"How can you not love this weather we're having?"

"I don't like the heat."

"You're a strange sort, Brophy." There was a pause for a few seconds, then McCall said, "Do you have your heart set on becoming DI if we get the upgrade?"

He sneered in disbelief at the question. "Where are you getting that out of?"

"I don't know. It's just that you don't talk about it like you used to. I thought maybe you were a bit anxious about it or something."

"Jeez, you're way off. Look, I probably shouldn't say anything until after this case, but I've made up my mind to pack it in after this one."

In a most uncharacteristic stroke, McCall lost control for a brief moment and swerved across the white lines on the road. She quickly regained control. "What the hell are you talking about, pack it in? You're not seriously thinking of leaving me alone with Bennett and his band of sycophants?"

"You'll be fine. I think you'd make a much better DI than I would anyway. My heart hasn't been in this for a long time."

"No shit, Sherlock. Everyone knows your heart hasn't been in it for a long time, but you've still got the best head for it I've ever seen. I hope you'll reconsider."

They pulled up outside the house in silence, not having said a word for the last ten minutes of the journey. Sure enough, the car Aidan drove on their first visit there was parked in the driveway. They got out of the car and briskly walked over to the gate and pressed the intercom. A full minute passed with no reply.

"Jesus, I hope he's not after doing anything to himself," said McCall. "Do you think we should climb over?"

Brophy took a few steps back to get a better look into the house but the large wooden gate and high walls impeded much of the view, including all of the downstairs.

"If he's heard about his father, he'll surely be wracked with guilt," said Brophy. "Here, my ankle is shagged. I'll give you a boost over the wall."

"What makes you think I need a boost," she said defensively.

"The ten-foot-high wall makes me think it."

McCall walked back to halfway across the road and eyed up the wall, ready to have a run and jump at it. Just as she leaned onto her front foot to accelerate ahead, the intercom buzzed to life.

"What the fuck do you two want? Haven't

you caused enough damage to our family?"

McCall rushed back to the gate. "Aidan, I don't think it's very fair to blame us," she said in a calm tone. "We're trying our best to find out who killed your cousin and kidnapped Seán, but we need to be clear on all the facts first. Can you let us in to have a chat, please?" She glanced at Brophy, a wishful look in her eyes.

Brophy was about to say something. She shook her head to ward him off. Then the gate clicked and began to roll back. When they reached the front door, it was left half-open. They entered, and Brophy called out to Aidan. His voice came from the direction of the living room, so he opened the white French doors and went in. The room was large and had expensive-looking plush furniture. The heavy curtains were drawn, blocking out the light. Aidan sat on an armchair facing the fireplace, a glass of whiskey in one hand, a glass pipe in the other. McCall goose-stepped past Brophy and snatched the pipe from Aidan's hand and examined it closely.

"I see you've already helped yourself."

Aidan turned his head in a slow laboured movement. "What difference does it make at this stage? Everything is fucked, and it's my fault."

Brophy sat in an armchair across from him, and McCall sat on the sofa on his other side.

"What makes you think it's your fault?" asked Brophy.

Aidan tried to direct his gaze towards where

the question came from but struggled to focus on Brophy.

"Is it because of the gambling debt?" said McCall.

"You're very pretty," said Aidan, a half-smile tightening across his gaunt features. "Is he your boyfriend?"

Brophy thought he looked like yet another young man who was probably very sporty in his youth but threw it all away on unbidden temptations and chasing the next buzz. He had an athletic frame that appeared to be in the early stages of hunching over into a crooked junkie posture. His Brown eyes were sunk deep, his skin pallid and sickly.

"Aidan, we really want to help you and your family, but you need to be honest with us," said Brophy. "How much did you owe, and who was it to?"

"Those scumbags set me up. They knew what they were doing all along."

"What scumbags?" said McCall.

"These little scangers from Coolock. They befriended me on my first week of uni. I thought they were genuine, you know? Like they really wanted to hang around with me. They took me to cool parties, loads of hot girls. Lines of coke covering every surface in the house. It was great for a while." He blasted out a shrieking pained laugh. "Then, the gambling started. They hooked me right in. Gave me credit any time I wanted it.

I started dealing to pay off my debts." Another laugh. "But I smoked half the gear and gave the rest to mates at uni. Thought I was the right 'ol gangster around the place. Till they turned on me and started demanding I pay all the money back in one go." He took a long pull from the whiskey, grimacing at the harsh aftertaste.

"How much did you owe at that stage?" said Brophy.

"Nearly a hundred grand."

"Did they ask you to approach your father for the money?" Brophy again.

"No. That came later. They cut off the drug supply but not the gambling. I made a few more high stakes bets, and that was it. Over a quarter of a million." He looked at McCall, tears streaming down his face. "Where was I going to get that kind of dosh?"

"It's a horrible situation to find yourself in," said McCall. "When did they make contact with your father?"

"I tried to kill myself, you know? Went back to my student digs one night, put a gym bag strap around my neck, and tied it to the top of a wardrobe. Piece of shit cheap Ikea crap fell to pieces and came crashing down on me." He laughed again. "Couldn't even get that right."

"Did you ever meet Frankie Doyle?" asked Brophy.

"Not directly. Talked on the phone once. That was about it."

"What did you talk about?"

"He told me I was cut off and that I'd have to settle my debts soon. He knew I couldn't, so he said he would have to pay a visit to my father's place of work."

"That must have come as quite a shock," said McCall. "What happened then?"

"Dad called me the next day, in a right state. He almost disowned me then and there. He broke down in tears on the phone. That was the worst part. I only ever saw him cry once. At my uncle's funeral."

"Maura's father?" asked McCall.

Aidan nodded. "But he got it together and told me he'd fix it. He'd just have to do one job for Doyle, and that would be it."

"But Doyle had other ideas?" said Brophy.

Aidan fumbled in his shirt pocket for a lighter, then brought his empty hand to his mouth before realising the glass pipe was no longer there. "Hey! Where's my...? Shit. You two are cops, aren't you? Are you gonna bust me?"

"Not if we can help it," said McCall. "You're not the first young man with useful family connections, these gangs sucked in like that, and you won't be the last."

"Did you know Jordan was associated with people like this?" asked Brophy.

"We had no idea. But later, we found out that Doyle used us to get at Quilty's business. He could have done what he did to me to any number of gullible suckers. No. It was all planned from the very beginning. Some big-shot Jordan knew caught wind of what was happening with us and said he'd help us out. All we had to do was deliver Doyle to him. He'd take care of the rest."

"How did your father react when he found out about Jordan's little sideline?" asked McCall.

Aidan scoffed. "I don't think he was too surprised. We all know he and Quilty went back a ways. Maura even mentioned him in passing a few times like it was nothing out of the ordinary."

"Did Maura know about Jordan?" asked Brophy.

Aidan's expression became stony and resolute. "Are you serious? Man, at times, it seemed like she was running the whole thing. Sometimes I wondered if it was her pushing him into it."

"Do you know the name of the big-shot who was going to help you?" asked McCall.

"I can't remember. Something unusual like Croyden or Clarence or something."

"And what was the plan?" said Brophy.

"We didn't get that far."

"Dinner on Thursday evening? You were supposed to discuss it then?" asked McCall.

"Yeah. But Maura cancelled last minute. Told us she'd catch up with us at the weekend. That obviously never happened."

Brophy asked, "Was this Clarence guy supposed to be at the dinner?"

"Yes. We were all going to sit down and talk it out. Dad was dead set against the idea. He wanted Maura to bring the guy here, but Jordan wanted us all together. Fucking prick that he was. He loved having this over Dad."

"Aidan, we think it's not safe for you to stay here. We'd like to take you in with us," said McCall. "We can keep you safe."

"Do I have to?"

"Well, no. But technically, we could do you for possession, but that wouldn't help anything. Please come in with us and give an official statement. It could really help your father. I assume you heard he was taken in this morning?"

"What? No, I didn't hear that. Why?"

"His lab was raided this morning looking for the meth. He's at the station now."

"C'mon. Come with us," said Brophy.

Aidan stood and walked to the French doors. "Are you coming or not?"

CHAPTER TWENTY-NINE

Brophy and McCall dropped Aidan off at an emergency outreach centre for displaced and troubled youths in the city. Peter Ducey, the man who ran the centre, was a friend of Brophy's, and he had great trust in Ducey to talk to Aidan and calm him down. He was to keep him safe until they had time to go back to the station and get to grips with how things had progressed with the raids and the arrests of Hughes and Donahue.

Aidan seemed to like the idea and was fast asleep in a shared room by the time they left. The station was only a five-minute drive from the centre. When they rounded the corner, they were confronted with a scene of mayhem. News vans and reporters took up every inch of space of the road and footpath outside the station. Assistants ran to and from the vans, grabbing camera and mic equipment and returning to set up facing the building's main entrance. McCall had to shout at two crews to unblock the entrance to the staff car park. As they shuffled away with a murmur of invectives, one of the photographers recognised Brophy and bee-lined to his opened window.

"Sergeant Brophy. Can you tell us if one of the men arrested is being charged with the double murder in Woodstown on Thursday evening?"

Brophy turned his head as the shutter clicked inside the oversized camera in the young man's hands. He felt like getting out of the car and smashing it on the road but knew the consequences would be far more of an irritation than the satisfaction he'd get from seeing the look on the photographer's face.

Before the thought finished, McCall was squeezing past the slow-moving crews.

"What in the name of God is this all about?" she said.

"Looks like the cat is out of the bag," said Brophy.

A minute later, they were in the crowded incident room. Detective Reagan sauntered in their direction, her shoulders drawn back, a grin of pride on her face.

"Where have you two been?" she said.

"Out looking for the kid," said Brophy. "What's happening here?"

"They've pressed charges against Donahue and Hughes."

"What charges?" asked McCall.

"Manufacturing and trafficking drugs, of course. What else?"

Brophy felt a shiver besiege his entire body, the cold dark walls closed in on his peripherals, and the ground rotated and slanted with nonrhythmic guile. He pressed a closed fist hard down on a tabletop and took a deep breath to stave off the oncoming descent into panic and possible collapse.

"They've just signed death warrants for these men and their families," said McCall, her tone on the edge of an outburst. "Why did they have to press charges so soon?"

"No one knows the details yet," said Reagan. "The Dublin lads interviewed them. I can only imagine they got some kind of confessions out of them. We could learn a thing or two from them, don't you think Brophy?"

Brophy was swaying on the spot now.

"Sergeant, are you okay?" said Reagan, puzzlement washing out her pride.

"Don't worry about it, Conal," said McCall. "There's nothing we can do about it."

Brophy regained a modicum of composure, ploughed headlong towards the door at that back of the incident room that led to the stairs, and barged out. He took the steps two at a time, for two floors, arriving at the fourth, where most of the private offices were located. Knowing the NBCI had set up shop in a disused room at the end of the hall, he almost galloped all the way down. He took a quick look through the gap left by the cardboard covering the small panelled window on the door and saw Leard and White inside. Without knocking, he burst through the door, gritted teeth and tense heaving breaths. Leard was sitting at the lone desk, talking on his mobile whilst reading something off the desktop computer. White stood by the window looking down at the reporters, satisfaction etched crookedly on his mug. Both turned with a start at Brophy's aggressive entrance.

"What have you assholes done?" he demanded through coarse panting.

"We've done our jobs," said White, taking a couple of steps towards the younger sergeant.

"You know as well as I do that those two men were coerced into doing what they did. And now we've let them hang out to dry. Do you know what could happen to their families?"

This question turned White's dismissiveness into something akin to rage.

"Do we know what could happen, you ask? Of course, we fucking know what could happen. We've lived with the consequences of doing our jobs too well for years. Seen every kind of vengeful acts played out on the streets of Dublin. Innocent people getting caught in the middle of the gangs' feuds. Unsuspecting parents learning that their children, barely out of their teens, were mixed up in the drugs trade, only finding out when we deliver the news that their son has been decapitated for saying the wrong thing to the wrong dealer. So, yes, Sergeant Brophy. We know what can happen, which is why we act quickly, which is why we've brought down most of these cartel players in the last few years. But I'm quickly beginning to realise that maybe you don't understand how these things play out. Makes me think we were premature in offering you the position we talked about earlier."

"I understand enough to know we could have waited a while until we had a better chance of finding the boy to press charges. We could have kept their names out of the newspapers. You've just severely damaged the chances of finding him with your agenda."

On the back of that comment, Leard sprang up from his chair and crossed the room to face off with Brophy. His eyes darkened, and he bit his lower lip.

"What are you gonna do?" Brophy said to him whilst involuntarily puffing out his chest and clenching his fists at his sides.

Leard's head was but a foot away, then brought in closer without seeming to move his body.

"Your little find in the woods today; I'm just off the phone with forensics. The gun used in the murders was in the bag. No prints, unfortunately, but at least we have the weapon and a pretty clear description that leads us right back to our man, Delaney. So, weren't we right to release him early?" he said the last part as a statement more than a question.

"So bleedin' what? Have you taken Delaney in yet? How about Veale?"

Leard's all but imperceptible flinch backwards answered the questions for him. "Yeah, I thought not. You two might go on like you have this one cracked, but as long as he's out there and the boy is missing, it's still sealed tight around you two dickheads."

"Okay, that's enough," said White, a hint of magnanimity in his voice. "Sergeant Brophy." Brophy turned his head slightly to face him. "We know you're fully invested in finding the boy and bringing down the shooter, but you have to get it into your thick head that there's a lot more at play here. There's a power vacuum left in the trade since we took down all the big players. Our battle now is trying to ensure that that space doesn't get filled by groups of headbangers who are even more lethal than those who came before them."

"I'm well aware of the situation in Dublin and Drogheda, and I get that there's a new generation of vicious little hardmen coming up, but that still doesn't justify sending these families down."

"They'll be fine," said Leard. "The people they were associated with are in prison or dead. We'll cut them a deal, and they'll be back to their patios and hot-tubs in no time."

Brophy never remembered his dislike for someone growing so quickly as it was for Leard.

"What has Doyle got to say for himself?" asked Brophy.

"Sorry, but we can't divulge that at this time," said White, "But rest assured, he had nothing to do with the murders."

"How can you be so sure?"

"We just are."

"Well, it seems to me like he was moving in on Quilty and Walters' operation and attempted to win over Delaney in the process. That would give him more than enough motive to get someone to pull the trigger."

"For now, our investigation is focused on Delaney. He was ID'ed in the woods with his piece of shit car burying a bag. He was also in the locality at the time of the shootings."

"But why?" Brophy said with a sneer. "Why would he eliminate his supply line like that?"

"We believe he got paranoid," said Leard. Brophy knew he was lying.

"So, it's gonna be like that with you two, eh? Bennett was right. You are just a shower of wankers."

Brophy turned and left the office in a cloud of bitter silence.

CHAPTER THIRTY

The roar of the engine, the screech of the tyres skidding underneath Brophy's Saab as he pulled out of the station car park, sent the reporters scattering away from the entrance they again blocked. The early evening sun offered little in the way of relief from the mugginess that clung to him since the woods that morning. The exchange with White and Leard had left him reeling, an unquenchable rage roiling his innards, the decision which direction to start driving was unconscious. Soon he found himself on the outskirts of the city, but instead of heading west towards his home, he headed north. The forty-minute drive went by like a hypersonic trip through a dark tunnel of fear and regret.

He came to, and his mission became clear in his mind as he trailed along the R448. The harsh bright sky like white light reflected off the River Nore, running parallel to the road. He crossed the bridge at Market Street and arrived in the centre of Thomastown within a minute. He crawled along the narrow hilly streets of the old market town for a few minutes until he turned onto the one he was looking for, Mill Street. Three-storey Georgian terraced houses lined both sides of the street, most of which had been turned into various businesses over the years.

The majority were painted in pastel colours, giving the appearance of a typical street in an Irish town. But the one he sought, situated at the end, was painted white with black trim and adorned with hanging lanterns and pristine flourishing window boxes. The name on the wooden sign hanging from an L-frame by two black chains sent a shiver down his spine, "Foylan's."

He drove to the far end of the building and found a large park full of cars that looked out onto the river. Business was good. Without a thought for the consequences or inconvenience, he parked in front of the exit, blocking any cars that might attempt to leave. He cut across the car park and entered the restaurant via the side entrance.

As soon as he stepped inside the door, a wave of loud chatter, traditional Irish music, and the aroma of freshly cooked wholesome food that the place was renowned for struck him. The restaurant was split into several rooms on two floors and after a quick scan of the dimly lit lounge he found himself in, he decided his mark was nowhere to be seen.

The hushed whispers from a table of two middle-aged couples in the corner edged surreptitiously towards him. Without a word they spoke registering in his mind, he knew they had recognised him. And then it hit him like a sledgehammer; the insult that followed him since that fateful day he missed the big game: 'Bottler.'

His whole body clenched, and the muscles in his upper lip conspired to create a deathly snarl. The red-cheeked overweight man who dared let the nickname through his lips became wide-eyed and shaky when he saw Brophy's darting glare. He was about to step over and confront the man when a waitress pushed the black panelled door open with her hip as she cradled three drinks in her hands. Brophy turned and took a step to the side to block her off.

"Where's the boss?" he asked the startled girl who looked no older than a school leaver.

She shimmied and struggled to regain control of the three pints so as not to spill a drop. "Síle?" she said as though it were the oddest question she was ever asked.

"No, not Síle. Brendan Foylan."

"He's either in the main room or in his office upstairs. I'll have a check for you as soon as I drop off these drinks."

"That won't be necessary," he said and swerved around her, headed for the black door.

He stepped into the main room, which was even noisier than the lounge. At least twenty tables took up every inch of floor space and were full of boisterous customers. He could sense burgeoning rivets of silence ripple over the din as others recognised the intruder in their space. Typical Kilkenny people still know who he was after almost twenty years since he was a no-show and their team won the All-Ireland.

His frustration was suddenly replaced by loathing when he caught a glimpse of Foylan. Across the room, he stood with his back to Brophy, chatting to a table of visibly charmed, laughing young ladies. Brophy marched across the room, the hum of merry punters lowering even more. He grabbed Foylan's shoulder and pulled him around to face him. The action drew an aggressive 'hey' from Foylan, but his demeanour flipped when it dawned on him who his accoster was. Foylan wore a navy blue blazer with brass buttons, white shirt and red tie, and beige slacks, a combination that further infuriated Brophy.

"What do you want? Get the hell out of here."

The thirty-year-old barely looked a day older than when he was under investigation for his girlfriend's disappearance twelve years before, with a shock of blonde hair and not a line to be seen in his face even as he frowned at Brophy. *Not a day of stress or bother since then.*

"Did you hear about your best friend, Scully?"

"Of course, I did. And I wouldn't exactly say we were best friends anymore," he hissed in a hushed tone at Brophy. "Maurice and I have drifted over the years."

"Yeah, well, you're almost home and dry. The last witness to what you did is almost out of the picture."

"You have a nerve, Brophy, coming here and saying that to me. And anyway, Maurice is going to be fine. He's responding well to treatment."

"You've certainly done well for yourself. Do you still not feel even a smidgen of remorse?"

"I've nothing to be remorseful for. She ran off, to England or America, just like I told you a thousand times." He turned back to the ladies at the table. "I hope you all enjoy your meal," he said to some awkward expressions.

He spun on his feet and headed across the room. Brophy followed. The restaurant was almost in complete silence. When Brophy pushed through a swinging door into the kitchen, a collective gasp was followed by the reemergence of loud chatter.

All seven or eight workers in the kitchen lifted their heads from their busy jobs to scrutinise the stranger in their midst.

"Max, you need to put more fresh basil in the soup," said Foylan to the tall, obese chef who stood in front of ten active hobs, sweat rolling down his red cheeks.

"Who's this guy?" said Max.

Foylan swivelled and said, "Would you ever get out of here. I have nothing more to say to you. Leave, or I'll call the guards."

Half of the workers ceased what they were doing and took a couple of steps towards Brophy, who was panting by the entrance. "I am the guards, so that saves you the bother," he said, more for the benefit of the workers, lest one may strike him and regret it later.

"She had a drug problem and took off with someone else. How many more ways must I tell you?"

"What about the photo taken the night she went missing?"

"What about it? There's no proof it was taken that night."

"Oh, there's plenty of proof. Just no one to back it up. You must have done a right number on your two pals."

"You're talking absolute shit again, Brophy. That's why you couldn't find her the first time. You fucked it up, just like you do everything."

"Boss, do you want us to kick him out," said one of the younger kitchen porters.

"Shut up, kid," shouted Brophy. "None of you are gonna do a damn thing."

"What's this all about, boss?" asked Max, clearly impatient at the kitchen work being stalled.

"It's nothing, Max. Get back to work, everyone. Our guest was just about to leave, weren't you, Bottler?"

Brophy dived across to the centre of the kitchen and grabbed Foylan by the scruff. Pots and pans clanged and crashed to the floor as a swarm of bodies rushed for Brophy. Screams of panic and dismay echoed around the furnace of a room as Brophy dug in hard and did everything in his power to get a shot off at Foylan.

Due to his enormity, Max managed to get his two arms around both Brophy and Foylan but lost balance and brought both tumbling down on top of himself. Brophy felt hands dragging at him from all directions, attempting to pin his flailing arms and legs away from Foylan. Brophy was momentarily stunned when the toe of a boot struck him on the top of his head.

"Jesus, take it easy, Mickey," squealed an unfamiliar voice. "He's a cop."

The struggle went on for another couple of minutes until a hoarse shouting, accompanied by the clatter of a metal table, brought things to a shuddering stop. All but Max scattered back to their work stations.

Brophy looked up from his prone position on the greasy red tiles and saw a local guard striking his baton on the table. He looked to be in his late fifties and had all the hallmarks and appearance of a local cop who's not to be crossed.

Foylan got to his feet, pleading with the new guest to arrest Brophy. Brophy rose slowly and told Foylan to shut his trap.

"Detective Brophy?" said the guard, "What seems to be the problem?"

"Just popping in on an old friend, Sergeant...?"

"Ryan. I think you've given your old friend enough of a surprise. Come outside with me, if you please."

"This is not finished," he said to Foylan as he brushed past him and tailed the guard out of the kitchen. He skulked across the main room and out the front entrance.

Sergeant Ryan walked along the front of the restaurant, towards the car park, stopped half-way, and turned to Brophy.

"What are you playing at?" he said, trembling with a scowl.

"I had some unfinished business with your friend back there."

Ryan edged in closer, his face constricting more with contempt. "He's not my friend. We all know at our station he should have been put away for what he did." Brophy was flabbergasted by this comment. At the time, he'd felt like he never had the full backing of the local guards. "But that wasn't on us. And I think we both know we were kept out of the loop for the most part so certain people could further their careers. How is that gobshite Bennett anyway?"

Brophy stood motionless, stunned to silence.

"I see you there, so preoccupied with yourself that you don't even remember me, do you?"

"Ryan? Ryan." He wasn't sure if he said the name twice or thought it, but a glimmer of recognition came back to him. "Garda Ryan. I remember you now. You almost had a confession out of Scully."

"That's right. Until your lot came in and pushed me aside." Brophy bowed his head, the onset of shame weighing on him. "I see her often, you know? Ursala Fanning, Mel's mother. All the rumour mongering and gossip eventually cracked her, and now she's holding out for her daughter to contact her from England or America. That's how cruel the aftermath of this affair has been."

"We could have a swipe at Scully together after he's discharged," said Brophy by way of apology.

"As much as I'd love to, I can't. I'd lose my job in an instant. This case still plagues the town. Has left a black mark on the place for twelve years. But that doesn't mean you can't have another shot."

Ryan looked vacantly over Brophy's shoulder as if contemplating saying something. "What is it?"

"Foylan always had a hold on those two boys. Both have single mothers who work for the Foylan's, just as half the town do. Scully feared that if he spilt the beans, the Foylan's would go after his mother and destroy her. She's already a very fragile woman as it is. Back then, I almost had him assured we wouldn't let them do a damn thing to his mother. That's your route in. But tread carefully. And I'm not sure if he'll get out of the hospital this time."

"What do you mean? Foylan said he's

recovering well."

"From what I heard, it appears that way, but apparently his liver is on its way out."

Brophy nodded, acceptance and gratitude welling in him.

"Now get out of here. Oh, and I have to file a report about this incident. So, deal with it."

The hour-long drive to his house on the Copper Coast drolled on as if the car was on auto-pilot. The late evening dusk of an Irish July sent waves of shadows cascading around the sloping green fields on all sides and cracked through the bulbous trees like shafts of dark matter subsuming everything in their path. The car swerved dangerously towards leaden ditches on sharp corners, and Brophy wondered if he was purposely toying with the danger of crashing, just to feel something. The sky blazed a molten mixture of red and orange, and an old saying he'd heard a thousand times as a child came to mind: red sky at night, shepherds delight; red sky at morning, shepherds warning. Tomorrow would be another scorcher. The thought of it gave further unease to his wrangled thoughts.

By the time he arrived home, the sky had descended to black, and the stars that speckled the voids with pinpricks of light seemed further away than ever. On entering the living room, his body screeched at him to shower and return to some semblance of normality, but his mind already at the precipice of exhaustion ordered him to throw down on the old couch and block it all out. Lying on his back, he looked up at the damp-stained ceiling, closed his eyes, and rubbed his temples. He was asleep in seconds. The numb descent into slumber did anything but brought peace.

A shattering creak followed by a crashing thump caused his eyes to spring open. After blinking in rapid succession, he rubbed his eyes, but still the room was in complete darkness. His neck was stiff. It took several attempts for him to turn enough to take in his surroundings. Still nothing. Then he noticed an echo emanating from a drip started from high above, wisping through the air until it made its landing.

"Hello?" came the voice of a terrified child. Was it his own voice?

"Who's there? I want to get out."

Muffled footfalls from way up drew closer, every contact with the ground a deafening beat in unison with what his heart was doing.

"I'm scared. I want my mam and dad."

"What's your name?"

"You don't even know who I am? How are you going to find me?" The boy began to sob.

The footsteps were now directly above.

A blinding shaft of white light blasted in the opening overhead. He was dazzled again but in another way.

The glimmer of something falling through the air was followed by a bone-crashing thump on the ground nearby. An ear-shattering crash of metal on metal made him jerk in his spot.

"Who is that? Can you help us out of here?"

Something dragged along the ground next to him. A shade of grey suddenly blanketed their entire surroundings. Light.

His vision slowly came into focus. The room smelled of coal and damp wood. A bunker.

"Can you help us? I want to go home now?" A girl's voice, older than the child's.

A sensation akin to paralysis held him firmly to whatever the flat surface he was laid on. A painful laboured exertion, and he turned his head to the side. He instantly regretted it. An eternity of darkness would have been better than what he saw.

One of her eyes dangled from the socket. A v-shaped dented into the top of her head oozed a thick syrup of blood and matter. Her mouth made an 'O' shape, but nothing came out. In a moment of sheer panic and dread, she flew towards him and came eye-to-eye.

Brophy sprang from the couch with a start, covered in sweat, the dawn light invading his gloomy living room.

CHAPTER THIRTY-ONE

Brophy gripped the sodden tabloid newspaper in his sweaty hand as he walked into the incident room. White and Leard sat at the big table next to Bennett and Kenneally. Most of the other officers worked pensively at their desks, no doubt ensuring they had their details straight should they be called on to give an update to the crowd that would soon assemble around the desk. A lot had happened in the last couple of days to shed further light on the case, yet the boy remained missing.

He approached his desk and stopped beside McCall who was focused on her computer screen, reading a report off PULSE.

Without looking away from the screen, she said, "I didn't take you for a Sun reader."

He flung the paper on her desk, the front page landing face up. The headline read, 'Waterford Labs Nabbed in Failed Experiment.'

"Jaysus, who writes these things?"

The split picture underneath the headline showed two men in suits being hauled out of their workplaces, distraught and unbelieving. Donahue looked as though he might have been crying, and Hughes's features appeared ashen like the pulp paper he was printed on.

"There's nothing we can do for them now,

Brophy. They made their choices, and now they have to live with them."

Her words faintly registered with him, his glare stuck on the smug-looking White, whispering God knows what to his lapdog. White eventually caught his sight and stared back. After a while, he turned back to Leard.

"Any word on Aidan?" He didn't answer. "Conal. Snap out of it." He looked down at her. "Any news about Aidan? Should we go and get him?"

"I called Ducey on the way in. He said Aidan was fine. He's well settled into the place. We can go and get him this afternoon."

"I'm sure he knows about his father being in the news by now?"

"Ducey said he doesn't think so, but if anything out of the ordinary happens, he'll give us a shout."

"Are you okay? You seem a bit distant. More so than usual, I mean."

"I didn't get much sleep again."

"Did you take one of the pills I gave you?"

"No, I forgot."

"You should try them. They worked a treat for me when I needed them."

A voice bellowed across the room from the big table. "Gather round everyone," said Bennett.

Most of those in attendance rushed to make a horseshoe by the table. Brophy and McCall barely took a few steps forward from their desks.

"Good morning, everyone," said Bennett, his lips pressed in a restrained smile. "Yesterday was a crucial day for our investigation, as you all know. We took down two big players right here in the city. So, good work on that, ladies and gentlemen. And we also found a small cache of firearms in a wood near Portlaw. The lab has been working overtime, analysing the guns, and they've come back with great results. Turns out, one of the guns is definitely our murder weapon."

Murmurs rose and settled just as quickly. McCall nudged Brophy with her elbow.

"Now, while there were no prints found on the murder weapon itself, there were several sets found on the others. And they've all come back as belonging to a sole handler. One Michael Delaney." A few gasps but mostly unsurprised nodding and tutting. "Our objective moving forward is very clear. Find Delaney by whatever means necessary. A warrant has been issued, so I want you knocking on the doors of every relative and associate of his. Shake-down all known users in town. Find that scumbag and bring him in fast. Find him, and we find the boy." This statement sent a shock down Brophy's body and alerted him to the task at hand. "Inspector White would like to say a few things before you all head out there." Bennett finished speaking and took his seat without looking at White once.

White grinned and scoffed at Bennett's

aloofness. "Firstly, I'd like to say how great it has been working with this team the last couple of days. Your due diligence has helped us bring down some major players in the never-ending fight against drug cartels in this country. For that, I commend you all. As I'm sure you all know by now, we tagged Harry Doyle yesterday and have strong evidence that he was in contact with Michael Delaney around the same time he made a deal with Barry Donahue to manufacture several kilos of methamphetamine. We haven't quite got a confession out of him yet, but it doesn't take a genius to work out that it was in his best interest to get Jordan Walters out of the way so he could corner the market. We believe they planned to use Waterford as a testing ground for this drug that has remained largely unpopular with users in recent years. We think they were experimenting with how to push the drug and create a distribution network before flooding the market in Dublin."

"What about Clarance Veale?" said Brophy in a raised voice.

White licked his lower lip and said, "Veale is not a priority at this time."

"Really?" said Brophy. "Even though he was working with Jordan and may-be the benefactor of the drugs we found at the crime scene?"

White's face reddened. "We're not suggesting he's not a person of interest, but like I say, Delaney is the sole focus for now. So everyone, let's not bottle this." Brophy flinched, knowing the word was used as a swipe at him. "Good luck out there today. And stay well hydrated. Looks like another glorious day today."

His comment raised a slight chuckle from the crowd before most of the gardaí dispersed amongst a chorus of action plans as they walked out the door.

White sat down again and continued his briefing with Leard. Brophy approached the big table.

"What can I do for you, Sergeant?" said White.

"I'd like to interview Donahue."

"That won't be necessary, Sergeant. You can read the transcript from our interview. I'm sure everything you need to know will be in there."

McCall joined Brophy at the table's edge, looking down at the two NBCI officers. "We have evidence that may prove Barry Donahue was forced into doing what he did."

"He never mentioned that to us," said Leard through a hideous sneer.

"Because he doesn't want his family hunted down by these people," said Brophy by way of retort. "He knows if he doesn't take the fall for this, his wife and kids will be in great danger, yet you took him in with this public circus nonetheless."

"What's this so-called evidence you think

you have, Detective McCall?" said White.

"Donahue's son."

This information silenced White. Out of the corner of his eye, Brophy noticed Bennett and Kenneally were fully attentive to the conversation at the other end of the table.

"Where is the lad, Brophy?" asked Bennett, rising to his feet.

"He's in a safe place, sobering up. We'll bring him in later to make a formal statement."

"You'd better let us handle that," said White defensively.

"I don't think so."

"I'm not asking, Sergeant."

"He hasn't broken any law, and he's not being charged, so I don't see why we should hand him over to you. I think you've caused enough damage as it is."

"Don't play this game with us," said Leard, getting to his feet. White followed him up and put his hand on his arm to settle him down a bit.

"Inspector Bennett. I'd like you to instruct your team to disclose the location of Mr Donahue."

Bennett beamed at Brophy. "Detective, would you like to inform us as to the whereabouts of Aidan Donahue?"

"No can do."

"Okay. Well, I guess that settles that, Inspector, unless there's anything else we can do for you."

Leard breathed heavily now, poised for conflict, likely of a physical nature, judging by his whole demeanour. White stretched his neck and rolled his head back around one time.

"If that's the way it's gonna be, then that's the way it's gonna be." He gave Leard a nod, and Leard reluctantly followed him out of the room, leaving the local officers stood around the table.

"I sincerely hope you know what you're doing, Brophy," said Bennett.

"I'm trying to protect that family from any more hardship."

"Maybe it's too late for that now," said Bennett.

"The boy laid it all out for us," said McCall. "He got in with a bad crowd in Dublin and worked up a massive debt. It was a set-up from the very beginning. Then Doyle paid his father a visit. I think you know the rest."

"These animals will do anything," said Bennett. "Well, good work finding the guns, Brophy."

"It was actually one of McCall's contacts that tipped us off."

Bennett glanced at McCall, the disdain clear on his face. "Let's not go celebrating quite yet. Delaney is still out there somewhere."

"Can we talk to Barry Donahue?" asked Brophy.

"What good will it do at this point?" said Bennett.

"We need to find out what his dinner plans were that night and why he didn't show up. Aidan told us they were all meant to have a sit-down and discuss everything with Jordan and Veale."

"You seem to have your mind set on this Veale character."

"There's no way he's not involved, and we all know they're protecting him because he's such a crucial informant to them."

"All right then. But it's better if just one of you go. That way, it won't look too official, and he mightn't try to lawyer up."

"Fine," said Brophy. "McCall can do it. I think he latched on to you more than me, anyway."

"No problem. I know what we need to find out," said McCall, smiling at Brophy.

"No," said Bennett. "It's better if you do it, Brophy. You'll have a better chance of warding off those two clowns if they come near the interview room."

"I really think-" started Brophy.

"He's right, Sergeant Brophy. It's better if you go. I can look into the forensics report while I'm waiting."

McCall skulked back to her desk, and Brophy and Bennett headed out the side door and down the stairs.

CHAPTER THIRTY-TWO

Brophy entered Interview Room One and found Donahue sitting with his head rested on his arms on the small table. He looked up as Brophy shut the door gently behind him. Brophy thought he heard him growl.

"You lied to me," said Donahue. "You said you'd help protect my family."

"I know, and I apologise for how this has been handled. It's not how I would have done things. But you lied to me too. And possibly cost us a couple of days in tracking down the killer and finding Seán."

Brophy sat across from him. Donahue looked as if he hadn't slept the previous night. His eyes were bloodshot and dry, his face plastered in specks of black and grey stubble.

"Had you been straight with us from the beginning, we might have been able to avoid this."

"Well, it's too late now, isn't it? Those other two pricks have made it very clear what's going to happen to me whether I talk or not."

"Why did you cancel your dinner plans with Maura and Jordan that night?"

The question caught Donahue off guard. He rubbed his chin, making a rasping noise that greatly irritated Brophy. "I didn't cancel. Maura called me and said they had a change of plans. Their associate, Veale, couldn't make it, so there was no point in getting together. She postponed it till Sunday. That way, Seán wouldn't be there, and we wouldn't have to tip-toe around our discussion in his presence."

"Did you have any idea how they were planning to help get you and Aidan out of the situations you were in?"

Donahue straightened a little and pushed out his chest. "What do you know about Aidan?"

"We met him yesterday at your house."

"Typical. He couldn't do as I said and stay with his mother in Clontarf. That kid screws everything up. But he's my son. My boy." A tear rolled down his cheek.

"He told us everything about how Doyle's foot soldiers lured him in and made him work up a huge debt. Listen, I know your hand was forced in all of this, and I promise I'll do whatever I can to help you and your family."

Donahue started and took a gasping breath. "Where's Aidan now?"

"We brought him to an outreach centre for troubled youths last night to sleep off a high. He's with a very trusted friend of mine there, so don't worry. But we'll need to take him in later, and it's imperative I have everything straight by then."

"He's suicidal, you know?"

"I gathered that. I can't imagine how

difficult it must be."

"He had everything growing up. Maybe we spoiled him a little too much. I always feared it would turn him into an arrogant adult. But he's not. He's incredibly sensitive and was never great at making friends. That's why those thugs were able to suck him in so easily. I had no idea about the gambling. Had he come to me earlier, I could have paid off the debt, and we wouldn't all be in this mess right now."

"There's no point laying that on yourself. These people had their sights set on you, and they likely would have found a way in, no matter what." Donahue shook his head and looked down at the table. "Have you ever met or spoken to Veale?"

"No. The dinner was to be the first time we met him."

"And what did they say he could do for you?"

Donahue considered the question warily then let out a long protracted sigh. "I'm not entirely sure."

"But you have to know something about it, or you wouldn't have agreed to meet him. So what can you remember? Were they planning to try to go into business with Doyle?"

"Go into business? God no. I don't think that's what they had in mind at all. Jordan suggested they wanted me to lure him in with a second batch, and I can only imagine what they would have done from there."

This information flicked a switch in Brophy's mind. Had they planned on eliminating Doyle, and in the already compromised position of his gang, take over everything? And did Doyle somehow get hold of this information and set up the murder of the Walters? These two cartels had been dead set on destroying each other for years, and now with the number of their key players so diminished, taking out one or two top people would tilt the balance in favour of one side for years to come.

"Who else knew about the planned meeting with Veale?"

"Just us. Myself, Aidan, Maura and Jordan, and Veale."

"How about Michael Delaney?"

"Who?"

"Budgie Delaney." Brophy scrutinised his reaction to the name and determined he was truthful in not knowing who Delaney was. "As of now, he's the lead suspect in the shooting."

"I've never heard of him. Who is he?"

"He's a local dealer we think may have been pushing the stuff Jordan was making."

"Then why on earth would he kill them if he was making loads of money off them. It doesn't make sense."

"Few things in their world usually does. What I don't get is why they would plan such a serious meeting and plan to have Jordan's sister and Seán there. What time did Maura let you know the dinner was postponed?"

"Early afternoon some time. Maybe twelve-thirty."

Around the time Ciara cancelled, Brophy thought to himself. Was there some deeper connection to the sister he was missing? "And you said you don't know Ciara Walters very well?"

"That's right. I've met her a handful of times. A few family events, that kind of thing."

"What do you make of her?"

Donahue thrust back his head in surprise at the question. "I don't know. She seems quite charming, if not somewhat distant and cold."

"Did Maura get along with her?"

"I believe so, but they were never very close from what I can gather."

"Did Jordan get on with her?"

"I presume so. I've never heard any different."

"Is it something Maura would have told you about?"

"I would imagine so. Maura was an open book. She didn't suffer fools, but she had a special way with people, and part of that was how honest and forthcoming she was."

"Why do you think she got involved in this?"

"I don't know how involved she really was. I think she was just used to being around that life.

It was normal for her."

"How did she find out about the situation with Aidan and Doyle? Did she come to you or you to her?"

Donahue squinted as he attempted to remember. "I think she came to us with the idea. But I'm not entirely sure if Aidan told her about the debt or if she found out another way. I'm sorry if that's not very useful."

"No, not at all. This is all quite revealing. Just a couple of more things. Where were you when Seán was being collected from hurling camp?"

"At the lab. Your people have already confirmed that. I was planning to stay until dinner, then go straight to Maura's. Aidan was meant to pick me up and drive us to Woodstown."

"So, Aidan had the Mercedes at that time?"

"Yes, but I can assure you he didn't collect Seán from camp."

"How?"

"How what?"

"How can you assure me?"

Donahue looked puzzled like he was second-guessing himself. "He told me he waited at home all day."

"Has your security camera footage been taken as evidence?"

"I don't believe so."

"One more thing. Did you think Doyle was

going to let you off with making one batch to pay the debt?"

"Not for a single moment," he said, a flash of rage clouding his features. "But I see what you're getting at. And the answer is 'yes.' I had more than enough reason to want him dead. But I never voiced that to anyone. Believe me, if you want. I don't see how it really matters at this stage. I'm screwed, aren't I?"

"Keep telling the truth, and you might come out of this clean yet."

Brophy got up to leave, gave Donahue a nod as he did so.

"Please take care of Aidan. And tell him I'm sorry."

Brophy left the shaken and battered man alone in the interview room.

CHAPTER THIRTY-THREE

When Brophy got back to the incident room, he found McCall at her desk, staring at the screen, tapping her foot fervently on the floor. She turned as he approached, a glum look on her face.

"What is it?" asked Brophy.

"I've just done a bit of digging, and it looks as though the planning permission for Jordan Walters' jetty was close to being approved."

"I don't think it matters much at this stage. Your new boyfriend is off the hook."

"Very funny," she said with a wry smile. "Anything new from Donahue?"

"Not much, but it was Maura that cancelled the dinner, at around the same time Ciara Walters cancelled."

That raised an eyebrow with McCall. "Do you think there's anything in it?"

"I'm not sure. Could be. The reason she gave him was that Veale had cancelled."

"Him again."

"They were planning to lure Doyle in with another batch and then dispose of him."

"You think he was on to them?"

"Very possible."

"Then made Delaney an offer he couldn't refuse, but there was one job he had to do first?"

"It would make sense. But how did he find out? And where is Veale?"

"Maybe Aidan can shed more light on it. You think he'll be okay to bring in now?"

"Yeah. We should go get him."

He took a step away from the desk, and McCall stood to follow him out. She picked up her mobile and lit up the screen for a quick glance. "Missed call from Dunford," she said." Brophy was almost at the door by now. She unlocked her phone as she strode quickly to catch up. She said, "You called me?"

To Brophy, she mouthed, "Dunford." After a few seconds, Brophy now heading down the stairs, she called after him, "Conal, stop."

"What's the matter?" He looked back and immediately tensed up seeing her shocked expression.

"They've just discovered a body in the river. We need to get there at once."

"Where?"

"Adelphi Quay. Near to where Aidan is staying."

Panting from the sprint down the two staircases, Brophy gunned the engine, releasing the clutch just as McCall was getting in. She let out a frightened yelp and slammed the door shut. "Take it easy. It probably isn't him."

"He's been suicidal a long time. Jesus, I hope

we haven't screwed up with this kid."

Within a couple of minutes, they were racing down Parade Quay weaving in and out of traffic as Brophy gripped the wheel tightly. They trailed along the Suir, swung around the bend at Reginald's Tower, and took a sharp left half-way around.

The Saab came to a shuddering stop when he slammed on the brakes, seeing two squad cars parked haphazardly on the road outside the traditional charter boat dock. A fire engine was parked as close to the dock as it could get. The brigade of eight men moved around like it was second nature to them, extending the engine's ladder horizontally, chaining a metal stretcher to it on the move. Brophy spotted Dunford at the edge of the wooden dock, peering over, with two uniformed officers doing the same. Brophy and McCall jogged over to join them.

"What's going on?" asked McCall on reaching the three gardaí.

Dunford turned to face her. "Was called in about twenty minutes ago. Someone said they saw a body caught on one of the pillars.

Brophy bent down and looked over. Directly beneath, he could make out the back of someone's legs. No shoes and black jeans. He searched his mind for what Aidan was wearing the previous day. He knew he was wearing dark clothes but couldn't remember the details. He cursed himself for his lagging perception of these things in recent years. Further reassurance, his mind wasn't on his job anymore. He tried to lean out more to get a better look. The upper body was at the other side of the pillar, under the dock. McCall joined him in peering over.

She gave him a grave look. "Aidan was wearing jeans just like these ones yesterday. Give Ducey a call, see if he's there."

"Wait till they pull the body out. They're about to lower themselves down."

The fire chief instructed all non-firefighters to move back a few metres whilst they lowered the stretcher with one man balancing on it. They used a purpose fitted winch to lower it slowly. Brophy watched on. He was a barrel of nerves, unsure whether he would crack if it turned out to be Aidan. He carried enough guilt with him already. He wouldn't be able to handle adding this to the pile. The darkness in his peripherals closed in, and he fought contemptuously to cast it off.

An ambulance pulled up, and two medics came rushing past the gathered onlookers. From the shouts of the five firefighters looking down at their comrade, he could make out the stretcher had reached the water level, and he was now attempting to pull the body from the water. An upsurge in volume indicated he, with the unenviable task was struggling to get it out of the water.

Brophy heard 'too heavy' on a couple of

occasions. Aidan was tall but not particularly heavy. Maybe he was caught on something under the dock. The wait was driving Brophy to despair. He was tempted to go over and tell them to get on with it or climb down himself and help. He knew he wouldn't get far, though.

The next few minutes passed in a cloud of disarray. The uniformed gardaí worked frantically to keep the growing crowds back from the eye line to where the body would be raised. Brophy's agony was compounded further by the arrival of a news crew, one he saw lingering outside the station for the last few days. It took both gardaí to keep them back, and even Detective Dunford had to assist and use his authority to hold them at bay.

On turning back to look at the firefighters, he heard "hoist" shouted up from the depths. A dull clang of metal on metal emanated from the chain rubbing off the winch, and each one caused a thud in Brophy's heart. The metallic taste of blood rose from his chest and assaulted his taste buds. The head of the firefighter emerged from below first, and when it came up another few feet, all hands reached down to pull the stretcher onto the dock. Brophy and McCall rushed over. They struggled to get a look in with all the firefighters encircling the stretcher. A medic moved in for a procedural inspection, but it didn't take long for her to determine the person was deceased. Brophy asked the two men closest to the head to move back. They complied.

The body was face down on the stretcher, and the first thing Brophy noticed was the ghostly whitish-green colour of the shrivelled skin. His eyesight flickered when the next thing registered. The head was shaved in a crew-cut just like Aidan's. The height and shoulder-width also looked consistent.

"Can you turn him over?" asked Brophy, conscious that his words came out in nerve-wracked staccato.

One of the firefighters gestured to the two at the feet end of the stretcher. Four of them took hold of him gently, and in a fluid movement, flipped the body around.

"Oh my god," whispered McCall beside Brophy. "Is that who I think it is?"

Focused fully on the fear-stricken opened eyes of the dead man, Brophy took a few beats to answer. "Delaney!" He turned to face McCall. "Send out an alert to call off the search."

She immediately turned and headed in the direction of Detective Dunford whilst pulling out her mobile. Brophy asked the firefighters and medics to move and let him examine the body closer. They hesitantly shuffled a few steps back and let him in. Brophy got down on his haunches and brought his head level with Delaney's. "What mess have you gotten yourself into now, Budgie? This is most inconvenient," he said, unsure as to whether in his mind or out loud.

He moved in close to the head, and eye to eye checked for any wounds that might suggest he was beaten before finding his way into the River Suir. He could see nothing of the sort and asked the one who fished him out to turn him a little so he could examine the back of his head. The young fireman did so, avoiding making eye contact with the corpse — nothing on the back of his head either.

McCall returned to Brophy's side. "Okay, I've let everyone know. This place will be swarming with our own soon enough."

"Good. Now let's go and see Aidan."

CHAPTER THIRTY-FOUR

When Brophy and McCall arrived at the outreach centre, they found Aidan in the living room chatting happily to another teenager. It sounded like he was giving the younger boy some advice on sticking with school and not dropping out, but the conversation came to an abrupt stop when he noticed the detectives arrive in the room.

Brophy was hugely relieved to see his spirits were a lot higher than when they found him at his house the day before. They had a quick chat, and Brophy informed him he'd just spoken to his father. Aidan admitted he'd seen the headlines that morning and was set on giving the gardaí a full and detailed statement, covering everything from his gambling and dealing to how it was his fault that his father was forced into doing what he did. Brophy was encouraged by this and felt like it could give his father a good chance at a lenient sentence.

On the journey back to the station, they talked him through how he should conduct the interview and not say too much that might give White and Leard a chance to incriminate both of them further. They also told him they'd arrange a solicitor to be present and have some time with him before the interview started.

"Just remember," said Brophy, "you're not being charged with anything. You're making a voluntary statement. If it feels like they're pressing too hard, you have every right to cut the interview short." Brophy felt like they were gaining the young man's trust. "There's just one thing I'd like to clear up with you first, Aidan, and I need you to be completely honest with me."

"Of course. What is it?"

"Did you pick up Seán from hurling camp on Thursday?"

Brophy gauged the reaction to the question and inferred Aidan was flummoxed by it.

"Why would I pick him up? I was home all day Thursday, freaking out about the meeting with Doyle. I even contemplated... Well, you know, if I'd had enough gear with me that day to end everything..."

He trailed off, and Brophy didn't see the need to press him anymore.

They dropped him off at the station and left him in the nice interview room with a coffee and a sandwich and instructions to wait for the solicitor before agreeing to talk. A mass search was now underway to find Seán Walters. Court orders were signed to enter the premises of family members and known associates of Delaney. Divers were scouring the river near where Delaney was fished out.

They learnt that White and Leard

accompanied a team to Tramore to search the house where Delaney's Polish girlfriend lived, the same place they knew Doyle had first approached him. There was no doubt the girl was the main target of the NBCI men. They'd attempt to get anything she might know out of her, and they had the skills and intimidation factor to have her spill her guts very quickly.

Bennett called Brophy and told him there was also a crew currently on the way to Woodstown to search Sam Harrington's property. He told Brophy to head out there and assist in the search.

Within twenty minutes, they were crawling along the long driveway of Harrington's place. Two squad cars were already parked outside the cottage. The front door was open, but no one was to be seen. They got out of the car and went into the house.

"Detective McCall, what is this madness? How is this even legal? I'm surely not a suspect," said Harrington from the end of the hall. He stood there looking on as gardaí ransacked through everything they could get their hands on, turning the place upside down.

"We're terribly sorry, Mr Harrington. You're absolutely not a suspect, but the investigation has taken on dramatic urgency due to finding the main suspect face down in the Suir this morning," she said whilst moving closer to him.

Brophy stayed at the foot of the stairs by the

front door, looking up to see who was shuffling around up there.

A few moments later, Sergeant Gough appeared on the top landing. "Ah, Detective Brophy, good to see you again," he whispered, coming down the stairs. "Sorry, it has to be under these circumstances. I've known Sam since I moved here a few years ago. There's no way he has anything to do with this. Why would they even issue a search order?"

With a hand shielding the side of his face, he whispered his reply. "There seems to have been some kind of a dispute about the building of a jetty on the beach. Harrington objected twice, but it looks like it was about to go through on the third try. It lends itself to a possible motive, so we need to check everything out. If it's any consolation, I think it's a waste of time too."

"I heard they pulled that Delaney character out of the river. Are they sure he was the shooter?"

"They think they're sure."

"You don't seem so convinced yourself."

"I can't say for sure, Sergeant. There's just too many holes in this. And Delaney's boss is still missing. Until we find him, I won't be convinced that Delaney pulled the trigger."

"Do you honestly think there's someone hidden in the Chesterfield?" said Harrington into the room, his tone just shy of an all out shout, grabbing Brophy's attention.

"Let's step outside," said McCall. "This will all be over very soon. Don't worry."

After a few seconds of contemplation, Harrington strode past McCall and down the hall. He stopped short of Brophy and Gough. "This is your doing, Detective Brophy, isn't it?" he hissed.

Brophy cut McCall a dirty look; it was she who'd discovered and reported the ongoing dispute.

"You're not a suspect, Sam," said Gough in a friendly tone. "We just need to rule everything out. As you're the closest neighbour-"

"They have to torment me with this nonsense," he said, his face turning red, white saliva droplets shooting out with his sharp words. He brushed past Brophy and out the front door, followed closely by McCall.

"Something I don't get, Detective," said Gough, "and tell me to mind my own business if you have to, but if it was one of these drug cartel fellas, then why didn't they take the drugs from the garage?"

"That's what I'd like to know myself. And it also doesn't explain why they took the boy."

"Where does this Veale guy stay when he's in town?"

Brophy raised an eyebrow at Gough's question. "I always assumed he drove down from Dublin and back on the same day. It's only a couple of hours, but you might be onto something." He rummaged for his phone in his pants pocket. "I'm gonna call that in right away, Sergeant. It's definitely worth looking into."

Brophy unlocked his phone as he walked outside and called headquarters to get someone to look into possible places Veale may have stayed on his trips to Waterford. After he finished the call, he walked across the gravel yard to where McCall and Gough were trying to calm Harrington. It looked as though they had almost reined him in until he saw Brophy coming, and his face twisted into a sour knot again.

"This is an outrage, Brophy. Everyone in the village will be talking about it," spat Harrington.

"No one's going to know we were here. And isn't it better that there's absolutely no doubt in the minds of people who might already be gossiping about the Walters' neighbour who likes to go out shooting?"

"No one had even suggested that, you little shit."

Brophy tensed and sidled up to Harrington. "You need to be very careful what you say to me, Harrington. The fact is, you're their closest neighbour. You were closest to the crime when it happened, and you have a years-long dispute with the family. The very kind of dispute people have been killing each other for hundreds of years in this country. So, it would be in your very best interest to step down and consider the consequences of your actions."

Harrington's nostril's flared, and he took in a heavy breath. "Sergeant Gough. Would you be so kind as to inform these two that there's no conceivable way I had anything to do with this crime?"

"I already have, Sam. They'll all be out of here shortly, and it'll be like none of this ever happened."

The two guards emerged from the house and gave Brophy a nod.

"Now that was easy, wasn't it?" said Brophy. "We'll be out of your hair now, Mr Harrington. Thanks for your cooperation," he said with a hint of a smirk and walked away towards the car. "You coming?" he called back to McCall. "I'll let you know where that enquiry leads us, Sergeant Gough, and thanks again for your help."

Brophy's car and one of the squad cars drove away and left Gough in a heated exchange with Harrington.

CHAPTER THIRTY-FIVE

On the way back to the station, Sergeant Kenneally called Brophy and told him he looked into the bigger hotels in the city to enquire if any guest named Veale had checked-in in the last week. All the hotels replied in the negative. He said he had an officer checking out smaller hotels in the area, and then he had the idea to call White and ask him if Veale ever uses an alias. White gave him two names Veale was known to have used in the past. Kenneally rechecked with the hotels he'd talked to earlier, and one of them came back with the name William Cliffe. The receptionist said he'd checked in on Wednesday evening, was booked and paid up for two nights, but never checked out and left some personal belongings in the room.

"Which hotel is it?" asked Brophy.

"The Tower," Kenneally replied.

"The Tower," said Brophy. He thanked Kenneally for his good work and rang off. "Veale was booked into The Tower for a couple of nights and never checked out," he said to McCall.

"The Tower? Jesus. That's right beside where we pulled Delaney out of the River."

"Maybe a coincidence, maybe not."

"Why wouldn't he check-out?"

"I don't know, but let's go and see if we can

find out."

As they spoke, they were at Passage Cross on the Dunmore Road. The roads were already busy with beachgoers, but it would only take a few minutes to get there. Hopefully, White and Leard were preoccupied with the Polish girlfriend, and they could be the first to see what Veale had left behind.

When Brophy pulled up to the main entrance of The Tower Hotel, a squad car had just parked in one of the spaces reserved for VIPs. The doorman began to protest at Brophy for leaving his car outside the main entrance, blocking anyone else who wanted to pick-up or drop-off guests. Brophy flashed his warrant card and barely looked at the now silenced man.

He approached the reception desk. McCall and the two uniformed guards hung back and scanned the lobby and lounge areas for any chance sighting of Veale.

"I understand our sergeant just called to enquire about William Cliffe," Brophy said to the red-haired receptionist.

"Yes. A guard called alright, asking about a guest who didn't check out. Is he okay? He seemed like such a gentleman. I hope nothing bad's happened to him."

"From what I understand, he left some possessions behind."

"Oh, he did, yeah."

"Can you take us to where you've stored

them then?"

"Of course. Step behind the counter there and follow me through the door right here."

She pushed open a door on the back wall of the reception area he hadn't noticed was there, one of those doors that looked the same as the wall, with the wooden trim going along the floor and a metre up. He gave McCall a nod across the lobby, and she briskly came to join him.

The room behind the wall was shrouded in darkness at first, then the receptionist flipped a switch and a florescent bulb bathed the small storeroom in white light. Metal stacked shelves ran along the sides of the room, partially strewn with bags and lost items. Most of the stuff in the room was covered in dust, some much more than others. A small round wooden table that looked like the kind found in almost every pub in the country, stood against the back wall. A mini black wheelie bag with a shiny exterior laid flat on the table. It was the kind one would use for a night or two away for a business trip or the likes. Brophy squeezed past the receptionist, who looked as though she was about to pick it up and hand it to him.

"Can you wait outside for us for a few minutes, love?" said McCall from behind her.

"Oh, I don't think I'm allowed to let you in here by yourselves."

"Don't worry about it. It's integral to an ongoing investigation that we check the contents of that bag then take it into evidence. A small forensics team will be along shortly to take it away."

"All right then, if you say so." She left the room, and the door clicked shut behind her.

Brophy snapped the rim of the second rubber glove he had now fitted and began feeling around the outside of the luggage. He gave it a small shake as McCall put on her gloves. Brophy knelt to take a closer look at the latch.

"Doesn't seem to be a combination lock." He glanced back at McCall for reassurance.

"Go for it?" she said.

He clicked open a latch at the side and one on top near the handle. Lifting the side of it open, he felt his heart pound against his chest. He flipped the lid and let it rest against the back wall. McCall edged in closer, rubbing her hip and shoulder off Brophy as she squished in.

"Eh, easy there," he said with a grin.

"Clothes?" said McCall.

At first inspection, the case looked to only have a few items of dark clothing; jeans, a couple of T-shirts, a jumper. Brophy gingerly moved the clothes over and back to see if there was anything important hidden between them. He found nothing.

"Take them out," said McCall.

He scooped his hands underneath the small pile of clothes and lifted them gently, holding them over the bag for McCall to check the bottom. She felt around the surface and sides of the case but still nothing out of the ordinary. She then examined more carefully to see if anything was hidden behind the lining but came up clean.

"Okay, you can put them down again."

He laid the clothes back down again, ready to close the bag, when he noticed a zipper on the open side. After unzipping it cautiously, he eased his hand in and felt around. "What's this?" He pulled his hand out slowly to reveal a small perspex case with a gold medal inside.

"Is that a medal?" asked McCall.

By now, Brophy had it close to his eyes, examining the inscriptions. "Wow. This is incredible!"

"What is it?"

"An All-Ireland final winner's medal."

"Are you serious?"

"From 1958. The last time Waterford won. This has to be stolen. No one in their right mind would give up one of these."

"How did a sex offender drug trafficker get his hands on it then?"

"I have no idea, but we have to get it back to the rightful owner." He turned the round-edged box over to look at the backside. "David 'Davey' Fraher. Jesus, Fraher was a legend. We all wanted to be like him, tough and hardy, but fast and skillful at the same time."

"Isn't that what they said about you?"

"They said nothing of the sort about me. I

couldn't hold a candle to Fraher. I know he passed away a few years ago. Some kind of brain cancer."

"What the hell was Veale up to?" asked McCall.

Brophy stood up straight, knew right away he had a grave expression on his face, the way she gazed back, furrowing her brow.

"God, what is it, Brophy?"

"Seán Walters was obsessed with hurling, wasn't he?"

McCall's face fell. "Do you think he used it to lure Seán in?"

"At that age, if someone offered me an All-Ireland medal from that legendary Waterford team, I'd definitely get into a car with them."

"And with a smile on your face."

"But why would he leave his stuff behind? And if he took Seán from hurling camp, why didn't his parents raise any alarm. They sat down to dinner that evening. Hardly the behaviour of parents who don't know where their child is?"

"Could they have thought he went with someone else and weren't worried?"

"Possibly, but we know Ciara Walters had already told them she wouldn't make it down on time."

"The only way to know for sure is to find Veale."

"If he hasn't already done a legger. Maybe he heard about the murder when he was out and got out of Waterford as fast as he could."

"That would certainly fit in with the theory of Doyle having Delaney do the murder."

"I just don't know. There are too many holes in this.

Before McCall had a chance to reply, the receptionist showed a tech officer into the room, and he made straight for Brophy and McCall.

"Is this the bag?" he asked, pointing at Veale's luggage.

"Get a bag for this?" said Brophy, holding up the medal. "And take care of it, will ye? It's invaluable."

Brophy and McCall exited, leaving the tech guy alone in the storeroom.

CHAPTER THIRTY-SIX

Shortly after departing the hotel, and on the way back out the Dunmore Road to see Ciara Walters, to inform her about developments and get more information about the day of the murders in the process, Brophy and McCall were called back to the station for a full briefing. Judging by the tone of the call from Kenneally, there was going to be an announcement later in the day to the media. Brophy didn't like the sound of it, guessed they were rushing into pinning the murders on Delaney before a full picture of events that day were laid out. Units across the city raided twelve premises that morning — still no trace of the boy.

The number of reporters seemed to have doubled since the day before; no doubt people piecing together the story of the body fished out of the Suir with the hunt for the killer. When they arrived in the incident room, the place was buzzing with excitement. It was packed with officers rushing from desk to desk, writing up reports, preparing for the adulation that would surely come the station's way. A rare sight indeed, Superintendent Russell sat at the centre of the large table, Bennett and Kenneally on one side, White and Leard on the other. His arms were crossed, a content air of satisfaction writ on his round blood-filled face. Brophy and McCall took their seats at their adjoining desks and took in the scene.

Minutes passed before Russell finally laboured to his feet. "Gather round lads and ladies, if you will," he said in his bellicose rasp of a voice. "We have a couple of announcements to make. I'm sure you have a fair idea of what we're getting at, but let's get the details straight, nonetheless," he said as everyone in attendance quickly formed the usual horseshoe. "Okay, settle down so we can start this thing before the media burst through the doors and drag the story out of us." He said this with no shortage of hubris, the first time the station had any kind of national attention like that; it was Russell's chance to shine.

Rumours had it he was always bitter for not getting a more senior position in Dublin, but this would surely make up for it. Bringing down the fledgling new drug business of two of the major cartels, possibly putting the final nail in their coffins, their domination of the trade in Ireland. Not only that notch on his bedpost, but now it appeared they also had the main suspect in the double murder. His corpse at least. All solved in less than a week. Validation, if ever there was any needed, to justify upgrading the Waterford station to the main headquarters for the South East.

"Firstly, I'd like to thank you all from the bottom of my heart for your fine policing in this case. Your hard work has helped to bring down major drug operations in the city and track down a career criminal who's been the bane of many an officer in this station. This morning Michael 'Budgie' Delaney was pulled out the river at Adelphi Quay. His remains are currently in University Hospital, awaiting a full postmortem examination, the preliminary results of which should be in later today. What we do know so far is that there was a small amount of methamphetamine found on his person, along with the type of glass pipe favoured by users of this particular drug. Also, there didn't seem to be any sign of injury on his body, besides the broken wrist he suffered when he dared get physical with our own Detective Brophy the other day." He said this last part smiling at Brophy and his words were followed by a small spattering of applause from those in attendance. Brophy felt truly uncomfortable by the comment and its reaction. "As of now, and unless it's proved otherwise, we are assuming Delaney felt the net closing in on him as our main suspect in the murders in Woodstown, panicked and took his own life. As you're all aware, Detectives McCall and Brophy were tipped off yesterday morning that a man fitting Delaney's description was seen burying something on a forestry site in Portlaw. The detectives quickly secured the location and found a gear bag buried where our friend was seen. That bag contained the murder weapon and several more illegal firearms with Delaney's prints. All this evidence, along with the sightings of him near the Walters' house the time the murders took place, leads us to strongly believe we have the shooter, the likely motive of which was the continuing, albeit severely compromised turf war that had been going on for years between the Quilty and Doyle crime families in Dublin.

"I'll be passing you over to Inspector White in a moment to give you more on that, but before I finish, I just want to extend my congratulations onto you all once more for your excellent work." A ripple of self-congratulatory applause rang in Brophy's ears. "And finally, I'd especially like to extend our warm gratitude to the two NBCI men with us today. Their knowledge and expertise of this ongoing war has been invaluable in bringing this case to a quick stop." Russell gave White and Leard a gracious nod, which elicited another shorter round of applause.

Russell settled himself back into his seat, then White rose and rounded the table to take up a position at its front, closer to the crowd.

"Thank you so much, Superintendent Russell," White said, looking behind him. "It's been a great pleasure and a refreshing change to work at a regional station like this, and I've already started drafting a letter of recommendation for this station to be made HQ for the South East. I truly believe that the country has suffered from a lack of decentralised power structures in recent years." Brophy observed Leard smirk at that comment. "And you are all fully deserving of breaking that trend. This case has garnered huge national attention as you can tell by the ravenous pack of hounds scurrying around outside." A loud chuckle rumbled up from the crowd. "Yesterday, we took in two major players who were manufacturing the meth in their labs in the city, and Inspector Leard and I have interviewed both men and got some very useful information from them that may lead to even more arrests. As of now, we are satisfied that Michael Delaney was the shooter last Thursday evening. Besides the evidence Superintendent Russell has just mentioned, the arrest of Doyle and the subsequent information we extracted from him has set out a clear motive for Delaney to carry out the murders-"

Brophy cut in before White had a chance to go on. "Will you be sharing that information with us?" He sensed the shared surprise at the bluntness of his question.

White was not perturbed. "Not at this time, Detective. For now, the information needs to be kept under wraps as it pertains to several ongoing enquiries regarding the operations of the cartels. But suffice to say, it proves Delaney was sent to Woodstown to confront the Walters, and no judge in the land would posit otherwise. We plan to tell the media of the evidence we've all built against Delaney, which we believe should be sufficient in convincing the public we have our man. The details-"

"What about the boy?" said Brophy, cutting White off mid-sentence and drawing a death glare from Russell. "He's still out there somewhere. Maybe we shouldn't be patting each other on the backs just yet."

"I couldn't agree more, Detective. And I'm sure the public and the relatives of the boy will have every confidence that the fine team assembled here today will do everything in their power to locate the boy."

"Are we to inform the media that he's presumed dead?" said Brophy, his voice rising a level.

Russell and Bennett shuffled uncomfortably in their seats. Leard licked his lower lip and gritted his teeth, poised for an offencive.

"Absolutely not. There's every chance the boy is still out there, unharmed. The search will go on until he's found."

"And Veale?" said Brophy. "What do we tell the public about him?"

White glanced back at Leard, and Russell cleared his throat as if he were about to interject. A few of the officers around Brophy tutted with displeasure. He was robbing them of their moment, but he didn't care. To him, it was a farce.

"There's no reason to suspect Veale has

anything to do with this. His name won't be mentioned publicly, and we-"

"McCall and I have just come from the Tower Hotel where he was booked in on the night of the murders. He never checked out and left his belongings at the hotel, including a coveted All-Ireland hurling medal. He was working closely with Jordan Walters to manufacture and supply meth, which was sold on the streets by Delaney. Now he's missing, vanished into thin air. And you say there's no reason to suspect he had anything to do with this?"

"That's enough, Sergeant Brophy," said Russell with no shortage of aggression in his tone. "I think we've heard just about enough from you."

"That's quite all right, Superintendent," said White, his perma-smirk wavering. "Detective Brophy has every right to raise his concerns, but what I can say for now is that we have our man and the evidence to prove he was the killer. Anything outside of that doesn't need to be made public at this time. Now, I'd like to make it clear to you all what you can and can't mention if asked at this time," he said, turning from Brophy, taking in the rest of the crowd.

The grimy dark walls of Brophy's consciousness closed in on his peripherals, only a star-speckled torrent of light obfuscated his tunnelled view of the desk and the senior officers. Taking in a breath was like sucking a straw in a crumpled plastic bag. He felt around for something to hold on to, so as not to lose balance and faint, likely losing what little regard the station had left for him at that point. There was nothing for him to hold, but he soon felt the warm touch of McCall holding his arm to keep him balanced.

The rest of the briefing passed by in a fit of muffled voices and earnest receivers of good news. By the time he came to, people were returning to their desks or heading outside for the day's beat. McCall guided him back to his desk and sat him down.

"Good on ye, Brophy. Someone needed to stick it to that smug asshole," said McCall, quiet enough not to be heard by a garda at the adjacent desk. "But I think you're in for a solid ear-bashing from Russell or Bennett, or likely both."

"It doesn't matter anymore. I'm done with this shit. It's all just a big contest, isn't it?"

Before she had a chance to reply, Bennett came crashing in the stairway door and roared over at Brophy, "What in the name of Christ, do you think you're playing at?"

Brophy sprang to his feet. Bennett moved in a few more paces, so they were all but face to face. "It's called detective work. You should try it sometime."

The half-dozen or so officers left in the room tensed to stillness, staring at the two men.

"You are way out of line," shouted Bennett. "What the hell has even happened to you, eh? You used to be a fine detective. Now you just float around like a fucking zombie, a shell of a police officer. This is by far the biggest case we've solved at this station, and you want to ruin it with your bullshit."

Brophy shouted back, "I don't consider finding a missing boy who may have witnessed his parents' murder as bullshit."

Bennett's voice came down to almost a whisper. "Neither does anyone else in here, you arrogant fuck. The boy will be our main priority for ages to come, but we have to face the fact that he's more than likely already dead, buried in a hole somewhere we'll never find him."

"Do you want to be the one to tell his aunt that?"

Bennett nodded, his expression softening a little. "You should have quit after the Fanning case ten years ago. You've been compromised ever since, holding back everyone here."

"You know what?" said Brophy. "I've been thinking the same thing. You'll have my letter of resignation on your desk in the morning."

Brophy brushed past him, almost knocking him over in the process. He rushed out the door, his head held down, feeling dizzy and nauseous.

CHAPTER THIRTY-SEVEN

The heat was unrelenting, and Brophy's ankle stung extra bad having taken the steps down from the incident room three at a time. Dying to get out of there as fast as he could, he sent a young reporter, who had somehow managed to get in past the car park and lay in wait at the back entrance, toppling to the ground as he barged past him with his shoulder lowered, man to man tackle style. The effort to catch him clean caused further pain to his ankle, but he felt it was worth it.

The clean-shaved reporter cried out in protestation from his embarrassing sitting position, but there was no one around to hear him. Brophy made his way over to his Saab and got out of there as quickly as he could. His world seemed to be closing in on him, and he was destined to go home and crack open a bottle of gin McCall had given him for his birthday months earlier. Never much of a drinker, he could hardly wait to get it down him and forget about the mess his life had become for a few hours.

All his failings flashed before him as he skidded out of the station car park: a university dropout, his girlfriend pregnant at twenty-three, missing the big game that still plagued him, his divorce, his heady rise towards the top ranks until the case of Mel Fanning created all sorts of disillusionment, and the subsequent years of caring less about everything day by day, the dark tunnel.

He gripped the steering wheel tight and zipped in and out of side-streets, attempting to reach the outskirts of the city as fast as possible so he could breathe again. Every so often, the dark shadows closed in on him, and he feared, as many a time before, that he would crash during one of these attacks he didn't have a name for.

On reaching the roundabout near the Viking Hotel, he was due to swing a right onto the road that would lead him to the N25, his route home, but caught sight of the signpost in the corner of his eye that pointed in the opposite direction. The sign read 'Dunmore East.'

An image of Ciara Walters popped into his head, and he realised he had promised to call out and give her an update of the past few days' events, so she wouldn't have to read between the lines of whatever the media was deciding to spin. A crushing stab of guilt recoiled in his stomach. *What must she be feeling right now?* Rumours were already well circulating that the imminent press conference would announce the main suspect in the murders was located. And yet no sign of her beloved nephew. It would be the most natural thing in the world to fear the worst. That Delaney likely took the boy after pulling the trigger on his parents, then realised there was nothing he could do with him, so probably took his life too and buried him somewhere he'd never be found. It was certainly what most of the officers in the station thought, even if they dared not say it.

After taking the left turn, his mood slightly shifted, and the darkness that had begun to subsume him subsided. He couldn't quite make out what was causing the sudden change but went with it. His thoughts cleared, and he was able to focus on what he should write in his letter of resignation. An idea that he should write it whilst tucking into the gin later brought a smile to his face.

Barely noticing the fifteen-minute journey go by, he soon pulled up outside Ciara Walters' house. The same 'D' reg white Skoda that was parked there the last day they came was unmoved. Getting out of his car, he looked down towards the bay and took a deep breath of sea air that felt cooler than the last two weeks, giving him hope the heatwave would soon ease up.

He walked up to the front door and rang the bell. The solid wood door had no window panes to give him an indication if someone was coming or not. A good thirty seconds passed, and a shroud of dark thoughts began to creep across his consciousness once more.

Then the deadbolt clunked out of its resting place, and his heart pumped an extra-strong beat. The door swished open, and the orange light of the hall cast a strange ethereal glow around her. She smiled on seeing Brophy, then fought it back just as quickly.

"I didn't expect you to come alone," she said. She wore a loose-fitting white linen dress and was barefooted, explaining why he didn't hear her moving through the house to come to the door.

His attention was rapt by her beauty, and he hesitated to answer. "Detective McCall had something to attend to."

"Is it something to do with the body they found in the river this morning?"

"As it happens, yes, it is."

"Oh, please come in, Detective Brophy. Where are my manners?"

"That's quite all right. I was just admiring how beautiful it is here," he said, looking down towards the bay again.

"Yes. Please, God, we find Seán soon, and I've decided to move here full-time so he can stay in the same school and not have his... Oh, what am I talking about? There hasn't been any sign of him yet, has there?"

"I'm afraid not."

Her face became grave and full of sorrow and loss. She turned and headed down the hall towards the kitchen. Brophy followed after her, closing the door on the way. He entered the kitchen and saw a glass of red wine and a half-eaten salmon salad on the island.

"I'm so sorry, I've disturbed your dinner."

"Not at all. It's been sitting there for ages. I can't bring myself to eat much these days. Will you have a glass of wine?"

"I really shouldn't. I'm driving, and I'm not much of a drinker."

"That must be rare in your profession," she said, gesturing for him to take a seat at the island and crossing the kitchen and reaching up to grab an extra wine glass. She turned back to face him, swaying the glass to and fro with a subtle wrist movement. "But I'd really like to not have to drink alone for a little while if that's okay?"

"Of course. Pour me one so. I know where the guards set up their breathalyser points anyway."

She chuckled briefly and sat close to him and poured him some wine. "So, what have you got for me, Sergeant? The news has been far too disturbing for me to watch the last couple of days," she said, nodding in the direction of the adjoining half living room. The TV on the far wall was unplugged, several black wires hanging down to the ground from its mounted position.

"I'm not sure if you heard about the raids yesterday morning?"

She waved her hand dismissively then took a big gulp of wine. "I know all about the labs being busted. I can't say I'm shocked about Hughes, but Barry Donahue is a different story. He always seemed like the straightest, most incorruptible type you could meet."

"We're not sure if it was entirely his choice."

"What do you mean? God, I hope you're not saying Jordan made him do it? That'd be all we need on top of everything else." She took another good sip of wine and refilled her glass in a hurry, causing it to splash over the rim, onto the counter.

"No. We don't think it was Jordan. In fact, it may have been Jordan helping him out."

Her brow folded in confusion. She took another smaller sip and encouraged him to follow suit. Her light blue eyes conveyed a coolness and assurance about her. He took a long drink and thoroughly enjoyed the feeling of it going down. He couldn't remember the last time he'd had a drink besides the sip of brandy at Harrington's place, but it was a while.

"I hope you don't take this the wrong way," he said. "But it's one of the more confusing things about this case. You see, that's what they were supposed to be discussing at the dinner on Thursday evening with Barry and Aidan Donahue. Apparently, when Jordan and Maura heard about a debt they had to a rival dealer, they wanted to help them out. So, they invited Clarence Veale to dinner as well, and they were going to come up with some kind of plan to help the Donahues out of their sticky situation."

He gauged her response. She looked as though this was all news to her but was numb to any kind of over-expressive reaction at that stage.

"And it's confusing why?" she asked.

"It doesn't make much sense that they would have such a serious meeting with a heavy hitter like Veale and have you and Seán present at the same time."

This last statement definitely provoked a reaction in her. She contemplated him for a few moments, her steely gaze cutting through his rugged and ready facade. "Are you suggesting that because I cancelled, the ultra-serious crime gang meeting was also cancelled?"

"Not at all. There's just too many loose ends here, and I'm trying to make sense of it all."

She smiled at him, but the smile was void of warmth. "What's your theory then? Aren't great detectives supposed to have wild theories about the crimes they're investigating?"

"Just as well that TV is unplugged. I think you've been watching too much of it."

She broke down laughing, drawing a rare smile from himself. She picked up her glass and clinked it off his, then took a sup. Brophy did the same.

"I probably shouldn't be telling you this, but Veale is also on the missing list."

"And you think he might have Seán?" she said, her hope irrepressible.

"It's a possibility."

"Where do you think he might be?"

"As of now, we have no idea. You see,

Jordan cancelled the meeting, saying Veale couldn't make it. But today we discovered that Veale was booked into a hotel for a couple of nights the time of the..."

"I see. Can't you track where he went next? Use his credit card or mobile phone or something. I don't know how exactly you do it, but surely he shouldn't be too difficult to find."

"Therein lies the problem. Veale never checked-out of the hotel and left his stuff behind him."

Her head swayed gently over and back, her eyes labouring on a thought. "Do you think he was the killer, and took Seán as he was leaving, after... you know what."

"It's a possibility I'm looking at."

"And I assume there's a search team out looking for him as we speak."

"Unfortunately not."

She turned boorish and said, "Why the fuck not? He's the main suspect in a double murder and kidnapping, and you're not out looking for him!"

"The body they pulled out of the river this morning, he was another associate of Jordan and Veale. A local dealer, probably the biggest in the city. He was seen around Woodstown the time of the shooting, and there's another few things that point towards it being him."

"That doesn't mean this Veale guy wasn't involved too, right?"

"I agree," he answered, starting to feel the burden of unloading all of this on her. "The thing is, the senior investigators are convinced they've got their man and aren't putting many resources into hunting down Veale at the moment. In fact, there's going to be a press conference soon, if it hasn't been on already. They're going to announce that they have the murderer."

"And then what? What are they doing right now about my nephew? He's just a boy. Jesus Christ, he must be terrified."

She brought her hands to her face, on the verge of breaking down sobbing. She managed to hold it back, got up, and went to the kitchen sink. She picked up a wet face towel and pressed it gently to her face.

Brophy couldn't help thinking how every move she made exuded a quality of such refined grace and elegance he could hardly take it.

She turned around and leaned back against the counter. "What do you really think, Detective? Is Seány still alive?"

"I truly believe there's every chance he's out there alive and well."

"But there's also another possibility. Please tell me what you're really thinking. It's clear you haven't even convinced yourself of the words you're saying."

"I think there's a strong chance Veale collected Seán from hurling camp. We found a rare hurling medal with Veale's stuff. I think

Veale might have used it to coax Seán into the car with a smile on his face. What hurling-mad kid wouldn't beam at such a thing? But after that, I really can't tell. Maybe Veale was onto the murders and was gone by the time it happened, and that's why he pulled out of the dinner."

"That would make some sense, at least. And do you think he took Seán to protect him from what was coming?"

"Maybe, but I really can't tell."

She walked back to the island and picked up her glass and beckoned him with her eyes to have a drink. He threw back most of what was left in his glass, and she gave him a refill. She sat down again and leaned in closer, moving her head around in a circle to relieve some of the pressure from her shoulders. "I trust you, Detective. I know you'll do all you can to bring him back to me."

"Call me, Conal."

She laughed lightly, and her gaze changed to one of restrained wonderment. "My, my. With all this madness, it's too easy to forget I'm sitting with a hurling legend."

"Ah, come off it," he said, blushing. "I had a couple of good seasons, and people don't stop going on about it."

She became serious and contemplative. "Do you find modesty gets you far in life?"

"Touché."

"Seán would love to meet you. He will meet

you, right?"

"I certainly hope so."

She stared at him for a few beats, her face softening again. "I've watched The Sunday Game with him a few times. He goes berserk when he sees your clip on the opening credits, diving through the air like Superman then springing up to score the clincher. Must have been an incredible feeling?" she said. He thought he sensed her, moving in ever so closer but his heightening nervousness robbed him of much of his sense of spatial awareness. His throat became dry, so he took another long sip of wine. "Aren't you gonna answer me?" she said with a flutter of a mocking laugh.

"It felt...good."

This time she didn't attempt to hide the derision from her laugh. "Good? That's all you can say? It felt good." Her impersonation made him laugh, and a wave of relaxation travelled down his body. "You score the winning point in the dying seconds of the game to get your home county into the All-Ireland for the first time in almost fifty years and it felt 'good.' C'mon, Conal Brophy. You can do better than that."

He nodded, paused a moment, then said, "It was like the climax of every boyhood dream I'd ever had exploded all around me in a cacophony of elated applause and worship."

"Worship, eh?` Now we're talking."

"It was the first time I ever felt truly alive.

Like nothing else in the world mattered if I couldn't get us to the final."

"What about the final, though? Didn't you go missing?"

"Let's not get into that." He looked down, breaking eye-contact, regret, and shame surging through him. "Something I've never lived down. It follows me everywhere I go."

"Oh, I'm sorry to bring it up."

He reengaged with her poised gaze.

"Tell me one thing, though, if you don't mind."

"What's that?"

"Did you want to play on the final, or was it beyond your control?"

"I still dream about what I would have done if I was there, how I might have altered the course of the game and help us win. But it wasn't to be."

"I can understand that. I always competed for Dad's love, but he seemed so focused on Jordan, I gave up when I became an adult and went my own way. It wasn't until near the end, when he was sick that I found out he only kept Jordan close because he was afraid of what he might become if he didn't keep an eye on him. But as it turns out, all his efforts were in vain. Good God, I'm so glad he didn't live to see any of this unfold. I can only hope he didn't know anything about it when he was still with us."

"You say he suspected Jordan always stayed

friends with Quilty?"

"It was kind of obvious. He went to Marbella a couple of times when that's where Bobby was hiding out. And trust me, Jordan isn't the Marbella type. More like Monaco, I'd say."

"He wanted to be a high-flyer?"

"Always believed he was. And as much as he was an asshole, sometimes, he didn't deserve this to happen to him." She closed her eyes to fight back a well of emotion and looked even more stoic and sublime to Brophy. One side of her blonde hair was pushed behind her ear, the other dangling over her face. She opened her eyes and smiled at him. "I wish I could have met you at a better time than this, Conal. I feel I can be myself around you. That's a rare experience for me."

His stomach knotted at the sound of her words. No idea had he she felt the way he was beginning to feel. At ease, ready to show himself to her. Something he hadn't done since the early years with his ex, before their doomed marriage. He took another drink of wine and enjoyed the moment just long enough before it might get uncomfortable, and said, "I won't stop until I find him. I promise you that."

She inhaled softly and blinked slowly, her head swaying gently. A thought crossed his mind that she was drunk, then it hit him like a hammer, the shock of his current reality. He was writing his letter of resignation tonight, and there he was, making a promise to her he most likely couldn't keep. He felt like a fraud, the type of man he despised, who would say anything a woman wanted to hear so he could get his way. His shoulders felt like a ton of pressure crashed down on them.

"I know you will. And that brings me great comfort. But I do know how these things can play out. With every day that passes, the chances of him coming back safely quickly diminishes."

"We have a great team at the station who will stay as committed to it as I do." Another lie. He hated himself. "I really should be getting on now."

Her shoulders slumped, her head tilted as she expressed her disappointment. "Oh, I thought maybe you could stay a little longer. How about one more glass?"

He clenched at anticipating the next words coming out as a stutter that would give away his deceptions and false claims. "I really shouldn't. I have an early start tomorrow."

He barely held back the shudder when her hand landed on his leg. "I understand. Thank you so much for all you've done. I feel a lot better to know someone like you is on our side. A lot of people will see my family as pariahs now."

"Don't mention it," he said and stood up. Her hand dropped from its position. They were almost face to face, albeit he a foot higher. Her head tilted up, and an unutterable silence pervaded the space around them.

"When this is over-" He stepped back as she spoke, and she reached out and held his forearm, lightly pulling him back. "When this is over, I'd like to get to know you."

"I'll try not to get in the way of that." A long pause followed. It took an embattled quenching of his will to hold back from moving in closer, her full lips like gravity dragging at him.

"Thanks again," she said close to a whisper. The scent of wine and lavender smothered his good sense. He edged in close, then a shock of clarity brought strength back to his legs. He pulled back.

"Thanks for the wine. I'll pay you back some time."

She nodded but didn't say a word.

"Well, bye. I'll let you know as soon as I find out anything."

Brophy headed for the door, glanced back once as he left.

Outside he got back in his car and sat in deep contemplation for a minute. Then he banged on the steering wheel, furious for thinking something could come of this, taking advantage of a bereaved family member of murder victims.

CHAPTER THIRTY-EIGHT

The towering occidentalis that flanked the long driveway were as overgrown as he remembered them as a child. The taller native trees that guarded the perimeter wall swayed overhead, creating a shadow dance atop the newly resurfaced tarmac on the balmy night. Having reached home and three glasses of gin into his drowning of self-pity and sorrow, on a whim, he went outside, got into his car, and made a speedy journey to his hometown. The events of the last week awakened in him the self-doubt that had followed him from childhood, doubt that he could see something through without cracking under pressure and letting everyone down, doubt that he was deserving of such opportunities. And now the meandering driveway also awakened in him the sense of adventure and danger he cherished as a child.

Gaining entry to the house was way easier than it should have been. A large window beside the back kitchen door was left ajar and easy to reach an arm in and unlock the deadbolt. Never his intention to make this visit in any way subtle, he gave no caution to entering quietly. He took in the room, had always wondered what the inside of the house was like, obsessed with it when he was young. An old, well-maintained redbrick fireplace stood on one end. Two armchairs faced it behind a glass coffee table. The floor, made of red quarry tiles, was coarse from over a hundred years of the giant room being the likely centre-point of the house. Three high sash windows filled the place with an outdoor quality, patches of sky, and stars visible beyond the trees.

Brophy walked to the fireplace and looked at a couple of old photos on the mantel. He only recognised one person in the family snaps, and that was his mark for the night.

A ceramic biscuit jar with a loose-fitting lid on top sat in the centre between the photos. He reached his hand up and cupped it behind the jar. With a flick of his fingers, he shoved it forwards and sent it crashing to the floor, smashing into a hundred pieces and sounding off an unmerciful clatter that echoed around the room. Within seconds, he heard shuffling around upstairs. Judging by the creak of the ancient floorboards, the bedroom was towards the front of the house.

Moments later, a rumbling sound rolling down the stairs was followed by a long silence that he guessed should have taken for someone to reach the door into the kitchen. Perhaps he was scoping out the situation before entering, or maybe he was calling the guards, in which case, Brophy would have a lot of explaining to do. At that point, he wasn't concerned. The resignation letter seemed almost to write itself in the half-hour it took to down the three gins. It wasn't like they could fire him for this stunt.

The door creaked open behind him, out of view from his position sitting in one of the armchairs. From the smooth sound of the footsteps, he assumed the person to be barefooted. The heavy breathing was louder. The figure passed three metres back from the chair, and the first thing to come into focus in his peripherals was the double-barrel shotgun the homeowner was holding firmly in two hands. He moved towards the back door, mesmerised and mistakingly not checking the rest of the room on seeing it wide open.

"The firearm won't be necessary, Mr Phelan."

He spun around frantically, his eyes dark and bulbous with fear. The gun was pointed straight at Brophy's head. "Who's there, and what do you think you're doing in my house?"

"Don't worry, Mr Phelan. I'm only here for a little chat."

Brophy's top half was in shadow, the moonlight from the large windows not quite reaching him at the far side of the room.

"What are you on about, a chat? You can't break into my house like this," he shouted, obviously gaining confidence in having the upper hand. "Now, who are you, and what do you want?" Louder that time. Then he brought the shotgun up to his shoulder and aimed it in a well-trained stance.

"I'm a little offended you don't recognise me."

Phelan sidestepped three times to get a more direct look at the diagonally faced intruder.

"Jesus Christ. Conal Brophy. Is that you?"

"Why don't you have a seat here beside me, and we can have that chat," said Brophy in a deep low voice, becoming of the situation.

"I'll do no such thing," said Phelan, sharpening up on his aim after easing off a bit on discovering it was who it was. "What do you want, Brophy? Are you drunk or something?"

"I won't lie. I've had a few, but that's not why I'm here."

"Why are you here, then?"

"I need to straighten something out with you, something that's been plaguing me ever since I was very young."

"I'm not in the mood for this shit, Brophy. Out the way you came, or I'm calling the local lads in to sort you out," he said, waving the gun in the direction of the open door. "I'm sure they'd take great pleasure in busting an arrogant knacker like you."

"Now, is that any way to talk to someone who's kept you safe and your reputation intact for many years?"

Phelan's hardened stance showed signs of abating. "What are you going on about? You don't have a thing on me."

"Please, have a seat, Mr Phelan. I'll be out of your hair soon enough, I promise. Just a few minutes of your time."

"Couldn't you have done this at a reasonable hour and used the doorbell? You had no problem ringing my bell when you were a kid, gallivanting around with those wild friends of yours."

"That was never me. I didn't want to fuck around with you like some of the others. I just wanted to see what this place was like. For some reason, this place was mysterious to me all those years ago. But now I know it for what it is."

"What's that, then?"

"It's a hiding place."

Phelan scoffed and lowered the gun. "What is it you're hiding from then?"

"More like what was I hiding from. I was hiding from the truth."

"What truth? That you're a thug cop, who can't hack the big moment?"

That stung Brophy, but he decided not to react with emotion as he'd ordinarily do if someone openly mocked him. "No. Not that. I've known that for a long time. So has everyone else." Phelan's face dropped at the unexpected answer. He lowered the gun to his side. "The truth I've been hiding from for a very long time is what happened to me here when I was a child. I'm sure you remember, I was locked into your coal bunker for over a day."

"Of course, I remember. You fell in there when you were trespassing on my property."

"Yes, yes. Everyone bought the story. I was running around like a wild tinker, couldn't keep my nose out of things, and I fell in there, and the door mysteriously closed down on the hatch and blah blah blah... The thing is, Mr Phelan, I don't remember it like that. I never did."

"What do you want me to do about it? Or did you just come here to have a whine about your childhood traumas? Coming from a family like yours is trauma enough, I'm sure."

Brophy didn't take the bait yet again. "What I want you to do about it is admit what you did to me."

Brophy thought he detected a slight twitch in Phelan's scowl but couldn't be sure given he was back-lit by the bright moonlit night.

"Listen, Brophy. I'm giving you one last chance to get the fuck out of here." He quickly brought the gun back up to his shoulder.

"Put the gun down, for God's sake. You're not going to shoot me."

"Are you sure about that? I could easily make it look like I had no choice. You came at me crazed and drunk, shouting about all the victims you've fucked over, coming to get you."

Brophy sprung up from the chair and beelined to Phelan. Phelan's finger clenched over the trigger, and the barrel began to shake in swirling movements.

"Go on then," shouted Brophy at the top of his voice, clearly sending the shakes down Phelan. "Do it. Finish me off."

Phelan shouted back. "Get out ye bastard. Would you ever just get out."

Brophy felt his face twist up in a salivating snarl. "Not until you confess to what you did."

"I didn't do a thing, right. You fell into that bunker and cracked your head off the ground. I don't know if I closed the door or not, okay. But I didn't know you were down there."

"Okay. We're getting warmer now. Because you definitely closed the door. And locked it too. But you knew I was there."

"I didn't know, I swear to God."

"You're lying."

"I'm not lying."

"Yes, you are. I remember it clearly. I was looking around the side of the house, trying to look in the window to see the living room, and you caught me. You flipped out and dragged me by the arm, and you threw me into that bunker, didn't you?" Brophy's eyes were bloodshot and frantic by now.

"So what if I did? You can't do a thing about it now."

Brophy dived at him, his arms outstretched, to grab the gun. He got his hands to it, and they tussled for control. Phelan fumbled to get his index finger on the trigger, so Brophy twisted it back and forth to make it more difficult. He changed tack and heaved forward, pushing Phelan back against the wall, knocking a framed picture off in the process.

Brophy whipped his arms downward and managed to get the gun loose from one of Phelan's hands. He then drove multiple shoulder charges at his right arm, and after three direct hits, Phelan cried out in pain and dropped the gun. It clattered off the tile floor. Brophy got his free forearm on Phelan's neck and pushed him into the wall with all his force whilst he kicked away the gun. Phelan let out an agonising scream, and his body seemed to wilt with the struggle. Brophy was momentarily impressed with the strength and stamina of the seventy-year-old man. It must have been a lifetime of working with horses.

"Tell me why you did it?" screamed Brophy.

"Because you were always pestering the life out of me, and I fucking hate children. I always have."

"And what were you planning on doing with me if they hadn't found me?" he said in a much more subdued tone, realising that was the question that had tormented him for years.

Phelan didn't answer him. He just stood there, resigned to his defeat, pinned against the wall, a look of terror on his face.

Brophy pushed him back even harder. "Tell me what you were planning to do with me?"

"The thought crossed my mind to kill you,"

answered Phelan, now starting to sob. "I might have even had a plan. But I couldn't go through with it. I wouldn't have been able to carry it to my grave. As much as I hated you, I'm not a monster."

Brophy eased up on his grip. Relief loosened his whole body, and a thought he couldn't quite discern threatened to surface. "I was a lost nine-year-old boy who you threw into a coal bunker and left for a day, Phelan. That's a monster in my books." He took a step back. "And I'm going to let you off with it but be warned that I'm going to be looking into you properly, and if I find any similar kind of incident around you, I'll get to the bottom of it."

"You won't find a thing," said Phelan, wiping the tears from his eyes. "I never did another thing like that in my life...I'm sorry."

"Go fuck yourself."

Brophy made for the open door, an idea nagging at his mind. He'd almost forgotten about Phelan by the time he got back in his car.

CHAPTER THIRTY-NINE

Freed of the burden of not knowing, Brophy was energised by finally getting a confession out of Phelan. A paralysing chip had been removed from his shoulder, and he revelled in the thought of having a proper night's sleep. The windows rolled down; he took massive gulps of the night air whilst snaking through the streets of his hometown. Soon he hit the N25 and was ready to cruise home on the twenty-five-minute journey. Yet something that festered inside him as Phelan was admitting to what he did gathered momentum as he drove past miles of farmland.

The full moon glimmered behind the top of the Comeragh Mountains to his left, creating the illusion of a vast wall of darkness bearing down on him. For a moment, he thought the image would break the ease of his current wellbeing, so he deigned not to look that way if he could avoid it. The inclined winding roads gently swayed him into a state fit for sleep, a calm repose before he changed the course of his life for good tomorrow. Maybe he'd return to university and finish his law degree. It's never too late for a change, as they say. Or perhaps something completely different. Sell the house and buy a thirty-five-foot sailing yacht and live off the grid as he'd always dreamed as a young man. The thought made him smile, and for a brief moment, he lost concentration and swerved the car on a bend in the road just before the village of Lemybrien. He regained control easily and audibly told himself to snap out of it; he could plan his life tomorrow.

To his dismay, the dark tunnel began to close in on him again. How foolish he had been to think it wouldn't happen anymore just because Phelan owned up to his crime. His lips tightened, he took in a long gulp of air, trying to fend off the attack by breathing, as had usually worked. A massive green road sign with five town names etched on, caught his attention. One of them was informing drivers to take a forked left turn onto the R676 heading for Carrick-An-Suir. Without thinking about it, he bore left, getting off the N25, his way home.

His breathing became heavy, his head fuzzy and light. Tim Phelan's words rang in his ears. "I wouldn't have been able to carry it to my grave."

Maurice Scully was on his last legs and carrying around the cross of knowing where Mel Fanning's body was hidden. Maybe Brophy could change his approach with him and plead to his conscience, to unburden himself of the cruelty that befell that young girl in the prime of her life. Maybe he could convince him that freeing his soul of such darkness would allow him some guilt-free last moments.

Over an hour later and on the verge of sleep,

Brophy pulled into the long driveway of Kilkenny General Hospital. The hospital looked almost abandoned, the car park empty, devoid of medical personnel running in and out like when he had arrived a few days before.

The third-floor windows were bathed in shadow, a few of them emitting faint green and yellow glows from some of the lifesaving equipment the patients were hooked up to. As he reached the main entrance, he contemplated how he would get past the reception nurse, and as soon as he began to think about it, he felt embarrassed at the decision to go there at that time of night. Of course, he wouldn't gain access to Scully's room. A stranger off the street at four in the morning with a smell of booze off him. They'd call security on him in seconds, or sooner if they recognised him as the trouble maker from the other day.

He entered the huge revolving door and shot out straight in front of the reception desk. Relieved it wasn't the nurse that was on duty the last time, he was greeted with curiosity by a heavyset woman with red hair, heavily freckled, and looked to be at an age near retirement. Her curiosity soon turned to suspicion as Brophy realised he'd been standing there for half a minute, staring at her without saying a word. What must he have looked like to her? A bum off the street looking for a place to lay his head down?

"Can I help you, young man?" she said in a tone that showed equal parts empathy and scorn. He hesitated for a long while, and the walls of the dark tunnel were not far off. "I see you've a bit of a limp. Have you hurt your leg?" she said with more compassion this time.

"Yes." He grimaced as the lie came out, partly from disgust, partly playing up the pain in his ankle.

"What happened to you?"

I got in a scrap with a drug dealer who's dead now and being blamed for a double murder he may not have committed. "I fell whilst hanging a picture of my daughter."

"At this godforsaken hour of the night?"

"Ah, no. It happened earlier, but I couldn't get asleep with the pain, so I decided to come in and have it checked out."

Her contempt was etched in her jaded pale face. "Well, take a seat over there then. I'll have the duty doctor take a look at it soon, but you won't be able to have an x-ray tonight. The radiologist isn't in till the morning."

"That's fine. If the doctor thinks I need one, I'll wait around until then."

She threw her eyes to the heavens and reached her arm out, handing him a clipboard. "Go over there and fill this out. I'll let you know when the doctor is ready to have a look."

Luckily for Brophy, the waiting area was next to the hall that led down to the wards. He should be able to make a break for it when she wasn't looking. He took a seat towards the far end of the fixed plastic chairs, drawing an over-exaggerated tut from the nurse. He began filling out the form, forgetting to put in a false name in the process. A couple of minutes in, he figured the nurse had all but forgotten about him, so he made a break for it. Within seconds, he was on the lift heading for the third floor.

He was relieved not to find Mrs Scully sitting outside the ICU. In fact, the floor felt almost deserted. An orange splash of light shot out from the small counter at the far end of the corridor. He assumed a duty nurse was there and would do her rounds regularly and again cursed himself for deciding to go there. But that thought was soon eradicated by the notion that this might be the last chance ever to put the case of Mel Fanning to rest.

Light-footed and pressed close to the wall, he made his way halfway down and stopped outside Scully's room. Focusing his vision amongst the medical equipment and lights, he saw Scully lying flat on his back, his breathing assisted by an oxygen mask. He thought he could make out his head slightly swaying over and back, his eyes blinking and his lips moving under the fogged-up mask. Brophy put it off to his lack of sleep and detoxing the alcohol that was leaving his system. He checked to see if the coast was clear, then opened the door gingerly and stepped inside. Scully looked a sorry sight, stocky and fit at nineteen when Mel Fanning went missing; he now cut a sorry shape of an addict on the cusp of his body saying 'no more; time to check out.'

Conscious of startling him and setting off all kinds of alarms and buzzers, he edged in slowly from the foot of the bed. First thing he noticed was that Scully's eyes were, in fact open, but instead of focusing on anything, in particular, they rolled around his head like shiny ball-bearings in mercury ponds. His heartbeat was forty-six, his breathing slow and laboured.

Brophy moved around the side of the bed and felt an unexpected shot of sadness at seeing the young man like that, robbed of his youth by a decision that cost the well-being of so many lives. A quick thought of how any one of Brophy's bad decisions could have turned him into something like what was laid out before him, made him grateful for the empathy he always felt was his lifeline out of the void. He spent years with a spiteful hatred of Scully and his friends. Clearly guilty of something during the investigation that lasted over a year, he failed at boring through the solidarity of the bond between the three young men. The kind of bond he felt for some of his teammates over the years.

"Cunt!" came out in a barely perceptible whisper.

"Maurice, you're awake?"

His right hand flapped up towards his oxygen mask, but he missed the mark, and it flopped down onto his skeletal midriff. Brophy was worried the catheter in his hand would get ripped out painfully, so he decided to help take off the mask. He reached out and pulled it down gently, leaving it resting on his neck. Scully finally formed a readable expression as he did so, and that was deep-seated disdain. He stared like that at Brophy for a long while, not attempting to speak again.

Brophy took the cue. "Maurice, I wanted to apologise for messing up the investigation into Mel's disappearance." Scully exhaled loudly through his nose. "I know now, I went about it the wrong way. I should have given you and Rob more assurances that if you cooperated and weren't the ones who killed her, you'd be treated more leniently. But truth be told, I let anger take hold and was determined to take down the three of you for what happened."

Scully tried to cackle at that, but it came out as a high-pitched wheeze instead.

"I know you feared, and still do, what Foylan can do to your mother, but the fact is, the damage is already done. Everyone associated with Mel's disappearance has been going around like the living dead for the last ten years. Mel's mother. Your mother. Rob. He arranged to meet me just before he took his own life but couldn't bring himself to do it in the end. But he wanted the truth-"

"Shut up, please. Just shut the hell up," said Scully, gaining a bit more composure now. "You have no idea what this did to people around here. I've been looked at like some kind of crazed psychopath in this town ever since she went and fucked things up." He gasped for breath after forcing out the words. "I'm gonna die soon, I know it. My mother will be all alone."

Brophy said nothing for a while. "She'll be protected, you know? They won't dare do a thing to her while I'm still around. The local guards want this ended as much as anyone, and they've assured me your mother would be looked out for."

"This has already destroyed her. There's no going back."

"But if you're the one to give everyone closure on this, I'm sure she'd be freed of so much of the mental hardship brought on by it."

Tears streamed down his sunken face. "I hated her, you know?"

"Who? Mel?"

"It was I who brought her into our group. We had a bit of a thing for a while. Only I wanted it to be more serious. She gave me the flick without a thought in the world and set her eyes on Brendan. He rubbed my nose in it good and proper for a while too. Fucking arsehole."

"What happened that night, Maurice?"

He closed his eyes for a few beats. When he

opened them, he looked out the glass wall and then glanced at the buzzer for calling the nurse to come and assist him. Brophy feared he'd blown his final chance to find out what happened to Mel Fanning. Scully began to reach for the buzzer but stopped a hand short of it. His face folded into a tortured grimace. He brought his hand back onto his stomach.

"It was just a normal Friday night. We were in Brendan's house, off our heads, having a laugh. His parents were in Greece, I think. After a while, the two of them headed off into one of the rooms as they always did. But this time it was different."

Brophy tensed up, shrouded in disbelief. He was finally hearing what occurred on that faithful night. "Why was it different? What happened?"

"We were all peaking on ecstasy, and they just started roaring at each other. I was so out of it; it was hard to pick up on what they were saying exactly. But I kept hearing them say 'pregnant' and something about 'keeping it.' I don't know how long it went on, but it seemed like forever. Me and Rob heard doors slamming, or that's what we thought it was. It went quiet for a while, then we heard this wailing sound. I thought it was Mel crying, and I guess I still felt something for her cause I got the hump and headed straight for the room. Rob was right behind me. I walked into the downstairs bedroom and found Brendan sitting on the bed with his back to us. It was him that was wailing. I was shocked. I'd never seen him come close to crying before. Through the haze of the high, it took a few moments to see what was in the far corner of the room. First, I saw the blood on the door frame. I looked down, and there she was, in a heap on the floor, blood all over her."

"Was she dead?"

"I puked, and I think maybe I collapsed and blacked out for a moment too. We were so off our heads and then seeing that. After a while, Rob went over and leaned down to check her. 'She's gonna be okay, lads. But she's barely conscious. We have to get her to a hospital,' he said. But Brendan freaked out. Started saying we had to get rid of her, or we'd all be fucked and our families with us. We pleaded with him, but he was always the dominant one. We didn't have a chance."

"Where did you take her?"

"The train track near the bridge. We used to play in a field beside the tracks when we were young. There's a yew tree, no grass around the base, so we dug a hole there. We spent hours digging whilst she was in Brendan's car boot. When the hole was finally ready, we went to get her." Scully broke down in explosive sobs and started to shout. "Jesus Christ, she was still alive. She was still alive, and we shoved her into that hole and filled it in."

As his last words came out in a tortured yell, the duty nurse burst in the door.

"Excuse me. What on Earth do you think you're doing in here?" She was young and terrified looking.

"Nothing. I was just about to leave. Don't worry," Brophy said, shuffling in his back pocket for his wallet. He pulled out his warrant card. "I'm a detective." He looked back down at Scully. "Thank you, Maurice. I promise nothing ill will come of your mother."

Brophy walked out of the room, leaving the nurse to tend to the devastated patient.

CHAPTER FORTY

Brophy sprinted out of the hospital, the desk nurses shrieking appeals not registering in his racing mind. Passing the main door, he came down hard on his injured ankle and let out a loud groan but didn't slow down a bit. Fifteen minutes later, he was bearing down fast on winding country roads outside Thomastown.

He fumbled with the GPS on his phone to get the exact location of the bridge and found he was only two kilometres away. The sun was readying its rise to the east behind him and his heart pounded rapidly. He couldn't believe his luck, after all the sleepless nights, the declining eagerness for the job, all because of his failures in this case. Now, he had what he'd become resigned to believing he would never know — the location of Mel Fanning's body.

A crushing thought took hold of him as the old arched stone bridge came into view; *what if Scully was lying again? He'd changed his story so frequently in the past. Why should now be any different?*

The bridge was on a sharp bend in the road, and he saw no place to park on the near side, so went through. He almost crashed when something sprung into view on the far side, a sprawling yew tree with manifold branches rising high, then curving down towards the dark earth beneath. He found a spot to park fifty metres up the road and ran back, half in awe, half terrified of the ancient tree.

He scrambled down an overgrown grassy ditch and landed in a stream of cool water at the end. Initially annoyed, the coldness was a brief respite from the throbbing in his ankle. Scaling the other side of the ditch, he grabbed a bunch of nettles, and as soon as he took his hand away, it began to sting and itch, in equal measure.

There was a stone wall on top of the bank, the style laid down hundreds of years ago in most parts, that had withstood the elements without budging. He stepped over the wall with great care, not wanting to displace a single rock, the remnants of a childhood superstition that said you'd have years of bad luck if you did so, surfacing from his subconscious. Finding himself in a clearance that circled the mesmerising tree, he could easily imagine the appeal of hanging out there with friends as a kid.

The outwardly growing thick branches offered good climbing, a place to sit and shelter from the rain that was sure to come. But its boyhood attraction soon turned to a sinister place of heartache and grief. The sun peered over the hills behind the yew tree casting an eerie predawn display of shadows lined with sharp golden edges. The branches began to reach further towards the ground, and for a moment, he felt like he was locked in a dark cell. To regain composure, he took a slow walk around the perimeter of the clearing. He estimated the entire area to be about a quarter of an acre. It could potentially take many hours to excavate and find the remains if they were, in fact, there. But he didn't care how long it would take. He would dig it up by hand if he had to. He wouldn't rest until he knew for sure it was or wasn't the final resting place of Mel Fanning.

The first call he made was to the local station in Thomastown. He explained who he was and the situation with Maurice Scully and was reassured to find the desk sergeant took him seriously from the start.

A squad car with two gardaí joined him ten minutes later. They tried to explain that they couldn't organise a crew to come out and dig until working hours, at nine o'clock. Brophy wasn't having any of it. Just shy of six o'clock, he insisted they get someone there with a digger within an hour, no matter who they had to wake up. By now Brophy looked a wily sight, wild bloodshot eyes and a glint that said he was ready to pop at any moment. The older of the two officers, a stout man in his forties, started calling around to people he knew in the town.

Forty-five minutes later, a flatbed truck pulled up with a mini-excavator on top. They had to drive a few hundred metres further up the road to gain entrance by the gate of the field. By then, six more officers had arrived, including Sergeant Ryan.

"I see you got him to fess up," said Ryan. He came across as nervous as Brophy felt.

Little was said between the small crowd assembled in the time it took to offload the yellow and black baby digger. Knowing McCall was an early riser, always getting in a run before work, he called her and explained the situation. She was ecstatic and cautious towards him at the same time. The reaction confused him, and she told him she'd get there as quickly as possible.

The digging started in earnest after a small argument about where to start first. They all agreed it would likely be on the far side to the road, the boys not wanting to be spotted committing such a heinous crime by passersby, even though it would be difficult to get a good view in. That left them with about a fifth of the entire area.

The burly local construction worker, O'Meara, who had brought the excavator, outlined a section a metre wide from the base of the tree to the edge of the grass, ten metres away. He started by loosening the topsoil along the area. A group of four officers, now dressed in white overalls, sifted through the loose earth with trowels and small rakes, a laborious task but necessary to see if there were any bone fragments or clothing before going any deeper and possibly damaging any evidence.

By the time McCall arrived at seven-thirty, they had gone five feet deep in that section and had decided to mark another one, closer to the bridge this time, an area that may have offered even more privacy in the dark of the night.

"Brophy, you look awful. What happened?" she said on approaching him after hopping over the stone wall like a nimble child.

"I've had a strange night, Christine. Something happened that made me want to have one more stab at Maurice Scully."

"And he talked?"

"Yes. He's probably not going to make it. This was truly the last chance to find her."

"Did he say what happened?"

"They were having a session in Foylan's house that night, as we already knew. Scully and Dalton heard Foylan and Mel arguing in the bedroom. They heard something about her being pregnant and about going to England to have it fixed."

"Fucking bastard! Killed her because he got her pregnant."

"It looks like it. They went into the bedroom and found her head had been smashed in. But she was still alive. They knew this place, so brought her here to bury her. That's all he gave me."

"Well done, Brophy." She took out a cigarette and lit it up, her hands shaking with rage. "Poor thing. What must she have gone through?" Brophy snatched the smoke from her and took a long drag. "Keep it. I'll light another one."

They looked on pensively, lost in the remorseful silence that pervaded the now brightly lit, dew-dampened field. The heat showed no signs of abating, if not even hotter than the previous few days.

What seemed like an age past until they were about six feet down on the second section. A few metres back from the tree, and one of the officers spotting the bucket as it dug into the soil, let out a ferocious shout. "Stop!"

Everyone rushed over to the spot. Two of them had jumped into the trench and were dragging the loosened earth away with their hands. It quickly became clear what they had seen. A foot-long section of black refuse liner was bulging out from the ground. All hands on deck, it took only a matter of minutes before the full length of the discovery was visible.

"Okay. Clear away, lads," said Ryan. "Time to call in the forensics team." He looked up from the trench at Brophy. "Detective, would you like to do a house call with me?"

CHAPTER FORTY-ONE

The interview room in Thomastown Garda station was a small stuffy, windowless room. The sweat cascaded down Brophy's back, his ankle throbbed a dull darting pain, and his eyes were forcing themselves closed despite his incessant attempts to ward off sleep. But all hardships aside, he sat there enthralled to finally get a chance at pinning the murder squarely on the one he never doubted had carried it out.

After the body was hoisted out from its grave of the last twelve years, it was taken to Kilkenny General for a full postmortem. Neither Brophy nor the entire crew of the local station had any doubts about who was wrapped in the black plastic coffin. During the investigation, they were blocked from doing a full forensics sweep of Foylan's parents' house. Insufficient evidence was the reason given, the photograph of the four friends together in the house that night not deemed concrete enough to prove she was last seen with them. He cursed the memory but was brought back to the moment by the local detective sergeant, Reid, entering the room and taking his place beside Brophy, facing the door.

"They're just about done booking him in. He'll be here any second now," said Reid, a man in his mid-thirties going prematurely grey, but with a youthful face.

"Thanks for letting me sit in on this," said Brophy. "I know you didn't have to."

"Are you mad, Sergeant? You just ended this nightmare for everyone here. I should thank you for coming."

Brophy gave a half-smile, and before he could say anything in reply, the door opened wide. A blast of sunlight burst in from the window on the other side of the hall, casting Sergeant Ryan and Brendan Foylan in a film of golden tinfoil. Brophy tried to focus on Foylan to savour the furtiveness of his defeated slouch, but his face was cast in shadow by the intruding sheet of light. Ryan guided Foylan to the seat and shoved him down much harder than was necessary.

"Hey, watch it," protested Foylan, hissing back at Ryan, who stared down at him with pure malice in his gaze.

Foylan turned to face the detectives, and his features came into focus at last. *Not a hint of remorse,* Brophy thought. *Just the same smug, arrogant expression as always.*

"What the hell am I doing here? You're all going to be in deep shit for this." Brophy and Reid knew to let him go on as much as possible before saying anything, in the hope his anger might make him say more than he should. "You're one desperate man, Brophy. Coming to my place of work, starting a fight, and now this charade."

Brophy and Reid ignored him and smirked at each other.

"So, what's the joke? Is this some kind of prank to humiliate me?"

"Have you been advised you can have a solicitor present?" asked Reid.

"I don't need one. But when I do speak to him, we're going to-"

"A body was dug up near the old railway bridge this morning," said Brophy. He let the words hang.

Foylan visibly fought to hold back the look of shock and fear, and it probably would have worked if he weren't talking to two seasoned detectives. They waited and waited, longing for Foylan to break the silence.

"So?" he said, the tiny word cracking up in his faltering voice.

"You see, I paid a visit to Maurice in hospital this morning. I regret to tell you, but he's close to the end."

"I know that. It's a terrible tragedy," he said, attempting to sound compassionate but failing miserably.

"He wanted to get things off his chest before he checked-out. It seems he's been afraid to say a thing about it for years, for fear of what might happen to his mother. But what we all know is that not a fucking thing will happen to her because of what's about to come out," Brophy said, his jaw tensing unnaturally as he spoke.

Sweat patches began to show on Foylan's underarms and chest. "What's any of this got to do with me?"

"Oh, please, Foylan. You know what's coming. Just admit what you did, and the courts might show some bit of leniency."

Foylan started to inhale massive shots of air through his nose. "It was him. He fucking killed her, the sick bastard."

Brophy slammed his hand down on the table, creating an unmerciful clatter. "Don't even think about it, you murdering scumbag. Forensics are on their way to your parents' house as we speak to examine the door frame of the downstairs bedroom. You're done for, Foylan. We have you."

"I swear on my mother's life. It was him. He was always intensely jealous of us, but he didn't have a hope, so it drove him nuts. He said if we didn't help him hide her, he'd tell you people we'd all done it together."

"You're a lying little maggot," said Brophy, almost fraughting at the mouth. "They were in the living room when they heard you two arguing in the bedroom."

"No, it was him with her in the bedroom."

"You just said he didn't have a chance," said Reid. "Why would he be in a bedroom alone with her, in her boyfriend's house?"

"We were buzzing off our heads. They were

just chatting or something. He probably made his move, and she rejected him. That's what happened," he said as if to convince himself.

"So, when the postmortem comes back, the results will show she was carrying Scully's baby?" said Brophy, unsure whether they could do such a test so long after her death.

Rage flashed across Foylan's face. He couldn't hide it.

"You don't have kids, do you?" said Reid.

"What's that got to do with anything?" Foylan was fuming now, almost ready to reel in.

"Maybe you despise the thought of having children," said Brophy. "Maybe you have from a young age. And that night, Mel told you she was pregnant with your child, and you flipped your lid. You wanted her to go to England and have it taken care of."

Foylan shouted, "That's not what happened, you bastard."

"You hate children so much, and the thought of having one with a girl from a council estate just didn't work for you. She refused to go, and you lost it. You drove her head so hard into the door, there was no turning back after it."

"Shut up," he roared, tears now streaking down his reddened face. "I'd never hurt a child. I wanted to keep it. It was that fucking bitch that wanted to kill my baby. She even had the ticket to England already bought. How could she?"

Brophy glanced at Reid. They had him.

CHAPTER FORTY-TWO

Later that day, Brophy arrived back at the Waterford City Garda Station. The reporters who had clung to the place like an infestation of mould in the last five days had all but vacated the premises. A new top story was taking over, a mere day after it had been unanimously decided that the double murderer was fished out of the River Suir with a pocket-full of the meth he was selling on the streets of the city.

Following the press conference the night before, people were already washing their hands of the dirty business, and now an even more dramatic story was unfolding just a forty-minute drive north. This time it wasn't some scumbag, thug dealer. This time it was a respected businessman from a 'good family,' whose girlfriend had gone missing twelve years earlier. A man who had been suspected by most as having something to do with her disappearance but was surrounded in a shroud of localised silence, no one wanting to be the one to feel the wrath of his powerful family. And most of all, his two best friends who had witnessed the murder and helped bury her body by a yew tree they all used to play around together as children, were stunned into silence in the years proceeding their wicked deed; one of them dead, the other soon to join him.

Brophy had been summoned to the top floor to meet with Superintendent Russell before reaching the outskirts of the city on his journey back from Thomastown. He knocked on the black metal door and was immediately hollered in. Inspector Bennett was seated in a swivel chair in front of Russell's desk and swung around to face Brophy as he entered. Both Russell and Bennett looked ruddy-cheeked, big smiles on their faces, half-drunken glasses of whiskey on the desk before them. Russell sat on his chair with his hands clasped over his substantial belly, an air of relaxation and contentment Brophy had never witnessed in him before.

"Have a seat for yourself there," said Russell, beaming with delight.

"You two seem jovial amongst all the carnage of the last week."

Russell chuckled, not a bit offended by the comment as Brophy had intended. "Now, now, Conal. There's no need for your flippant remarks. We've heard it all before."

Brophy sat next to Bennett feeling slightly deflated by the current situation but still light and composed having cracked the case that had dogged him for the last decade.

"I just want to say, Brophy, you're one of the finest investigators I've ever seen on the job," said Russell, trying to sound serious through the merriment smudging his features into a crooked smile.

"Thanks, Superintendent."

"Great job, Conal. Seriously. No one ever thought Mel Fanning would be found. There'll be a book written about it one day," said Bennett.

Brophy cringed at the thought.

"It was made official about twenty minutes ago. I think maybe your work in Kilkenny put the final stamp on it," said Russell.

"What are you talking about?" asked Brophy.

Bennett cut in. "We're the new Garda headquarters for the South East region. It comes into full effect in October.

Russell shuffled around one of the drawers at his desk and pulled out another tumbler. He slammed it down on the desk close to Brophy and said, "Will you not have a drop to celebrate with us, Conal?"

"I really shouldn't. I haven't slept in two days," he replied as Russell, heedless, poured him a generous measure.

"It's gonna mean a major upgrade of this place, and there'll be promotions to be had," said Russell.

"And there's many fine people who I'm sure will do a great job in those roles," said Brophy.

"Ah, here now, Sergeant," said Russell with an expression that attempted to come off as solemn but failed miserably through his glassy eyes. "I hope you weren't serious about this resigning business?"

"I've been considering it for a while, and I think now might be as good a time as any."

"Jesus, Conal," said Bennett, incredulous. "Don't you know what we're trying to say here? You're a shoo-in for detective inspector. This is as good a time as ever to stay and do what you're good at."

"Thanks for the vote of confidence, but I've my mind pretty much made up. I think McCall would make a much better DI, anyway."

Bennett scoffed at the suggestion and took a sip of his whiskey, an irrepressible scowl sagging his features.

"Christine McCall is definitely in the running too, Sergeant, but the fact remains that you have a lot more experience than her."

"And more respect," cut-in Bennett, scorn twisted into his voice.

Brophy made firm eye contact with him in an attempt to decipher what was behind his disliking of McCall. "What have you got against her? She's a great detective. Everyone here loves her."

"Maybe she doesn't love everyone back the same way, though," said Russel with a mischievous grin.

And then it clicked with Brophy. Although Bennett was married with three children, he had a reputation for trying it on with most new female recruits. He just never imagined he had

had a try with someone so out of his league.

Bennett was stony-faced now. "There's also the matter of the missing boy. Don't you want to know what happened to him before you ride off into the sunset?"

Brophy almost yielded to his manipulative remark, his initial instinct to bark back at Bennett, but managed to rein himself in. "Of course, I want to find the boy. I didn't say I'm leaving today, did I? I think there's every chance he's still out there, unharmed. To be honest with you both, I think there's a chance the killer is still out there too."

"Ah, don't start on with that, Sergeant," said Russell. "We got the killer. It's obvious it was Delaney. And I've every confidence White'll get a confession out of Doyle sometime soon. You just have to have a little faith."

"Do you not think it's strange that Veale hasn't been heard from in all of this? He just disappeared into thin air."

"White assured us that Veale was well clear of Waterford. On the run like many a time before," said Russell.

"What about the hotel? He never checked-out and left his personal belongings behind."

"Leave it alone, Conal," said Bennett, with a hint of disgust in his tone. "We got our man, and now we can focus all our resources on finding the lad. Shouldn't that suit you better?"

"It's not about what suits me. It's about

finding the people responsible."

"Which we've already done," said Bennett emphatically.

"Who was the other person supposed to be at dinner that night?" asked Brophy.

"It must have been Delaney," said Bennett.

"Come out of it, for God's sake. Do you really think a family like the Walters would have a street dealer over for casserole?"

"Why not if they were talking business?" said Bennett.

"There was supposed to be a meeting between the Walters, the Donahues, and Clarence Veale to sort out the problem of Aidan Donahue's debt to Doyle that night. Maura Walters had already started preparing dinner for a large group. Veale cancelled, according to Barry Donahue, so the meeting was called off."

"So what?" said Russell, his furrowed brow hinting that Brophy had piqued his curiosity.

"So why would Veale have cancelled? He was in town, booked into a hotel for that night, and the following."

"Maybe he caught wind that something was going to happen and got out of here as fast as he could," said Bennett. "These cartels are full of snitches and double-crossers. One of Doyle's people could have tipped him off."

"That still doesn't explain why he'd leave his stuff behind. If he knew what you're saying, wouldn't he want to check-out early and have it on record? Then be seen somewhere in public when the shootings happen. That's their usual M.O."

"We have the killer," said Bennett. "Along with all the evidence that puts him in the area, the guns he hid, and a motive. Why are we still even entertaining this-"

Bennett was stopped in his tracks by Russell, raising a hand, palm out, in his direction. "What do you think really happened then?" he said.

"I'm not sure. And I acknowledge it very well could have been Delaney. But there are too many unanswered questions. And if we don't find those answers, I don't see how we'll find the boy."

"So, what do you want to do?"

"Firstly, I'd like to interview Barry Donahue and get more details about the dinner that night."

"That's gonna be difficult," said Bennett. "He has a high-priced hawk of a solicitor, and I don't think you're his favourite person at the moment."

That one stung deep. Brophy felt intensely guilty about Donahue's arrest, after assuring him he'd be treated leniently, maybe even protected.

"Let me have a try. I think it might help if I was able to go in there with some kind of a deal if the information he gives me could lead to us finding the boy."

"Can't see that happening," said Russell. "The big boys want to put him up as a poster boy for the new breed of white-collar cartels on the go now."

"You know he was coerced into it, though, right?"

"And he'll have every chance to prove that in court."

"By the time he's in court, the Doyles will have so much fear put into him, that I doubt he'll do anything but plead guilty."

"What is it you think you can get out of him at this stage?" asked Russell.

"I'm not sure. I still haven't ruled out the possibility that he or his son collected Seán from hurling camp and hid him to keep him safe."

"The family and their properties have been checked out thoroughly," said Bennett. "I can say with all certainty none of them are involved."

"What about Walters' sister? What's her name?" said Russel.

Brophy became self-conscious his face might be reddening at the question. "Ciara. McCall and I have spoken to her. That's another thing that doesn't quite fit with their version of events. If Veale and she hadn't cancelled, she and the boy would have been there during the meeting. Hardly the scene for a child."

"I don't think these people have any reservations about that kind of thing," said Bennett. "They are drug dealers, after all."

"There were messages deleted from Maura Walters' phone that day. I think that might hold the answers."

"Tech team said it could take weeks to retrieve those if they can at all," said Russell.

"There was also the neighbour, Harrington," said Brophy.

"What has he got to do with anything?" asked Bennett, sounding more impatient by the second.

"Maybe nothing, but he did have a dispute with Walters about planning permission for a jetty."

"Okay, this is getting out of hand," said Bennett. "You're making things out of nothing here. Delaney was put up to it by Doyle. He had a way into their house as he sells their gear for them. He pulled the trigger then took the boy. Why can't you just accept that and concentrate on finding him?"

"That's exactly what I am doing. I'm asking questions, probing. It's called investigating. You should try it sometime," said Brophy with a jagged edge in his voice.

Through gritted teeth, Bennett replied, "How dare you speak-" but before he could finish, Russell interjected.

"Okay, that's enough, you two. This investigation is not over yet." Bennett sunk back into his seat. "But until I know otherwise, Delaney is our shooter. You do what you have to do, Sergeant. But keep your theories on the down-low for now. I'll try to set up an interview with Donahue, but as I say, I wouldn't get your hopes up. And I need you two to be on the same page when the inspectors come down from Dublin in the months to come. They're gonna want to see that we run a tight ship here, so I can't have you two sniping at each other every chance you get."

Brophy and Bennett sat there with bated breath, sulking.

"Is that understood?" said Russell firmly.

"Yes, Superintendent," said Brophy after a short silence.

"Yes, Sir," said Bennett.

"Off with you now, Sergeant. Get some sleep. The least you deserve is the rest of the day off."

Brophy didn't need to be asked twice. He got up to leave. As he took a few steps away, Bennett called after him.

"Conal." Brophy turned to face him. "Well done on getting that bastard."

Brophy nodded with a faint glimmer of a smile. He turned and left the office.

The incident room was a lot more sedate than it had been the last week. People weren't banging into each other, rushing out to follow up leads in the case. Now was more a mixture of hushed voices on phones, making enquiries and responding to tip-offs from the public as to the whereabouts of Seán Walters, and gardaí gossipping about the rumoured decision about the new South East headquarters.

Brophy trudged over to his desk, rivulets of sweat creeping down his back. The air was a lot heavier than it had been recently. He thought a cooling thunderstorm would nicely top off what had been an eventful couple of days. The plan was to have a quick chat with McCall, then go home and sleep for at least twelve hours.

Their adjoining desks were vacant when he reached there, so he took a seat and assumed McCall would be back at any moment. The initial impulse was to go online and have a look at what some of the national papers had to say about the two cases. On shimmying the mouse around and bringing his PC's screen into life, he quickly decided against it. Surely, he'd come across an article or opinion piece that speculated wildly as to the inner workings of the cases, likely naming him, the 'former hurling star turned missing person specialist,' and no doubt have a jibe at him being an expert at disappearing acts for a very famous reason.

Instead of putting himself through that, he switched off the monitor and sat back in his chair, getting as comfortable as he could. His eyes grew heavy and the urge to sleep overpowered him. Just as his eyes clamped shut, a vision of Mel Fanning presented itself, a laughing young lady, vivacious and poised at the prospect of a long and exciting life ahead. What it must have been like for her to lie in the back of that car as her childhood friends, having wrapped her in plastic sheeting, drove her to her final resting place. The adulation that came his way was well misplaced, but he was relieved to put it to rest finally.

All of a shot, he was jolted out of his slumber by the sound of a familiar voice behind him.

"Sergeant Brophy? What are you still doing here?"

He turned slowly; his movements laboured and heavy. Garda Mallon's smile was captivating, her pop-star good looks a rarity on the force. "Garda Mallon. I was just having a little rest while I waited for Detective McCall. Thanks for your concern," he joked.

"Well done on today. Everyone's well proud of you," she said with a broad smile. "But shouldn't you go home? She could be gone for hours."

"What do you mean, hours? Where's she gone?"

"She left about half an hour ago, out to Woodstown to see some guy, Harrison or something. I thought you knew."

"Harrington, you mean. No, I didn't know. Did she say why she was going to see him?"

"He called her earlier about something to do with his initial statement, I think. To be honest with you, I think she's a little smitten by the guy. I could make out she was blushing on the phone to him from the corner of my eye."

"I should hope it was out of the corner of your eye. You don't want her knowing you see a soft spot in her."

Mallon laughed, her green eyes glazed over, iridescent and calming.

"Thanks for the little pep talk before we saw those bodies last week," she said, becoming serious. "It really helps to know that even someone with your experience has been through the same thing."

"Don't worry about it. You're going to make a fine officer. Everyone says so."

She lowered her head, blushed, and bit her lower lip. "Well, I have to go now. I'll see you tomorrow."

"Bye, Garda Mallon."

She turned and walked across the room to the main entrance. Brophy's gaze followed her all the way there, and he had to check himself that she was far too young for him. He suddenly remembered that he'd left his phone in his desk drawer before going to see Russell and Bennett. On taking it out, he noticed he had a couple of missed calls and a message from McCall. He checked the message first.

McCall: *Gone to Harrington's place. Said he saw something Thursday he didn't think to include in his statement. Fill you in later. Good night.*

Brophy tried to call McCall back, but there was no answer. He left a message for her to call him as soon as possible. His interest was furiously stoked. What if Harrington had some important information that could lead to finding Seán or Veale? Then his heart momentarily sank as a darker thought took hold. What if he was, in fact, the shooter and was luring McCall out for nefarious reasons? He quickly buried that thought as highly unlikely. But a battle still raged inside him, should he go home as everyone was suggesting, or should he head out to Woodstown to meet McCall and find out what was going on?

Sleep can wait another few hours.

CHAPTER FORTY-THREE

On the journey out to Woodstown, he made several attempts to reach McCall and became anxious that she wasn't answering. She usually left her phone on vibrate mode, especially if she was out on the job, and it seemed strange that in the twenty minutes since he'd left the first message for her, she made no attempt to call him back. The thought of Harrington somehow involved in the murders kept creeping into his mind, but as much as he tried, he couldn't connect the minor issue of the jetty with such a brutal act of violence. Maybe he had missed something, though.

He cursed himself for not looking into Harrington more, his background, and family history. He never even checked if he'd had any past convictions or warrants. All kinds of scenarios played out in his mind; if Harrington attacked McCall, would she be able to fend him off? If he had taken Seán, was he still alive? If Harrington was involved in the drugs racket, would they be able to pin it on him at this stage? *Why isn't she calling back?*

His heart, already unsettled from sleep deprivation, was now palpitating like an automatic machine gun. It was so apparent to him there was more to the case than Delaney and

Doyle wanting the Walters out of the way so they could take over their business. Waterford was a relatively small market for hardcore addicts, hardly worth risking life in prison for. Just as the dark tunnels began to shroud his peripherals, his phone lit up in the dashboard holder and revealed McCall's name. He was on the outskirts of Woodstown when the call came in. He tapped the answer button and followed it with the speakerphone.

"Hey. What's happening? I've been trying to call you."

"Okay. Keep your shirt on. No panic. I'm at Harrington's place. He called earlier, saying something had been bothering him the last few days. He wasn't sure if he should say anything. But it's probably nothing anyway. I'll check it out in a while."

"What did he say?"

"Remember we asked him if he'd seen any fancy-looking 'D' reg cars in the area around the time of the shooting?"

"I remember. He said he hadn't."

"That's the thing. He was thinking along the lines of dodgy looking characters driving around looking shifty. It didn't occur to him until later that he saw a black 'D' reg BMW shortly after the shit hit the fan. He was shaken up and drove to the local pub after getting back home from reporting the shooting."

"So, where did he see it?"

"Look, it's probably nothing, but he saw it parked in the driveway of the local station."

Stunned at this revelation, he looked around and got his bearings whilst driving along the country road. He guessed he was only a couple of kilometres from the station, so decided to head there instead of meeting McCall. Gough clearly said he hadn't seen such a vehicle.

"Okay. I'm close to there now. I'm going to head over and see if Gough is in. I'm sure it's nothing, but probably worth checking out, all the same."

"No worries. Give me a shout if it's anything interesting."

"Will do. Bye."

Brophy turned onto the road where the station was situated. He'd be there in seconds, so slowed down and jogged his memory for anything that might connect Gough to the goings-on of the last week. Gough seemed like a solid guard, through and through. There was no way he was aiding in the distribution of drugs. But then again, people could often do the direst things for reasons most others couldn't contemplate. Brophy knew little of Gough's past, only that he was stationed in Drogheda before being assigned to the small countryside station he now ran alone. Drogheda had its fair share of criminal activity in the last few years, which hadn't really been in the public eye until the murder of Detective Ross O'Malley. Brophy wondered if Gough had known O'Malley, assumed he had.

He parked in the clearing across the road from the station. As he turned off the ignition, a few raindrops splatted onto the windscreen. Thick clouds hung low in the sky, and it was all about to collapse onto the seared land that had been baking for the last three weeks. Down the road, a blanket of heavier rainfall was barrelling towards him. He got out of the car and slammed the door shut in a single fluid movement and ran across the road to the station.

The squad car sat slightly crooked in the single space, so Brophy assumed Gough was in. He gave the door three thumping raps of his fist then pressed his ear against it. No sound came. He took a couple of steps back and had a look at the upstairs window. He knew these old stations sometimes had a cell upstairs if the downstairs was taken up by reception and office space.

Tattered white netted curtains, along with the lowering light, made it impossible to see inside. No telling what the rooms were. Brophy's shirt began to stick to his skin with the heavy drops coming down now. He stepped back in towards the door and gave it another solid knock. As his fist repelled after the third strike, the door swung open. Gough opened it all the way, resting it against the hallway wall. His eyes shone glassy and bloodshot, but the moroseness of their last visit was nowhere to be seen. He looked elated at seeing Brophy.

"Detective," he said warmly. "I wasn't expecting you, but I'm glad you're here, all the same."

"It's good to see you too, Sergeant. Could I come in for a quick chat?"

"Of course. Where are me manners? Come in there." Gough stepped aside and let Brophy pass him. "Down the hall to the back room. I think you know the way."

Despite the lingering taste of liquor off his own breath, as he passed Gough, the stench of booze was overpowering. "Is there a cell upstairs in this shop?"

"There is, indeed. Not that it gets much use these days. More of a storage space for dust now." Gough laughed at his quip, and Brophy followed suit out of politeness.

Brophy entered the same room where he and McCall had chatted with Gough the last time he visited. A half-drunk bottle of Jameson was on the table beside a stack of case files neatly piled.

"Have a seat there, Detective. I'll be right with you."

Gough disappeared into the adjoining room and reemerged seconds later, wiping another glass with a dry dishcloth. Brophy cursed silently that he had to have another drink. The last twenty-four hours was the most he'd drunk in over a year. He sat on the chair adjacent to Gough's and came down much harder than he'd aimed. Lethargy was kicking in, his body gasping for energy whilst his mind raced on.

Gough plonked down on his seat, topped up his glass, and poured Brophy a hefty measure. Straight away, he picked up his glass and held it out to Brophy for a toast. Brophy knew he couldn't get out of it now. He picked up the glass.

"I just want to say, Detective, what you did today, nabbing that piece of filth in Thomastown, was a great thing. Sláinte!"

They clinked glasses, and whatever way Gough was considering him, Brophy felt a surge of pride from the moment. "Thank you so much, Sergeant."

They sipped with eyes locked, willing each other to keep going. Soon the glasses were completely drained. Brophy grimaced and broke down laughing.

"It's been some week, alright. You know the night before the murders, I had a nightmare about Mel Fanning."

"Is that right?" said Gough, deep interest etched in his face.

"It happens quite a lot. But now I hope..." he trailed off and didn't finish but understanding radiated the air between them.

"I know how it is, Detective. I have them as well. All the regrets of the job, the things you reflect on and know you could have done a little differently; you could have saved someone some pain."

Brophy nodded, and there was a long silence.

"And Delaney as well, huh?" He poured two more drinks. Brophy protested to deaf ears. "Let's just hope Seán Walters doesn't enter those dreams," Gough said gravely. The rain was now pelting off the windows and roof.

"Did you know Ross O'Malley?" asked Brophy.

Gough's whole demeanour stiffened. His eyes darkened. "I did," he replied with a quiver in his voice. "I knew him very well. Everyone on the job in Drogheda and surrounding areas did. He was well-liked and even more respected. Why do you ask?"

"I'm sorry. It just popped into my head on the way over here when I was trying to remember where you were stationed before."

"I see." Gough became more tense.

Brophy was apprehensive about his approach and hoped not to offend Gough by the next question.

"I hate to ask you this, Sergeant, because I know there's nothing in it, but during our enquiries, we asked people in the area if they'd seen any black Mercedes or the likes, with Dublin registrations in the days leading up to the shootings." Gough's face crinkled, and his head tilted in a quizzical turn. "No one seemed to recall seeing any at the time of questioning. Then, this afternoon a local got in touch with us to say they remembered seeing a black BMW with a 'D' reg right after the murders happened." Brophy paused to gauge any flicker of recognition or fear in Gough's eyes.

His expression was unchanged. "Okay. And where did they see it?"

"That's the thing. He said he saw it parked in the driveway of this station."

Gough beamed. "You've got me, Detective," he said, stretching out his arms, his large white palms facing his guest. "I have a sideline as a door to door vacuum cleaner salesman." He laughed at his joke and shot up from his seat all of a sudden.

Rust framed the filing cabinet Gough walked across the room to. He opened the top drawer and ruffled through the manila folders. He looked over his shoulder to Brophy. "A bit old fashioned, I am. I like to have things printed out and not just stare at a screen all day. Worse than any drug, those devices everyone's glued to these days." He pulled out a thin, fresh-looking file and returned to his seat. "Now let me see," he said, examining the two pages contained within. "Ah, that's right. I'd almost forgotten about this, what with all the cartel action and murders in our little village here. The car was left in the car park of the pub for a couple of days, so they asked me to come and have a look. Last Tuesday, it was. Went over and found the door was left unlocked, the key in the ignition. I ran the plates and found it was owned by one Alex Gibbons, from Foxrock in Dublin. His family has a Summer house in Woodstown, and he was on a bit of a bender for a few days."

Brophy sensed what he was hearing wasn't entirely true. For the first time, he knew Gough was hiding something, and he dreaded what may come.

Gough held up the pages for Brophy to take. "You can have a look if you want."

"That won't be necessary," he said with a wave of his hand.

"Gibbons came by the day after the incident, and I wasn't in much of a mind to quiz him, as you can imagine. He took off fairly quickly."

"Did you get any information from him?"

"Like I said, it was the last thing on my mind at that point. He came by first thing in the morning, and I'd had a hard night of it," he said, gesturing his head at his glass. "He was just another yuppie from Dublin down here to live in the wilds during the hot weather."

"It's just that that's the exact kind of car we were following up in our investigation. I know you didn't know that by then, but maybe you can give me his number, and I'll give him a call."

"Sure, don't we have the killer? What the fish left us, at least."

"But we don't have the boy," said Brophy, feeling more ill at ease with the situation.

Gough closed the file and laid his hands across the top of it. He took a deep, audible breath, letting it out through his nose. "You know, I think there's nothing in this, so maybe I should just put it away."

"I'm afraid I'm going to have to ask you to put it into evidence. We'll look into it further in the city."

Gough smiled, and Brophy detected a hint of menace in it. What he did next surprised Brophy. He got up and returned to the filing cabinet, put the file back in its place, and slammed it shut a little too hard. A wave of anger was surfacing, one Brophy couldn't quite place but resolved to keep his composure.

"Have we a problem here, Detective?" asked Gough.

"I'm not sure."

"How did it feel?"

"How did what feel?"

"Finally, getting the one who got away?"

"Truth be told, a little anti-climactic, as it always does. The girl is still gone, and now I know how brutally it was done. Many lives were destroyed because of that one act of madness, and we have to try to put it behind us and roll onto the next human tragedy. That's all this job ever is."

Gough stood with his back to the filing cabinet. "I know how it feels. To have a case that crushes your confidence in the job, that you feel was your fault for messing up. For an opportunity, after all these years to set it straight, must be euphoric."

"Which case is it that plagues you?"

"Ah, there's no need to get into that. But let's just say if the culprit ever raised his snakey head out of the grass, I'd pounce on him with all my might."

Distant thunder echoed ever closer to them. The room was cast in darkness even though it was still late afternoon.

"Are you sure there's nothing you'd like to confide in me, Sergeant? I understand how this life can fill you with demons. Seeing the worse humanity has to offer on a daily basis."

Gough's laugh sounded like the thunder drawing nearer. "Not on a daily basis out here," he said, pointing out the window. "This station had been idyllic the last three years. Until this dreadful affair with the Walters, that is."

"What do you think happened to the boy?" asked Brophy.

Gough rolled his head back and around to loosen the tension in his neck and let out a long sigh. "I believe he's still out there somewhere. But it pains me to think of the situation he might now find himself in."

"What do you mean by that?"

"You know the statistics. Human trafficking, the sex industry." Gough's face twisted into a venomous snarl on saying the last part. "Some real fucking animals out there. And they need to be stopped by whatever means necessary."

"Within the confines of the law."

Gough scoffed. "Obviously, that's what I meant. But you have to admit; our hands are tied too tight on certain matters. Take your case with the Kilkenny businessman. Everyone, including his own parents, knew he had a hand in the girl's disappearance, yet we couldn't act on it."

Brophy's stomach knotted. "I might have been partly responsible for that. I made mistakes in the investigation,"

"Ah, that's nonsense. You were following the rules set out by people who have no idea what it's like dealing with the lowest of the low. They had more powers to deal with things properly back in the day. Then the world grew eyes and got all political. Now we have to suss it out from these damn files half the time."

"Things are improving recently. They were able to bring down the cartels after all."

"Very little conviction in those words you speak. And don't tell me anything about bringing down those gangs. The top guys are still out there, living the Hollywood lifestyle, and they seem to have chosen Waterford as their new drugs lab. I'd say they're far from brought down. And look what happened when the last families were nabbed a decade ago. They were replaced by much meaner bastards, and the next crews will be worse still. There's a power vacuum out there now, and it'll get filled by whoever is willing to go the furthest. And we know what that means, Detective Brophy."

"Maybe you're right. But that doesn't mean we stop trying."

Gough stared out the window. The low light cast his round face in soft shadow. "Do you mind if I ask you something personal?"

"Ask away."

"Why didn't you show up to the big match?"

The question had evoked bitterness and sometimes anger in him when he was asked in the last sixteen years. This time he decided not to let it be a shackle and ball dragging him down. He would lay it all out to this troubled colleague.

"I was just a couple of years on the job at that stage. Everything was great in my life: a beautiful young daughter, a fiancé who I adored. And reaching the pinnacle of the sport I'd loved since I first picked up a hurley and started swinging it around when I was two years old. Then-" Brophy's head shot up towards the ceiling, his gaze fixed on a spot directly over Gough's head. "What was that?"

Gough's upper teeth bit down on his lip. "It's only rats, Detective. Don't mind it. Carry on."

"Have you someone up in the cell?"

"I told you, it's just rats. They get all over the place this time of year."

This time a quick secession of three thuds

sounded down.

Brophy shot up from his seat and made for the door.

"Detective, I wouldn't do that if I were you," Gough shouted after him.

The impact of the sudden increase in volume stopped Brophy before he reached the door. He turned to Gough. "What's going on here? Who have you got up there?"

"That's none of your concern. You need to stay out of it and leave right now." Gough moved slowly towards him. Brophy expected his sheer size would be way too much for him. Gough must have been twenty kilos heavier and had fists like bowling balls prized and ready to strike.

Brophy grabbed the door handle, fumbled for a few seconds, and Gough quickened his pace. He felt Gough's hand graze on his back as he raced out the door towards the stairs down the hall.

"Stop it right now, Brophy, or I'll shoot you down."

At the foot of the stairs now, he stopped with his foot raised to take the first step and looked back at the oncoming behemoth, fully expecting to see a gun pointed at him.

"You can't go up there. This is my station, my rules." Gough's hand was behind his back, reaching to take out the gun.

"I'm going up there, Sergeant. This ends

now."

"I'm afraid I can't let you do that." He was only a few steps back now.

"Where's your gun?" said Brophy.

Gough brought his hand out from behind his back. It was empty, and he waved both hands before him. "I don't have one because I'm not going to need one."

He swung a swooping right hook towards Brophy's head. Brophy dodged the punch just in time but fell backwards onto the bottom few steps. Gough reached down to grab him. He looked delirious as his eyes bulged and his bulbous cheeks became red and sweaty. The wind and rain whipped off the house from every angle.

"Get off me, you bastard," shouted Brophy as Gough made his move. He kicked out and struck Gough right in the face, sending him toppling back. Brophy let out a loud groan, having forgotten that was the leg with the sore ankle.

Gough rose to his feet quickly. "Don't go up there," he roared as he headed up the stairs.

But Brophy was too fast for him; he was already halfway up by the time Gough made it to the first step.

Brophy found himself on a dark landing, two doors on the left and one on the right.

Gough came trundling up the stairs. Brophy threw out another unsuspecting kick, landing squarely on his chest and sending him tumbling back down to the bottom step. Gough shrieked in pain.

Brophy checked the first door on the left. A small dusty bathroom with only a sink and toilet. He walked down the hall cautiously, looking back to see if Gough was in pursuit. The next door on the left was newer than the white wood-panelled door of the bathroom. He reached out for the shiny silver handle and pulled down. It wouldn't budge. Brophy cursed that he'd have to fight Gough to get at the keys.

He knocked on the door and called out, "Hello. Who's in there?"

No reply came.

He heard Gough scamper across the hall beneath him. He looked around, trying to think of another way, when he saw a key on a piece of string hanging from a hook near the top of the door frame. Grabbing it without hesitation, he slotted it into the lock, and in one movement, pulled down the handle and pushed the blue door wide open. A putrid stench struck him and nearly knocked him over. Human waste, sweat, and fear smothered the thick air.

The room was darker than any other in the station, but he could make out the outline of a person crouched over on the ground in the far corner. The cell was otherwise empty. No bunk, no toilet.

Conscious of his rapid blinking, he tried to

allow his eyes to adjust to the darkness as quickly as possible.

"Hello. Who are you?" he said whilst waiting for better visibility.

Still no answer.

"Seán? Is that you?"

Brophy took a few sidesteps towards the person, keeping at the ready for Gough to come barrelling in at any moment. His eyes adjusted more to the glum foulness of the dark cell.

The person sat with his back against the wall, half crooked over as if he could barely hold himself up in a sitting position. Brophy's hopes were soon dashed when he discerned the person was too big to be a ten-year-old child.

The man's head bobbed up, a painful struggle to keep it in position. A tiny slit reflected the shallow slip of natural light that made it into the cell. His other eye was completely shut, bruised, and infected looking, puss seeping down the outer side. Now he could make out his entire face was a mass of swelling and cuts. The shaved head was matted with dried blood. His t-shirt, which was probably white originally, held different shades of dark brown and red. He was clearly clinging to the last vestiges of life.

"Clarence Veale?" said Brophy. "What the hell happened you?"

The single slit of Veale's sight focused on Brophy as much as it could. It appeared as though he was trying to speak, but only a trembling wisp of air came out.

Brophy moved in closer and was repulsed at the hideous sight of the battered criminal.

"Hang in there, Veale. I'll get you to the hospital."

Brophy reached into his pocket for his phone and cursed that he'd left it on the dashboard holder again. He contemplated helping Veale to his feet and bringing him downstairs and outside so he could make the call. He'd be a sitting duck for Gough, though.

Before he could think of an alternative idea, the sound of creaking steps taken cautiously reached them in the cell. Gough was on his way back up.

Brophy went back to the door. On stepping outside, he came face to face with the barrel of the gun, Gough held aloft towards him. He gestured with the gun for Brophy to go back into the cell.

"I'm not letting you lock me in there. You'll have to shoot me first."

"Don't think I won't, Detective. I've little left to lose at this stage." He brought his other hand up to hold the gun, pointed it straight at Brophy's head. He kept coming at him, so Brophy back-stepped into the cell, not wanting to tempt fate.

Gough flicked a switch on the wall beside the door, and the cell lit up with yellow light from an incandescent bulb. Brophy glanced at

Veale and was even more repulsed at the sight. It was as if no part of him had escaped a disfiguring grotesque injury.

"This is insanity, Sergeant. It's not the way to do things."

Gough stood at the doorway, the gun held firmly in Brophy's direction. "The way to do things?" he said and scoffed. "These little scumbags know how we do things just as well as we do, and they've spent years using it against us, bending the system so they'd get away with their crimes. Well, I'm having no more of it." Gough was wild-eyed as he spoke, gun pointed at Brophy, but not taking his eyes off Veale like he expected him to pounce at any moment. Brophy doubted Veale could so much as struggle to his feet in his current state.

"Did he kill the Walters?" asked Brophy.

A gurgling exhalation of air came from Veale's direction at hearing the question.

"Him. Him", he managed to force out.

Brophy couldn't believe it. "Tell me it wasn't you who shot them, Sergeant?"

"They were in the process of infecting your city with their poison. You know exactly what would haven happened if I didn't stop it. Not only that, but that little posh bitch had the nerve to threaten me if I didn't join up with them."

"You were the fourth guest?"

"I went over to the house that evening to have a word with this one. And when I went in, she propositioned me to help them out in building their little empire. Even went as far as to say that if I didn't, 'bad things would happen.' So, I showed them bad things."

"Put the gun down. Let me take you in before this gets any worse than it already is."

"It can't get any worse than it is. And I'll go in as soon as this toerag answers my questions."

"What do you want to know?"

"I want to know who shot down my best friend in cold blood. And he's going to tell me where that boy is."

"Was Seán at the house when you went there?"

"No, he wasn't. It was just him and the Walters, having a right laugh about all the business they were doing."

Brophy turned to Veale. "Where's the boy?"

After a disconcerting bout of coughing and wheezing, Veale managed to squeeze out, "I don't know. I swear."

"Why did you have the all-Ireland hurling medal?"

"Gift." More coughing and gurgling. "For the kid."

Gough moved in and pushed Brophy out of the way, sending him crashing to the other corner. He sidled up to Veale and crouched down, jammed the gun to the side of his head. "Where is he?" he shouted in a guttural roar.

"Shoot me, you fucking pig."

Gough grabbed his neck and drove his head hard into the ground. He put a knee on his neck to hold him down and pressed the gun into the back of his head with two hands.

Instinctively raising his hands in a gesture of peace offering, Brophy rose to his feet and approached slowly. "Let him go, for God's sake. We can do this properly; take him in and find the boy."

"Stay back there, you," said Gough, then pressed the gun harder into Veale's temple. "Now, I'm gonna give you one last chance, you little maggot. Where is Seán Walters, you rotten paedophile?"

Nothing but strained gasping came from Veale.

"Get off him, Sergeant. He's no good to anyone dead."

"I disagree. I like the idea of him dead. They can pull him out of the river like Delaney."

"Jesus Christ. That was you too." Brophy thought about the guns, the meth in Delaney's pocket, the tip-off from Gough to check the hotels. It was all him, right from the start. But that still didn't explain the disappearance of the boy.

He took a step closer to the hideous sight of a guard resorting to these measures to get a confession. Suddenly aware of his presence, Gough swung around and pointed the gun at Brophy. "This doesn't end until he tells me who shot my friend. Now back off."

Brophy didn't budge from his position. "Look, I know how it is, these lowlifes getting away with so much and shoving it in our faces, but it needs to end here. Every cop in the country will understand. I'm sure you'll be given a lenient sentence."

Gough laughed. "Sentence? You actually think I'm gonna let them lock me up for this? No. That's not how this is going to end. You shouldn't have come here today, Brophy. It's a most unfortunate thing, but you're in it now."

A chill travelled down Brophy's body. If Gough was capable of killing three people in cold blood, what else was he capable of? Would he take down one of his own to cover it up?

Gough put his hand in his pocket and pulled out a four-inch flick knife, never taking the gun off Brophy. He flicked the knife open and brought the tip of the blade right up to Veale's fully closed eye. "Time to give you the gift of clarity. Hopefully, you'll remember more then, huh?"

Veale began squirming but gave little resistance to the much bigger man on top of him. Gough eased the blade into his smoothed over, bulbous eye. A squirt of blood shot out.

"Mano Dunne," whispered Veale.

Gough pulled the knife back a hand's length. "What's that?"

"Mano Dunne. He shot Ryan."

"Bullshit."

Brophy recognised the name from the news a couple of years back. Dunne was a member of the Quilty family who was shot down in a park in Dublin in broad daylight whilst walking his six-month-old baby.

"I swear to you. It was Dunne."

Gough once again placed the blade close to his eyelid. At the same time, he lowered the gun to his side, possibly forgetting he needed to keep Brophy at bay. Brophy didn't hesitate and made his move. He dived forward. He pushed his bodyweight at Gough to knock him off Veale, grabbing the arm holding the gun at the same time. He succeeded in forcing Gough back off Veale but missed his attempt to control the gun arm.

A frenzied scuffle ensued. Gough twisted around and came down hard on Brophy. Brophy felt the wind gush out of him and let out a thumping groan. He brought his knee up hard, causing Gough to roll off him, cursing as he went. Brophy sprang to his feet and jumped on Gough's back, grabbing his wrist with the gun and shouting for him to drop it. Gough back stepped quickly and drove Brophy into the wall. Brophy felt like his ribcage had folded in but never let go of Gough's neck and wrist.

"Drop the gun, Gough," he shouted with what felt like his last breath.

He tightened his grip on Gough's neck and

felt him starting to weaken. Suddenly, Gough stumbled forward, driving Brophy into the wall once again. With the power from the hit, Brophy sensed his consciousness slipping away. After a few more seconds, Gough crumbled to the floor, his air passages blocked for long enough to render him immobile. Brophy came down on top of him and gasped for breath. He checked for the gun, which was now beside Gough on the floor.

A dark flash cut across his vision, and he thought he was going to pass out. Then he realised the flash was Veale escaping from the scene of his forced imprisonment. Brophy cursed that he'd now have to give chase just after that draining struggle with Gough.

He heard Veale trundle down the stairs and thought if he managed to get into one of the cars outside, he might get away and not be found again. He stumbled to the door, feeling pain all over his body. When he got to the cell door, he looked back to see Gough getting up. He slammed the door shut and locked it with the key still in its place.

He almost lost his footing on the stairs and had to hold the banister with both hands to get down. He rushed to the front door. The wind and rain lashed at the station and the trees overhead. A quick scan around the front of the station and no sign of Veale. He headed to the side of the building, which led into an uneven plot of dense woods.

Already soaked in the three seconds it took him to get there, he spotted Veale easily, stumbling through the trees, falling several times as he did so. It took Brophy under a minute to reach him, and when he did, Veale put up little struggle. He fell to the soaked foliage, life slipping from him. Brophy couldn't help but feel a pang of pity for the battered man.

"Do you know where the boy is?" he asked.

"I have no idea."

"Why did you have the hurling medal?"

"She asked me to get it for him."

"Who? Maura?"

"No...Ciara."

Before he had time to process the revelation, a gunshot rang up from the old converted cottage and sent a couple of crows fluttering up from the chimney into the blustery dark sky.

CHAPTER FORTY-FOUR

Brophy crouched uncomfortably in the darkness, his body drenched in sweat after the heat had returned following the day of stormy weather. His vain attempts to settle into a less painful position resulted in a loud clank of metal dimpling and springing back into shape. McCall smirked at his disposition and gave him a look to say, 'it won't be long now.' A live video feed came through to an iPad that was placed near their feet, giving them both a view of the car park entrance.

Following the arrest of Clarence Veale, Brophy and McCall did their best to extract information from him at his hospital bed. A mixture of medication, semi-consciousness, and stubbornness made him resistant to their probing. It was made clear that because of his past record with minors and his close proximity to the family at the time of the murders, he would be charged with the abduction and possible murder of Seán Walters if he didn't comply. That made him a little more forthcoming with some answers, but still, he remained guarded.

His solicitor had already assured him they had very little on him in terms of the murders and the production of the meth. If he was cleared of any involvement with the missing boy, he would likely go free as soon as he recovered. *Then he'd be left out for the dogs.* He wouldn't last long after all this.

Veale continuously denied any knowledge of the drugs, claiming he was merely old friends with the Walters, taking them up on a dinner invitation as he often had. Brophy eased into the main subject that was on his mind.

"You said Ciara Walters asked you to procure the medal for Seán?"

Veale blinked and attempted a sly grin that only resulted in sending a shock of pain down his battered face.

"If I didn't know any better," said McCall, "I'd say you were afraid of her."

Veale's eyes darted back and forth, anything to not make eye contact with the two officers towering over him.

"Was the meeting with Donahue called off because she couldn't make it?" asked Brophy, not giving him time to recover from the previous question.

Veale raised his mangled, bandaged hand a couple of inches, likely forgetting three fingers on it were broken, as he tried in vain to flip off Brophy.

"I'll take that as a 'yes.' She's behind it all, isn't she?" he said with more force. "She's also the one who informed Sergeant Gough what was going on with her brother and sister-in-law."

401

Veale was visibly startled by this revelation. "So, what does that tell you, Veale? That she had your back? That she sees you as an equal partner?" Behind the firmness of the swelling on his face, Veale was grimacing. "You see, she was hoping Gough, in his unstable state of mind, would also take you out of commission, leaving her as the only one from the upper-echelons of your organisation to run the show in Ireland. But things went wrong. No one was meant to get killed. She only planned on you all getting busted, but instead...Well, you know the rest."

"Fuck you!"

"The way we see it, you have two choices. We can release you back into the path of the hounds, or you can go into protection with your pal, Doyle. Maybe you can share a bedsit in Birmingham." Brophy and McCall sniggered. "I'm gonna ask you this once; where would she run to?"

McCall used her foot to tickle Brophy's ankle, and again he squirmed and banged his head off the side of the twenty-year-old Opel Corsa van combo.

"Jesus. Why couldn't they give us a regular-sized van to hide out in?"

"Yeah? Why not just one of the big white ones with Garda written across it in big blue letters?" She gave him a teasing smile.

"Whisht a second. What have we got here?"

They both stared intently at the screen as a black C class Mercedes eased into the entrance of the car park. The next flight to Doha was in just over an hour. If it was her, she was cutting it close. It was the fourth day in a row they hid out at Dublin Airport's long-term car park in the poky van combo; all other avenues to track down Ciara Walters having been exhausted. Most of the team assumed she had already left the country, but Brophy wasn't giving up. It was only the two of them on the stakeout and one detective garda staking out the check-in counter, but Brophy's success in the past week bought him as much time as he needed.

As the car backed into a space on the second floor, they could make out two people, one in the driver's seat and one passenger. The woman had wavy black hair and wore oversized sunglasses; the passenger was hidden from view, obscured by the concrete column they parked next to.

"Not a sound," whispered Brophy. "Wait till they get out and move away from the car."

McCall gave him a look as if to say, 'don't dare patronise me.'

The woman got out of the car and went straight for the boot, facing away from the camera lens that pointed downward from a yellow emergency sprinkler system pipe. She had put on a beige sun hat and wore a knee-length green dress. She opened the boot, which took her more out of view. Brophy's pulse raced, and a feeling in him grew that this was her.

She emerged seconds later with two large black cases, carry-on bags attached. She came around the car, keeping her head down, looking in at her companion. She gave a slight knock on the window. They could just about make out the corner of the door-frame as the passenger side swung open. A few heart-stopping moments passed, and Brophy began to think the pair headed in another direction they knew to be in the blind-spot of the cameras. But that was unlikely. How could they possibly know?

The woman walked to the front of the car, followed seconds later by a young boy dressed in blue jeans and a grey hoodie, his face obscured by a black baseball cap. She put her arm around the boy's shoulder and seemed to be hurrying him along. They had their backs to the camera now, each wheeling their luggage behind them. Brophy gave McCall the signal, still not sure if it was them.

They got out of the van as quietly as they could and headed for the couple who were almost at the lift.

"Excuse me!" said Brophy, a decibel short of a shout.

The woman kept her head pointed to the lift door. She began pressing the button multiple times. The boy turned to see who was behind them, and instantly Brophy knew it was Seán Walters.

"Ciara," he shouted. "Stop right there."

McCall ran towards them and reached them in seconds. She grabbed Ciara Walters' arm and swung her around.

"What are you doing? We're late for our flight," she protested in a futile display.

Brophy had now caught up. "The game's over, Ciara."

"Aunty Ciara. Who are they?" said the boy on the verge of tears.

"Are you Seán Walters?" asked Brophy as a formality but wanting to hear him say it to prove he wasn't dead.

"Yes. Who are you?"

"Don't say anything, Seány. Don't believe a word they say," she said, becoming hysterical. McCall proceeded to handcuff her.

"Don't worry, Seán. We're the guards," said Brophy.

"I don't want to go on a plane. I want to go home to my mum and dad. Do you know where they are?" he said, tears welling up in his innocent eyes.

CHAPTER FORTY-FIVE

Brophy followed McCall as she marched down the corridor towards Interview Room Two. They had waited anxiously in the office for two hours after returning to the station with Ciara Walters to get a chance to question her about her involvement in recent events.

Seán Walters was in Interview Room One with a representative from child services; they waited for the arrival of Meabh Donahue, Barry's wife, so she and Aidan could break the news to him about his parents, together. Brophy was grateful he didn't have to be there.

The NBCI had long since left the city but would no doubt be on their way back to take over things again, and block Brophy and McCall out of proceedings. Both left their phones in the desk drawers after seeing incoming calls from White. Bennett ignored a further two calls from him as he and Russell joined them in the office to congratulate them on bringing Ciara in. Russell intimated there was no way he would deny Brophy and McCall their opportunity to get the full story out of "Ms Walters."

McCall reached for the door handle and looked intent on barging in, a tried and tested technique for shaking up an arrogant, above-it-all suspect who had been waiting around, stalling the inevitable for as long as she could. But before McCall pulled the handle, she turned to Brophy with a broad smirk.

"You sure you'll be able to keep your heart on the task?" she said and raised an eyebrow into a mocking arch.

"Get lost, you. I said there was nothing there."

McCall dropped the eyebrow and down-turned the smirk into a grimace. She barged in more dramatically than Brophy had expected, letting the door swing fully open and crash off the wall on its backside. When Brophy stepped in a couple of seconds later, his stomach knotted as he saw Ciara visibly shaken by the sudden intrusion. Her solicitor sat beside her, whispering something, probably not to react to the detectives' bellicose act.

McCall plonked down on one of the two seats on the near side of the tattered table, and Brophy lowered himself in a more measured manner, never breaking eye contact with Ciara. Her lips tensed several times in a way that usually precedes tears or a smile.

"Detectives," said the solicitor, who was dressed in an expensive blue pinstriped suit and barely looked old enough to drive, let alone defend a client in such a big case. Brophy cottoned-on there was no way Ciara intended for him to ever reach a courtroom with her but would be fired at a later stage for a contrived conflict of interest, another delaying tactic of those who could afford it. "I demand you release my client at once or press charges. As far as I can see, you have nothing on her. She's a bereaved victim in all of this."

McCall overemphasised her scoffing sound. "Oh, please, Solicitor...?"

"Hunt."

"Mr Hunt, that nonsense isn't going to work here. We have mountains of evidence against Ms Walters," she said, staring straight at Ciara, who met her eye contact without hesitation. "And that's before we even get to the fact she was about to board a flight to Doha with a missing person, using fake passports. So, with all due respect, pipe down. Do your parents know you're skipping school, anyway?"

Hunt's face reddened, and he wound up to let loose when Brophy intervened.

"Why did you lie to us when we asked you if you knew who picked up Seán from hurling camp?" he asked.

Her nostrils flared. *Anger or grief,* Brophy wondered.

"I didn't know who to trust. And I had to protect him, no matter what. If I have to go to jail for that, then so be it."

"You're not going to jail," piped Hunt.

"Shush," said McCall in as patronising a way as could be imagined.

"So you did this to protect him?" asked

Brophy.

"Yes." A tear rolled down her cheek. "I knew those monsters were around him. I was gonna do whatever it took to get him away from those people."

"Is that why you sent Sergeant Gough to the house?"

He detected a sudden change in her.

"There is absolutely no evidence of that," squealed Hunt, losing control of his emotions.

"Let me rephrase the questions, then, if you will. Did you invite Gough to dinner that night?"

"I've never spoken to the man before in my life," she said coolly. "And why on earth would I invite anyone to my brother's house?"

Hunt touched her arm as if to signal not to ask unnecessary questions.

"Because you knew Veale would be there, seeing as how you invited him to help out with the Aidan Donahue situation. Then you cancelled last minute, knowing Veale was already in town and would still have dinner with your brother and sister-in-law."

"That's preposterous," said Hunt. "You'll never make such a fanciful theory stick."

"I don't think I'll need to. I think Ms Walters will eventually plead guilty to the charges we bring against her."

Ciara's expression stiffened.

"Why would she do that?" asked Hunt. "Gough was a cold-blooded killer. No one has any sympathy for him."

McCall's chair screeched a couple of inches across the tiled floor as she shuffled in her place. Brophy heard her increasingly loud breathing. He understood her frustration and also felt like diving across the table and grabbing Hunt by the neck.

In the days since Gough's suicide and since the circumstances of his actions became clearer across the country, a great deal of public sympathy was shown to the fallen sergeant's family and his demise. Politicians and members of the public alike were all but saying, whilst his actions were not justified in any way, his reasons for reacting were understandable. Vicious debate pervaded over whether he should be given a proper police burial with a full Garda salute. In the end, it was decided he wouldn't, and was laid to rest in a small service attended by his family and closest friends.

Many sectors of society fumed at the decision and saw him as a vigilante hero who brought down a burgeoning drug empire. Brophy and McCall agreed with this in private but dared not say it aloud. Having Gough's name besmirched by a weasel like Hunt was almost too much to bear. But they had to grit their teeth and hold their peace.

Brophy laid his hand on McCall's leg under the table to stop her tapping her foot and calm her down.

"We can hold you for twenty-four hours before charging you, so I'm gonna tell you exactly what I think your role was, and you can sleep on it, and we'll discuss it further in the morning," said Brophy. "Is that understood?"

Ciara nodded.

"I believe you're a lot closer to Quilty than you let on. Maybe even closer than Jordan was."

Her expression remained passive.

"For some reason, you wanted your brother and sister-in-law out of the way. Why? I'm not sure yet, but I'm guessing it's because you wanted to control everything yourself. You arranged for this dinner with Veale and Donahue to ensure he'd be in the house, and you also invited Gough, informing Jordan, Maura, and Veale you already had him on their side, a new recruit into your growing little empire."

Ciara's lips parted slightly.

"You told Maura about Gough using a burner phone, one we wouldn't be able to trace back to you. I guess she wasn't fazed by this, as she knew all too well how involved you were with running the business. I'm guessing you knew Gough was close with Detective Ryan and would love the chance to take Veale down. So, you gave him that chance. But you only expected him to arrest them and find the meth, then you'd probably get custody of Seán, and the whole missing person thing wouldn't have happened. One thing gets me, though."

"Yeah," said Ciara, indignantly. "What's that?"

"Even after it all went haywire and your only sibling ended up dead, you showed little remorse. The scene outside the house that night was a great act and fooled us all for a while. But a couple of days later, you were baking cookies and, from what I understand, you never asked when you could have your brother's body to have a funeral. That's a first for us when a family member died tragically. Usually, it's one of the first things people ask."

Ciara's eyes were like rising tides, waiting to spill over. When they eventually did, she let out an unmerciful wail and buried her face in her hands.

Brophy looked at McCall who gave him a sly smile.

"Let's get out of here, Sergeant," said McCall. "Maybe she'll be ready to talk after a sound night's sleep." She got up and headed for the door, much more calmly this time.

"Seán will only ever be truly safe if you help us take down the right people," he said with forced compassion. "We'll see you tomorrow." He nodded to Hunt, who was now pale and gob-smacked.

Brophy rose from his seat and headed for the door.

"Conal," called Ciara through the tears and sobs.

He half-turned to see her looking pleadingly towards him, moving her lips but nothing coming out. She lowered her head again.

"Just one more thing I'd like to know?" She looked up at him again. "Sean's Dublin jersey was found in the woods near the house with blood on it." She gave a half smile. "Did you put it there?"

Composed again, she said, "He put it there himself when when we dropped out to get clothes for the weekend. He didn't want his parents arguing over his fighting again. He'd grown terrified of their incessant raging arguments."

Brophy turned, walked out and closed the door gently behind him.

McCall was waiting at the far end of the corridor, leaning with her back against the wall. He reached her within a few seconds.

"Looks like you got her, Detective. Fancy a celebratory drink?"

"I'd love to, but another time if that's all right. I'm taking my daughter for a driving lesson when there's still a bit of light left in the day."

"Okay. Well, soon, I hope. We need to celebrate."

Brophy headed for the stairs, leaving McCall behind.

"I saw that letter on your desk earlier," she said, turning serious. "Will you even be here

413

tomorrow?"

"We'll see, Christine. We'll see."

Brophy walked down the steps slowly, unsure of what the future held, but fine with that for the first time in a long while.

Printed in Great Britain
by Amazon

21607900R00241